THE CALLING CHASE

Also by Cap Daniels

THE CALLING CHASE

CHASE FULTON NOVEL #30

CAP DANIELS

ANCHOR WATCH
PUBLISHING

** USA **

The Calling Chase
Chase Fulton Novel #30
Cap Daniels

Published by:

ANCHOR WATCH
PUBLISHING
** USA **

13-Digit ISBN: 978-1-951021-67-2
Library of Congress Control Number: 2025931842
Copyright © 2025 Cap Daniels – All Rights Reserved

Cover Design: German Creative

Printed in the United States of America

The Calling Chase

CAP DANIELS

Chapter 1
Shooters Will Be Shooters

Summer 2014 — Sea of Cortez, Baja California, Mexico

"Is obvious. Someone must kill her, so please let me be person to do this."

Anya Burinkova, former Russian SVR assassin, among other things, glared through the glass at the woman locked securely on the other side, but hers were not the only eyes boring through the one-inch-thick pane partially designed to eliminate any outside noise from penetrating the chamber. The woman's imprisonment was the justifiable result of years spent earning exactly what she was now enduring. Everyone who knew her felt she of all people deserved nothing less than practical entombment in the prison of her own making.

The grownups in the room were watching with barely controlled anticipation of what the woman would do next, but Gator, the youngest shooter on my team of tactical knuckle-draggers, gawked more than studied the meticulous movements, expressions, and apparent anxiety of our subject. Gator obviously saw the woman exactly as Anya did, but killing her was not what he had in mind.

He moved a few steps to his right, apparently to improve his angle and increase his visibility. "She may be one of the most beautiful women on Earth."

Anya threw up her hands. "Yes! This is why I must kill her. *I* am supposed to be most beautiful woman inside every room."

I turned to face the Russian who'd once been the woman I believed I'd love until I drew my dying breath. "Technically, the two of you aren't in the same room, so you're still winning."

Anya tilted her head and turned on the smile that had melted hearts, destroyed resolve, and crushed security clearances all over the world . . . including mine. "*Spasibo*, Chasechka."

Skipper, the finest intelligence analyst in the business and practically my little sister, slapped my arm. "Chase Fulton, that is *not* acceptable behavior. You're a married man, and Penny would *not* approve."

She was right. My wife would most certainly not approve, and I was working on the element of my personality that needed the most improvement—keeping my mouth shut. That particular skill had never been my strong suit.

Skipper wasn't finished with her flurry of admonishment. In a blatantly self-serving effort, she shoved Gator. "That goes for you, too. Stop looking at her like she's a piece of meat."

He protested. "What did I do? I'm not married."

Skipper huffed. "It's still not cool."

Mongo, our resident giant in both stature and intellect, growled. "Would you guys please shut up? Some of us are trying to learn something new."

I glanced across my shoulder at the largest human I'd ever met. "You want to be in there with her, don't you, big man?"

Gator spoke up before Mongo could open his mouth again. "*I* want to be in there with her, but only if this window has a curtain."

That earned him another shove from Skipper, but he caught himself before going down.

He said, "What? I'm just saying I think I could learn more from her if I were in there with her and there was a curtain or some blinds to block out you bunch of voyeurs."

"Yeah, I'm sure that's exactly what you meant," Skipper said. "You know what? I'm going in there alone, and you can stand here and watch."

The young gunslinger leaned close to Skipper's ear and whispered, "If you go in there, she won't be the most beautiful woman in the room anymore."

The analyst didn't blush, but it was obvious she was finished scolding the young operator.

Mongo leaned toward the glass. "There she is!"

Everyone who'd been watching the beautiful, remotely operated vehicle pilot instantly redirected their attention to the massive display filling most of the wall in front of her, and silence consumed the space.

"Is that a baby dolphin?" Kodiak asked.

After two decades underneath a green felt beret in Army Special Forces, Kodiak was the grizzliest survival expert on the planet. No one knew more about negotiating with Mother Nature than the man behind the bushy red beard that made him look way too much like Yukon Cornelius.

Mongo spoke as if in the hallowed halls of a great library. "That's a female vaquita, the rarest animal in any ocean anywhere in the world."

"And that's what we've been chasing for three weeks?" Kodiak asked.

I wasn't as captivated by the marine mammal as Mongo was, but she was, indeed, a magnificent sight. "No, that's not what *we've* been chasing, but it is what Masha, the marine biologist you bunch of Neanderthals have been drooling over for three weeks, has been chasing. *We* are chasing a grant to purchase the equipment required to capture and relocate a pair of breeding vaquitas."

Kodiak tugged at his beard. "I'm just a grungy old trigger-puller, so somebody's gonna have to explain to me what a team of door-kickers needs with a machine to catch baby dolphins."

Without looking away from the monitor, Mongo reached behind him, took Kodiak by the collar, and shook him. "Would you please stop talking?"

The former Green Beret yanked himself free of the big man's grip, and just as instructed, stopped talking.

A moment later, Mongo planted two enormous hands on the glass and gasped. That captured everyone's attention, but only for an instant. The scene unfolding on the monitor suddenly became impossible to ignore.

A slightly smaller vaquita swam into the frame and nuzzled the first, brushing against her as if he wanted to play.

Mongo said, "I'm going in."

I caught his tree trunk of an arm in one hand. "If you interrupt her, it could cost us the grant."

He groaned and turned back to the glass. What happened next took everyone by surprise, but none so much as Doctor Masha Turner, PhD. Her delicate hands fell from the controls of the undersea ROV, and she froze in place.

We stood in silent awe until the pair of mammals parted ways and swam for the surface to catch their breath.

When the monitor was empty, Dr. Masha Turner spun in her custom seat to face the glass from the other side. Tears fell from her eyes, leaving streaks of indescribable emotion streaming down her flawless face. Even Kodiak appeared to be moved.

When the moment passed, Masha stood and unlocked the chamber hatch, then emerged and stood before us as if she were a surgeon delivering news to an anxious, waiting family. She cleared her throat and spoke softly with only the hint of a Hungarian accent in her English. "Do any of you realize what just happened?"

We stared back at her in dumbfounded silence.

She wiped an invisible tear. "For the first time in human history, we just witnessed a pair of Phocoena sinus breeding in the wild. Not only has it never been observed by human eyes prior to today, but we now have the entire encounter on high-definition video and audio. I am the first and only marine biologist to ever observe the most endangered species on Earth beginning the cycle of life."

She faltered, and her knees buckled beneath her petite body. Singer, one of history's deadliest snipers and the gentlest man I've ever known, caught her before she collapsed, and he cradled her in his arms as if she were his own child. The scene was almost as emotionally moving as what we'd witnessed through the eighteen lenses of the ROV's camera array.

Kodiak caught my elbow and leaned in. "This means we're getting the grant, doesn't it?"

Shooters will be shooters, and that will never change, but I had to admit that I thought exactly the same thing when Masha stepped out of the control room.

"Yeah, I think it does."

When Masha regained her composure, Singer gently placed her back on her feet, and she ran immediately into my arms. "I can never tell you what this means to me. You are the reason this species will not become extinct in our lifetime. I can't thank you adequately. I'm . . . I don't have words."

I returned her embrace. "You're being too generous, Masha. You made the discovery. You captured the footage. It was all you."

"No, Chase. Without your ship, I could have never done any of this. I would be an orca trainer at Sea World without you. You don't understand what you've done. You've changed the future for an entire species."

I appreciated her gratitude, but the species I devoted my life to pre-serving walked upright, created language and the atomic bomb, and found innumerable excuses to hate each other.

I smiled down at her. "It's just a boat."

She laughed. "It's so much more than just a boat. It's the Research Vessel *Lori Danielle*, the ship that saved a species. It'll never be forgotten."

"That's not why we're here," I said. "We just—"

She reached up and pressed a finger against my lips. "I know what you do, Chase. My grandfather and my father told me what you are, but today, you are not killers. Today, you are saviors."

We left Masha and reconvened in the combat information center, where I took the floor immediately. "Well, that was an interesting way to spend the morning. I'm ashamed to admit I'm not smart enough to understand the magnitude of what happened down there from Dr. Turner's perspective, but now, it's time to talk about what it means for the rest of us."

My handler, Clark Johnson, a man who taught me almost everything I know about staying alive when the whole world is trying to kill me, popped up on the monitor behind me. "Hey, College Boy. I hear we're adding a groovy new toy to the arsenal."

I spun to face the camera. "How could you possibly know that already?"

He lit a Cuban, stuck it in his mouth, and mumbled, "It's best if you always assume I know everything. Gotta run. It's time for my first massage of the day."

"Your *first* massage? Does that mean . . ." But he was gone before I could finish my question. Shaking my head, I turned back to my team. "I'm really looking forward to retirement."

Everyone laughed, and Mongo said, "No, you're not. You love a good gunfight just as much as the rest of us. You'll never leave this gig. Now, tell us about the groovy new toy."

I leaned against the console. "Skipper, go ahead and bring up the pictures."

A collection of four photos filled the screen where Clark's face had been only moments before. "Gentlemen, and ladies, allow me to introduce the deep-sea remote exploration autonomous manned utility platform. Her friends call her DREAMUP. She's the brainchild of our very own technical services officer, Dr. Celeste Mankiller. Everybody, please give Celeste a big hand."

The genius designer, inventor, builder, and dreamer appeared on a second monitor beside the first. She offered a small, humble bow, and said, "Thank you. I'm sorry we weren't able to keep you in the loop on this one, but to be honest, I never dreamed it would be possible to actually build, test, and field this thing. That's why I've kept it under wraps for so long. I've been fantasizing about this magnificent machine for years, and Chase tells me we're on the verge of getting the funding to actually bring it to life. I've sent complete specs to each of your tablets, and I encourage you to learn everything you can about the DREAMUP. Ask a billion questions if you need to. If the funding actually comes through, we're going to build it, and you guys will be my personal crash test dummies."

Mongo was first to raise a finger. "I've got a question already. If this thing doesn't exist yet, what does Dr. Turner think we're going to do to save her vaquita?"

"I'll take this one," I said. "The mechanism required to relocate a pair of breeding vaquitas is expensive to build and impossible to pay for without massive grants—just like the ones Dr. Turner's find will guarantee. We're going to modify the *Lori Danielle* to safely collect, protect, and relocate at least one breeding pair of vaquitas. Modifying our existing ship costs a tiny fraction of what it would cost to build a custom ship to move the mammals. That's called 'overrun' in spending parlance, and that overrun is what we'll use to build and test Dr. Mankiller's DREAMUP."

Mongo furrowed his brow. "Why do we need a deep-sea exploration vehicle?"

"We don't," I said. "But you're just looking at the first half of the DREAMUP. The U and P stand for *utility platform*."

Mongo's eyes widened in obvious understanding. "It's a weapons platform."

I nodded once. "Among other things . . . Imagine being able to silently and undetectably move weapons, intelligence-gathering technology, and even warriors like us anywhere in the world that touches the water."

Instinctually, everyone in the room turned to stare at Shawn, our resident SEAL, and he grinned from ear to ear. "Where's the clipboard to sign up? I want to be the first to ride that thing to the bottom of the ocean."

Chapter 2
My Guardian Angel

We dismissed our little gathering in the CIC, but Mongo lingered. He pulled up a chair when the room was empty of everyone except Skipper, him, and me.

The analyst asked, "Do you guys need the room?"

Mongo said, "No, no. It's nothing like that."

Skipper turned back to her work—whatever that was—and pulled on her noise-canceling headset.

"What's up, big man?"

Mongo could've taught quantum physics at MIT or played for the NFL, but the Army got their claws into him at seventeen and turned him into a warfighting machine on the outside. However, deep beneath that scarred, battle-worn exterior, beat the heart of the meekest man I've ever known.

He almost looked like a child on the verge of asking his mother for a new toy, so I said, "I'll bet I can guess."

He looked at me with a sheepish smile. "You probably can."

I nodded. "And you already know the answer. Of course you can move into the lab with Dr. Mankiller for the project."

I surrendered the lair back to Skipper and headed down to the bowels of the vessel. My first stop was the moonpool, where we launched and recovered our SEAL Delivery Vehicle, a flooded submarine capable of carrying the team several miles at six knots below the waves. The sub's only limitations were battery power, depth limits, and the inability to fit

Mongo inside. I tried to imagine what the space would look like when modified to carry a happily married pair of vaquitas ready to repopulate the world's oceans like a modern-day, post-Flood, family of Noah.

Undoubtedly, the space would become a flooded tank of some sort, rendering our ship incapable of launching and recovering the SDV without detection. We'd still have the ability to hoist the sub from the stern deck with one of the ship's cranes, but the covert nature of our work didn't often lend itself to showing all of our cards.

I ran a hand across the length of the sub and thought about the hours I'd spent inside the metal tube, shivering like a freezing puppy and anxious to hit the ground running. There was no way to predict how long the *Lori Danielle* would be relegated to bio-marine service, but I hoped she'd miss me as much as I'd miss her in our time apart.

My next stop was the control compartment for the ROV operation, where I found Dr. Masha Turner with a phone receiver pinched between her ear and shoulder and both hands on a keyboard, in a perfect impersonation of Skipper. She glanced up and pointed to a chair that I promptly accepted.

Masha pulled her fingers from the keyboard and pressed the mouthpiece of the receiver under her chin. "I'm on hold. Can you believe what we did this morning?"

I took a long breath and slowly allowed it to escape. "I'll be honest, Masha. I don't really understand the significance of what's happening around me, but I'm proud to be part of it."

She yanked the receiver back to her mouth. "Hey, yes, I'm still here." She listened for a moment and said, "Okay, great. Thanks."

A few seconds later, she said, "Hey, Gloria. It's Masha. Have you heard? . . . I know! Can you believe it?" Once the jubilation receded, she asked, "Where are we on the grant applications?"

I listened closely, but I couldn't hear the other end of the conversation.

Masha said, "It's all done. I uploaded the data, video, and audio a few minutes ago. You should have all of it. I covered this in the email, but do *not* release anything yet. I'll publish the white paper in a few days, but we need to keep this under wraps for now."

A few more minutes of high-pitched celebration ended with Masha returning the receiver to its cradle. "The grant proposals have been written for months. Gloria just has to update the supporting data with my report and evidence of this morning's sighting, and they'll be ready to go."

"Go to whom?" I asked.

Her face brightened. "The whole world! The biggies are The Lerner-Gray Fund for Marine Research, Schmidt Ocean Institute, Rockefeller Foundation, World Wildlife Fund, World Wide Fund for Nature, and the biggest is the National Science Foundation."

"How much money are we talking about?"

She seemed to shrink in her chair. "Close to a billion dollars."

"What about the Smithsonian?"

She shrugged. "I've never heard of them offering grant funding for a project like this, but maybe."

"They fund a lot of things you've never heard of." I paused. "Well, that's not entirely true. A lot of things you've never heard of were funded *through* the Smithsonian, but not *by* the Smithsonian. Do you understand what I'm saying?"

She said, "When the grants come in, that will mean you don't have to pay me anymore. I can live off a stipend from the grants as long as the project is underway."

"Let's not worry about you getting paid," I said. "You're an employee of the Bonaventure Historic Trust as long as you want, and as long as we have a ship, she's all yours to conduct research wherever you want, with only a few exceptions."

She cocked her head. "Why are you doing this for me? You don't even know me."

I rolled a few inches closer and lowered my tone. "We know your family, Masha, and that's what makes you one of us. Your father and grandfather told you a tiny piece of the truth about who and what we are. You may not know this about them, but they aren't exactly what they appear to be either."

She bowed her head. "Yeah, I got that impression, but we've never had that conversation."

"I don't know your father," I admitted. "I only know his reputation."

She huffed. "From my point of view, his reputation isn't great."

"I'm sure it's not, but he wasn't just an embassy diplomat. He was a great deal more."

"He was a spy, wasn't he?"

I swallowed hard. "Listen, Masha. I promise I'll never lie to you, but because of the nature of what we do, there will be things I can't tell you. Do you understand?"

She chuckled. "That means he was a spy."

"He was an intelligence officer under diplomatic cover in Eastern and Northern Europe."

"That means spy, right?"

I redirected the conversation. "Your grandfather, Hank, is an entirely different story. He's an American hero. I'm sure he's too humble to tell you what he did in the wars, but suffice it to say, he's part of the reason America still exists."

She grinned. "You're right. He doesn't talk about it, but Nagyanya showed me his medals and told me about him flying in the war. I don't really know which war, but you'd never believe he was that guy once. To me, he's just Nagyapa."

"I assume that's Hungarian for *grandfather*, right?"

"Yes, and Nagyanya is *grandmother*."

"I'm afraid I'm running out of room to learn new languages, but I'll pick up a word or two from time to time. Anyway, back to your salary. One of the things we do is take care of family, and you more than meet that qualification."

She pressed a finger to the corner of her eye. "You're going to make me cry again."

"It's okay to cry for the right reasons, and what you did this morning definitely falls into the category of right reasons."

She slowly shook her head. "Chase, you just don't know. I'll be the envy of every marine biologist in the world. This never happens to a biologist fresh out of school. It's practically a miracle."

"Maybe they picked you," I said.

She narrowed her gaze. "What?"

"Maybe the vaquitas picked you. Maybe they knew you'd take better care of them than anyone else. Or maybe they're exhibitionists and just wanted to show off."

She giggled. "I doubt either of those things is true, but you have a way of making everything all right."

"That's kind of what I do. I just don't get to publish white papers about it."

"I bet it's exciting, though, isn't it?"

I said, "Not as exciting as being the only marine biologist who's ever seen a mating pair of vaquitas. By the way, is that word like *sheep*? Is it already plural?"

Her giggling continued. "Yes, it's already plural, but since there are fewer than three dozen left on Earth, it almost feels like we don't need the plural."

"You're going to take care of that, though."

She grinned. "Yes, I am."

"There's just one more thing I'd like to talk about if you have three more minutes."

"Of course. What is it?"

I said, "I know you're loyal to the University of Miami Rosenstiel School, but I'd like you to consider submitting the grant applications through the Bonaventure Historic Trust. We set up the trust specifically for this project and to give you a place to work on whatever you want."

She squirmed in her chair but didn't speak.

"There are several advantages associated with using the trust. First of all, you'll have full, unfettered access to the funding without asking a board of regents or trustees—whatever they have. The research is yours. You don't have to share the byline with anyone else. And perhaps the most important reason to apply through the trust is that we have attorneys on payroll who can fast-track the applications, especially the NOAH, Smithsonian, and NSF ones."

She leaned toward me. "Is that all legal?"

I relaxed. "Yes, it's one hundred percent legal and fully transparent."

"What kind of fast-tracking are we talking about?"

"I can't say for sure, but definitely weeks instead of months or years."

"Seriously?"

"Yes. In fact, it could be a matter of days."

She sighed. "That doesn't sound legal."

"You're right. And it probably shouldn't be, but that's how our political system works these days. Learning to play the game is the only way anything meaningful—like saving your vaquitas—ever gets done."

She stood and leaned toward me with her arms extended, and I wrapped her in mine.

She whispered. "It's like you're my guardian angel or something. You're going to get tired of hearing me say it, but thank you a billion times."

"You don't have to thank me. We're just doing what the world needs. And I told you I only needed three minutes, but there's one more thing."

She nestled back into her seat. "All that's on my schedule is to fly your ROV the rest of the day."

"That's part of what we need to talk about." Her perfect features morphed into the epitome of concern, so I said, "No, don't worry. It's not bad. I just need you to understand what's going to happen with the ship."

She continued frowning. "I thought you said I could use the ship for all the research I wanted."

"I did, and that's what I meant, but here's the plan. I'm going to take the *Lori Danielle* through the Panama Canal and into Grumman Shipyard in Pascagoula, Mississippi, where she'll be refitted to serve as your relocation vessel for the vaquitas. It could take thirty months or more to construct a purpose-built ship just for the move, but retrofitting this ship can be done in weeks, and I've already made the call. They're preparing a dry dock for us now."

She still looked concerned. "That means I can't stay here with the vaquitas."

"That's what this conversation is about," I said. "I've got some feelers out for a vessel we can lease so you can stay here with your vaquitas while we're in for retrofit."

She covered her mouth with both hands. "Oh, Chase, that would be amazing. All of this is a dream come true."

I stood. "Go play with your fish. I'm headed up to talk with the captain."

She looked up at me with disappointment on her face. "They're mammals, not fish."

I turned for the door. "I knew that. I was talking about the ROV. I like to call that thing 'a fish.'"

"Sure, you do."

* * *

Captain Sprayberry was on the starboard bridge wing with two junior officers, each holding a sextant and staring at the sun. I stood back and listened to his class for several minutes before he noticed me and patted one of the young officers on the back. "Call celestial noon and calculate our longitude against the ship's clock."

The pair answered in unison. "Aye, sir."

The captain motioned for me to follow him inside. "How's it going, Chase? I heard that girl found her vaquita this morning."

"She's a PhD, Captain. It's not politically correct to call her a girl."

He poured two cups of coffee. "When you've been on the planet as long as I have, you can call anybody younger than forty a girl."

I accepted the offered cup and took a seat. "How long will it take us to get to Pascagoula?"

He took a sip. "It's forty-six hundred sea miles. How fast do you want to get there? It'll take us six days plus the canal. I'll have to book a slot."

"We're going to put the old girl in dry dock for the refit we talked about, and they'll be ready for us in ten days."

"What do you want me to do with the crew?" he asked.

"Send most of them home,."

He laughed. "To most of them, the ship is their home."

"We'll put them up in Biloxi if they don't want to go to their real homes. Of course, we'll keep you and the engineers through the process."

"Makes sense. When do you want to set sail?"

I motioned toward the phone. "See what you can get for a canal slot."

He spent the next ten minutes on the phone speaking two different languages and arguing with somebody. Finally, he hung up and said, "Five days. Will that do?"

"Sounds perfect. One more thing. I'd like to lease a vessel or space on a vessel for Dr. Turner to continue building rapport with the vaquita she found."

He snapped his fingers. "Now, that I can do. I've got an old ship-mate friend of mine who just happens to be looking for work. How big does the tub need to be?"

"Big enough to support an ROV operation and keep Masha from getting seasick."

He waved a dismissive hand. "Sooner or later, that girl's gonna have to grow a pair of sea legs if she's gonna spend her life on a boat. I'll see what I can do."

Chapter 3

Face-to-Face

An hour later, Captain Sprayberry called my cabin. "I found your girl a boat."

I said, "She's a PhD, and she's about to be the most famous marine biologist on Earth. She's not a girl, and she needs a ship, not a boat."

He huffed. "All right, then. I'll call him back and tell him your marine biologist girl doesn't want his four-hundred-foot boat."

"Wait! Don't do that. A four-hundred-footer isn't a boat."

He said, "It is to me. He'll be here in twelve hours. It's not as nice as our tub, but it ain't bad. He's got his own ROV setup on board, but he said yours should be plug and play . . . whatever that means. Do you want him or not?"

"I want him."

I found Masha exactly where I expected, but unlike her last session flying the ROV, she hadn't locked herself in. The relatively sound-proof door lay ajar, so I made myself at home. "Any more sightings?"

She looked up from her monitor. "Yeah, two new ones this time."

"Another mating pair?" I asked.

"No, they were both females, but it looked like they were on the prowl for a boyfriend."

"I've got some good news," I said. "The captain has a friend who runs a four-hundred-foot vessel that already has an ROV. He'll be here in less than twelve hours, so it looks like you're getting kicked off the *Lori Danielle*."

She grinned, and for a moment, I thought she might never stop. "That's amazing news. Thank you so much. But until we get our grant funding, we can't pay for another ship."

"Don't worry. It's taken care of."

She said, "It's starting to feel like *thank you* isn't sufficient, but that's all I have."

I motioned toward the monitor, and Masha turned with a girlish chirp. "That's another male."

I leaned in. "It looks like he wants to play with the ROV."

"It's believed that the males are very playful and curious while the females are far more aloof."

"Have you ever seen one eye to eye?"

She said, "You mean, like, in real life? Not on a camera?" I nodded, and she said, "No. Of course not. Very few people have . . . except for dead ones. The reason they're going extinct so quickly is because of the gill nets. They get trapped in them and drown."

I scanned the status screen of the ROV. "Do you want to see one face-to-face?"

She furrowed her brow. "What?"

I pointed at the screen. "The ROV is twenty-six feet deep in eighty-six-degree water. We just happen to have some of the best dive gear on Earth right here on this ship. You're certified, aren't you?"

Her mouth dropped open. "Are you talking about diving with the vaquitas?"

"Why not?"

She suddenly looked deeply concerned. "Interacting directly with a species that's as threatened as the vaquita is . . ."

I motioned toward the monitor again, where the male was prodding the camera lens with his snout and performing barrel rolls.

Masha stared in wide-eyed wonder and disbelief. "Yeah, I want to go."

After a call to the bridge to coordinate the operation, Masha, Shawn, Anya, and I sat on the edge of the moonpool in the belly of the ship, fully kitted out with rebreathers, full facemasks with comms, and serious anticipation.

I said, "Comms check. Can everyone hear me?"

We continued the checks until all four rigs were confirmed to be working perfectly.

I gave Masha a pat on the shoulder. "Are you sure you don't want to take a camera?"

"I'm sure. Some moments are too big for a camera."

"I like that," I said. "You go first, and we'll follow."

She said, "Stay close to me, okay? I've only done a little rebreather training, so this is new for me."

"You'll be fine. Just don't hold your breath. We'll be right behind you."

She slipped from the edge of the moonpool and into the subtropical water. I followed and watched closely as she established her buoyancy to remain stable in the water. Her inexperience was showing, but she wasn't plummeting to the bottom or corking to the surface. A little time and patience were all she needed to learn to hover like the ROV.

After a few minutes of fidgeting, we swam from beneath the ship and into the open water of the Sea of Cortez. I rolled onto my back and swam below Masha, looking up at her. Her brilliant smile flashed through the facemask when she spotted me, and I asked, "Are you doing okay?"

Her smile exploded. "This is amazing!"

"Whenever you're comfortable, you can lead us to the ROV. It's still hovering where you left it."

She spun around and surveyed the world around us. "Uh, I'm a little ashamed to admit this, but I don't know where we are or where the ROV is."

"It's all right. I'll lead the way. Just hold the back of my left leg so I know where you are, and follow me. Shawn and Anya will stay behind us in case you let go."

She laid her gloved hand in the bend of my left knee, and we began our swim to the starboard side of the ship.

The ROV came into sight in minutes, and I pointed toward it. "See the lights?"

"Is that the ROV?"

"Yes, it is. You take the lead, and I'll follow."

She moved ahead and swam toward the lights. When we reached the ROV, we hovered and watched for the return of the vaquita. As I slowly turned, I caught a glimpse of Anya in a rare moment of playfulness. She was performing some sort of aquatic ballet while Shawn and I watched in wonder. She was as graceful underwater as she was deadly on the ground. I'd known her for almost two decades, but the dichotomy of Anya Burinkova never stopped fascinating me. When most of the world saw her, they saw a beautiful, elegant woman who likely spent her life on the fashion runways of Paris and Milan, but for the unfortunate few who looked into her face and tasted her wrath, beauty was not the memory they took away from the encounter . . . if they survived.

While trying to look away, I heard Masha gasp. "Oh, my God!"

I spun to see a vaquita resting motionless only a few feet in front of the biologist. Both of them were frozen in a moment of mutual astonishment.

I remained as still as possible and whispered, "Breathe, Masha."

The two mammals moved in unison toward each other as if they were teenagers at the prom, neither knowing exactly what to do next but each knowing they wanted to dance.

I found it necessary to remind myself to breathe as well. Although I'd never have the appreciation for the experience as Masha had, I was conscious enough to recognize it as an unforgettable moment between marine mammal and marine biologist. Perhaps they needed each other equally and neither fully understood their own need for the other. Masha would devote the coming years of her life to saving the species that lay just beyond her fingertips, and the curiosity of the vaquita seemed to meld with its own silent cry for help as it appeared to understand Masha's purpose.

I never remember experiencing a more beautiful moment than the instant when the vaquita waved his tail and propelled himself against Dr. Masha Turner's body. To my surprise, Masha didn't reach for him. She merely relaxed and allowed the vaquita to move around her.

It would've been impossible to know what she was thinking in that moment, but seeing her simply exist beside the vaquita was soul stirring and unforgettable.

After a dozen passes brushing against her, the vaquita positioned himself eye to eye with Masha, and they drifted silently, staring into each other's hearts until a flash of red appeared from below and the vaquita darted for the surface.

Masha stared up as he swam away. She clearly hadn't seen what the vaquita and the three of us saw approaching from the darkened depths. In an instant, a creature wrapped Masha in its tentacles and tugged with all of its might to carry her into the abyss.

I kicked with all my strength, extending both hands to free Masha from the creature's grasp, but I was too slow. She was descending faster than I could dive, and the bottom of the sea lay a thousand feet below. Whatever had Masha was far more capable of surviving in those crushing depths than any human, and no matter how hard I kicked, she was growing smaller by the second.

Shawn, the SEAL, rocketed past me with a gleaming dive knife in one hand and his fins cycling like a machine. The commotion was disorienting and terrifying, but I forced myself to focus and continue downward.

To my disbelief, the vaquita that had played with Masha soared by me as if I were sitting still, his tail pumping harder with every stroke, propelling himself toward the scientist and her attacker.

Shawn's chugging breath echoed in my ears between Masha's shrieks of terror until bodies, noise, and motion collided in a mighty cacophony of sound.

Unsure what I'd do when I reached the scene, I continued kicking as hard as my legs would stroke, paying no attention to my depth and desperately chasing whatever lay beneath me.

I never caught them. Instead, Shawn and Masha passed me on their way upward. Masha's cries of pain and obvious fear echoed inside my mask, but Shawn's determined voice cut through the chaos. "If we black out, get us in the chamber. I don't know how deep we were, but she's going to bleed out if I don't get her back on the boat now."

I turned and followed them back toward the *Lori Danielle* resting peacefully above.

Anya appeared in my periphery. "What happened?"

"I don't know. Something attacked Masha, and Shawn saved her. They were deep, and she's losing blood."

Shawn spoke through powerful breaths. "We're in . . . the moon-pool . . . Make sure . . . you decompress . . . on the way up."

I checked my dive computer. It showed one hundred ninety feet with a max depth of two hundred twenty-eight. We were definitely in decompression depth. Returning to the ship without allowing time for the nitrogen to escape our bodies would leave us with a life-threatening case of the bends.

I took Anya's hand. "We have to off-gas. I was deeper than you, so we'll deco by my computer. Are you okay?"

"Yes, I am fine. Was it shark?"

"I don't think so," I said. "Let's get up to one fifty."

We leveled off at one hundred fifty feet for a short decompression stop before slowly stairstepping our way back to the surface, allowing plenty of time for the nitrogen to leave our tissue. I'd been bent once before, and I never wanted to experience that pain again. I was blown to the surface by an explosion near the Bridge of the Americas at the southern end of the Panama Canal and survived only because of the recompression chamber aboard the original *Lori Danielle*. I didn't want to repeat that ordeal, but everything inside me cried out to know how badly Masha was hurt and what had attacked her.

As Anya and I decompressed together, she continually scanned below us for any sign of a second attacker. "This is very strange situation, no?"

I laughed. "You can say that again."

She said, "Skipper would not approve."

I cocked my head. "Approve of what?"

She smiled through the clear facemask. "Of the two of us being alone together without chaperone."

"We're wearing wetsuits and rebreathers. I'm pretty sure your chastity is safe."

"This is true, but you are still holding my hand."

I let go. "I didn't realize I was doing that. I'm sorry."

"Never be sorry for this, my Chasechka. You may hold my hand anytime you like."

My dive computer beeped and displayed the next deco stop depth, and we slowly rose through the water. Lights appeared from above, and I turned to see the ROV making its way toward us. Although we had no way to audibly communicate with the ship, the ROV's cameras gave us a one-way channel to let the surface know we were alive and well.

Anya and I flashed the okay signal, and whoever was operating the ROV flashed the lights. We spent the next twenty minutes decompressing in slow increments, and the ROV stayed with us through every stop. I couldn't stop imagining Skipper at the controls of the robot and watching every move Anya and I made in our self-inflicted imprisonment in the deep. We didn't need a babysitter, but we had one.

When we finally reached the moonpool, Anya and I climbed from the water and pulled off our masks. A trail of blood ran from the edge of the pool, to the hatch, and into the corridor system of the ship. If Masha was alive somewhere up those ladders, she was undoubtedly in the early stages of severe decompression sickness and possibly dealing with a potentially fatal wound from the closest thing I'd ever seen to an actual sea monster.

Chapter 4
What Is Life

I expected a welcome party in the moonpool when we surfaced, but instead, Anya and I were entirely alone.

She leaned toward me. "What did we see down there?"

I shucked off my gloves and began the long process of peeling my wet suit from my body. "I wish I knew. It all happened too quickly for me to understand any of it."

She ran a finger through a small puddle of blood on the deck. "This is good sign."

"What? How can blood on the deck be a good sign?"

She examined the crimson liquid clinging to the pad of her finger. "People stop bleeding when heart stops beating. She was still alive when she was taken from this room."

"You have a strange way of looking at the world."

"Is not strange. Is only different from your way."

I helped Anya from her wet suit and pulled a towel from the bin.

She took it from my hand and smiled. "It has been many years since you have undressed me, Chasechka. I liked this better when—"

"Stop, Anya. We're not going down that road. That part of our life is behind us, and I'm happily married."

She glanced over each of her shoulders. "Where is happy wife? If you were husband to me, I would not be in state far away. I would be with you to make for you even happier marriage." She stepped from her one-piece bathing suit and dried herself carefully, ensuring every cobblestone on memory lane was laid bare to remind me exactly how dangerous she was without drawing a blade or raising a hand. As I had done so many years before, I once again turned my back on the woman who would've been my undoing had my feet dared to tread on those ancient stones better men than me had stumbled and fallen upon.

What is life if not a collection of opportunities for a man to fail when the better road lay just around the coming bend in the pathway to Hell?

The medics I'd expected when Anya and I emerged finally arrived just in time to see my dive partner sliding herself into a T-shirt and shorts. The professionals they were ignored the show that was never meant for them and approached with stethoscopes in hand. They took our vitals and measured our oxygen saturation levels. I didn't enjoy the penlight shining in each of my eyes, but the exam was routine and reassuring.

I asked, "How are Shawn and Dr. Turner?"

One of the techs draped his stethoscope around his neck. "They're both in the chamber."

"So, she's alive?"

He said, "Her heart's still beating, if that's what you're asking."

"Can we see her?"

"Sure. Follow me."

We made our way to sick bay and stepped through the curtain and into the compartment where the ship's pair of recompression chambers stood side by side. Shawn lay in the first tube with a pillow behind his head and another beneath his knees. He offered a half-hearted salute when I laid a hand on the chamber.

He pointed toward the handset, and I stuck it to my face.

Before I could say a word, he asked, "How's Masha?"

I turned and couldn't believe my eyes. Inside the second chamber, Masha wasn't alone. Her petite frame left just enough room for Dr. Shadrack to lie on his side next to her inside the tube. The remnants of several suture kits were scattered inside the chamber, and a bag of blood hung from a hook at the top of the airtight enclosure.

I pressed the handset to my mouth. "It looks like the doc has her patched up and she's getting a couple units of blood."

Shawn strained to see across the six feet that separated his confinement from hers. "Hmm. I didn't know you could give somebody a transfusion in a chamber. I guess you learn something new every day."

"How are you doing?" I asked.

"I'm fine. We're just crushing some nitrogen bubbles. I should be out in another hour or so."

"How deep did you go?"

"Dive computer said two sixty, but who knows? That thing is only certified to one ninety."

"You saved her life, you know."

"Not yet," he said. "I just carried her body back to the surface. If any saving gets done, it'll be the doc who does it."

I glanced back at Dr. Shadrack as he pressed his fingers against the soft flesh of Masha's neck. A few seconds later, he gave me the okay sign.

"It looks positive," I said.

Anya pulled the handset from my grip. "What was creature who took her?"

I leaned close to hear his response through the ear cup. "No idea. It was dark down there. I just felt around until I found the part that didn't feel human, and I sliced it open. Whatever it was, it let go, and you saw the rest."

"So, you never saw it at all?" I asked.

He said, "I could've been in nitrogen narcosis, but the thing had tentacles like an octopus. Its body didn't feel like an octopus, though. I guess at the time I was more worried about killing it than identifying it."

The sutures on Masha's arm and shoulder told a story of wounds no octopus could create.

I said, "None of her wounds are from your knife, are they?"

"I don't think so. It was a little chaotic, and like I said, it was pretty dark down there. I just wanted to kill that thing and get Masha out of the water."

Anya left, leaving me alone in the room with two of the most sophisticated recompression chambers on Earth. I felt fortunate to have what amounted to a trauma center aboard our ship. Without it, most of my team would've bled out countless times.

Minutes passed at an agonizing pace until a nurse came in and lifted the handset for Masha's chamber. She read off a series of depths and times. I couldn't hear Dr. Shadrack on the other end, but his expression was one of satisfaction. The woman turned several dials, and the needles on the gauges fell to zero. She opened the hatch at the foot of the chamber, and the doctor squirmed out.

He stretched and rubbed his neck. "I hate tight spaces. How are you feeling, Chase?"

"I'm fine. Your medics checked us out, and we apparently passed their screening. How's Masha?"

He helped the nurse pull the gurney holding Dr. Turner from the chamber. "She lost a lot of blood, but fortunately, we had plenty of O-negative on hand. What bit her?"

"I don't know."

He leaned down to inspect the sutured wounds. "It wasn't a shark. Those aren't teeth marks. I've never seen anything like it. Whatever it was, I don't want to get tangled up with it."

"Is she in a coma?"

He said, "No. I gave her a mild sedative so she wouldn't wake up inside the chamber and panic. I thought I'd let her sleep awhile. Her body has been through a great deal of trauma. I'm keeping her on IV antibiotics until we know what attacked her. Nobody on the ship knows more about marine life than she does, so maybe she'll remember the attack and be able to give us some answers when she wakes up."

I helped pull Shawn from the chamber, and he sat up on the edge of the gurney. The doctor checked his vitals and asked a few questions to rule out lingering neurological symptoms.

"I'm good, Doc. Thanks for blowing me back down. I'll come down in the morning so you can have another look."

Dr. Shadrack said, "Light duty for the next twenty-four hours, understand?"

Shawn patted him on the shoulder. "Sure, Doc. Whatever you say."

The SEAL stepped around us and leaned down to examine Masha's injuries. Apparently satisfied with what he saw, he kissed her on the cheek as if she were Sleeping Beauty and headed for the door. "Give me a shout when she wakes up, would you?"

Dr. Shadrack said, "You bet. Get some rest, Frogman."

Whether it was the kiss, fresh air, or the conversation in the room, something pulled Masha from her slumber, and she squirmed.

The doctor stepped beside her and examined her eyes. "How do you feel, Dr. Turner?"

She smiled. "You're the doctor. I'm just the scientist. Is Shawn okay?"

"He's going to be fine," he said. "How do you feel?"

She stared down at the wounds the doctor had sutured closed. "How would *you* feel if you'd just been attacked and dragged to the bottom by a Dosidicus gigas?"

Dr. Shadrack said, "I have no idea how I'd feel because I don't know what that is."

Masha said, "It's commonly known as a Humboldt squid. I've heard rumors about how aggressive they can be around humans, but I never thought I'd find out firsthand. How much blood did I lose?"

"Too much, but we're working on that. We'll have you refilled by morning, but you'll need to stay with us for a while for observation. Do you know anything about the toxicology of the Humboldt squid's mouth?"

"If you're worried about infection," she said, "you can relax. The giant squid's beak is cleaner than your scalpel."

"I doubt that, but even if it's true, I'm keeping you overnight for continued transfusion and observation."

She turned her attention to me. "Did you see what the vaquita did?"

"Yeah. He was Johnny on the spot."

She tried to smile. "From what I remember, Shawn and the vaquita hit us simultaneously, both with the same mission."

"But the vaquita didn't have a razor-sharp dive knife."

She frowned. "Did he kill the squid?"

"Who? Shawn or the vaquita?"

"Either."

I said, "I don't know. Shawn said he sliced it open, so there probably wasn't much left for the vaquita to attack. It is cool, though, that he came to your rescue."

"Shawn or the vaquita?"

"Both."

She tried to sit up, and I could almost see the stars circling her head. Dr. Shadrack encouraged her to lie back down, and she obeyed. "Wow. That was a terrible idea."

The doctor said, "Let's get her off the gurney and onto a more comfortable bed."

The nurse managed the transfer as if she'd done it a million times, and soon, Masha was resting peacefully in a quiet room of her own under the watchful eye of the nurse.

* * *

Evening chow aboard the Research Vessel *Lori Danielle* is less of a naval mess and more of a family dinner around the old kitchen table. My team and I ate, laughed, and even had a few meaningful discussions as the hour passed.

Gator said, "Hey, Shawn. I heard you killed a kraken this afternoon."

The SEAL dismissed him with a wave.

"No, seriously," Gator said. "Was it really a giant squid?"

Shawn swallowed a mouthful of something and wiped his chin. "I guess so. It happened pretty fast, but that's what Masha said it was."

Gator demolished another bite. "How was the chamber ride?"

"Same as always," Shawn said. "I've been bent so many times, I should have one of those chambers installed in my room."

Skipper took the opportunity to chide Anya and me. "You two certainly looked cozy on your decompression stops."

"It was not cozy," Anya said. "It was frightening. Masha had just been attacked, and we were forced to decompress inside water because both chambers on board ship were full. I think maybe you would be also afraid in same situation, no?"

Skipper shot back. "I wouldn't know. No one invited me on the dive."

Gator surprised all of us by snatching a bite of cornbread from Skipper's plate and saying, "I'll go diving with you anytime you want."

Skipper snatched the morsel back from his fingertips. "That's sweet, thank you. But after today's little field trip into the abyss, I think I'll stay on the ship until we're in friendlier waters."

Chapter 5
Moments of Weakness

The Research Vessel *Southern Cross* lay abeam the *Lori Danielle* when the sun melted beneath the western horizon from my vantage point on the weather deck, and it was a facepalm moment for me. The Cuban Cohiba hooked in my index finger had yet to drop its first ash, so abandoning my smoke wasn't in the cards. Going in search of the person responsible for not calling off the *Southern Cross* would be a fool's errand since I was smoking with the responsible party and I was all alone.

Dr. Masha Turner was in no condition to transfer ships. For that matter, she probably needed some time ashore in a bed that didn't roll with the ocean's swells. I'd been on Earth long enough to have learned my lesson about making decisions for women, so I held my position, stuck the Cohiba back in my mouth, and hummed an old Michael McCloud tune about moments of weakness.

Sneaking up on a mostly deaf, one-legged man on the deck of a ship in fifteen knots of wind is something a marching band could pull off, but a sense stronger than sight or sound told me I wasn't alone. I checked across my left shoulder first, and my pursuer slipped to my right and plucked the fifty-dollar cigar from my mouth with her long, thin, Russian fingers. Instead of reacting, I relaxed even further into my chair and hummed the second verse.

She said, "I thought I would find you here. I can join you, yes?"

I didn't want to look at her. I wanted my cigar back, and I wanted to be alone, but it was quite likely that neither of those things were in the cards for me.

She exhaled the first stream of aromatic white smoke from between pursed lips. "Ballet dancers, tobacco, and AK-forty-sevens are only things communists produce well."

She wasn't wrong, but I wasn't in the mood. "What do you want, Anya?"

"I want to give to you apology for what I did today inside moon-pool. It was childish and foolish, and I will not do it again."

I pulled a new cigar from my shirt pocket, punched one end, and toasted the other. On the first draw, the absurdity of the moment took me, and I choked on the combination of laughter and Cuban smoke.

"Are you okay?" Anya asked.

I gathered my composure. "Yeah, I'm good. I was just thinking about how ridiculous it is for someone who looks like you to apologize for being naked."

"Someone who looks like me? Does this mean you still think I am beautiful?"

I examined the veins of the tobacco wrapper. "There's not a man on this planet or any other who doesn't think you're still beautiful."

She said, "This is opinion based only on appearance and not on reality, no?"

I finally turned to face her. "Do you ever wish you hadn't given Penny part of your liver after the accident?"

She grabbed the cigar that would've fallen from her lips when her jaw dropped. "No, of course I do not wish this. Please tell to me you do not wish it either. This is terrible thing to say."

"It came out wrong," I said. "No, I don't wish that either. I guess what I meant was . . . Ah, forget it. Let's not ruin a nice evening with what might've been."

She said, "It was cruel thing for me to say today when I asked where happy wife was. I should not have said this to you. I am also sorry for this."

I didn't answer, and she didn't probe. We sat side by side, staring into the night, each of us probably wondering what the other was thinking.

Finally, I pointed toward the *Southern Cross*. "See that boat? She's costing me almost ten grand a day. Masha is supposed to be on that ship, and we're supposed to be steaming for the shipyard in Pascagoula."

I could count the number of times I'd heard Anya laugh on my fingers and toes, but one more episode was added to the tally that evening. "You forgot to tell other ship to turn around and go home, no?"

"That's exactly what I did."

"Is okay, Chasechka. You were distracted. I have sometimes this effect on men." She lowered her voice to a husky whisper. "I like that I still have this effect on you. Good night. I believe I will go to bed and have beautiful dreams of what might have been."

After twenty more minutes alone, I checked my watch. Being in the same time zone as Penny was a rare treat, so I pulled my phone from my pocket.

She answered on the fifth ring. "I wasn't expecting to hear from you tonight. Is everything all right?"

"It's good to hear your voice," I said. "We had a little excitement today."

I told her about the vaquita and the giant squid.

"That sounds terrifying. Is Masha going to be okay?"

"I think so. Things will grind to a halt until she's back up and running, but she's young and fit. She'll bounce back in no time."

She said, "I'm sure you're right. Listen, I have a thing at eight, so I need to run."

"A thing?"

"Yeah, it's a studio function. I really have to be there."

"I understand, but before you go, when do you plan to be home? It'd be nice to see you. It's been too long."

"I really have to go, Chase. Call me tomorrow, okay?"

"Sure. I love—"

But the line was dead.

I finished my cigar and watched the world turn from dusk to dark. The RV *Southern Cross* lost her shape and morphed into a collection of lights half a mile away. As I tried to remember the lines of her profile, I wondered if the people I loved would watch the same thing happen to me when the sun finally set on my life. Would I fade into that formless collection of distant light and waft farther away with every passing sunset?

As I pressed my palms against the arms of my chair to stand, a gentle hand rested on my shoulder, and the baritone voice of my moral compass said, "Mind if I join you?"

I'll never understand how Singer knew exactly the right time to sit down beside me, but I feel sorry for anyone who doesn't have a Singer in their life.

"Please do."

He nestled into the chair that had been Anya's moments before and let out a long sigh. "It's been a long time since we crushed any bad guys or blew anything up. I think the natives are getting restless."

"Our natives?" I asked.

"We're not exactly the save-the-whales type. What we're doing is fascinating for the big brains like Mongo and Dr. Turner, but the rest of us need a trigger to press."

The fingernail of the moon appeared as a low cloud drifted past. "I don't go in search of work very often, but I could give Clark a call and see if he has anything coming up for us."

We sat in silence for a moment before he said, "I'm not suggesting you go in search of something new. I just don't want any of us to forget who and what we are."

There was no way for me to know the lesson I was about to learn, but I knew beyond any doubt a lesson was coming.

When he held up a finger and closed one eye, I watched as he moved the tip of his finger from one spot in the sky to the next several times.

"Is that some kind of sniper thing you're doing?"

He dropped his hand. "You know, scientists say we can look through space and time for almost fourteen billion years, and most of the stars we see right now burned out millions of years ago. All we can see is the lingering light from those stars still plowing its way through the cosmos."

"You don't believe that, do you?"

He smiled. "No, but what I believe or what scientists think they can prove is far less significant when the ultimate question is asked."

Inside, I was an impatient second grader dying to know what the ultimate question was, but I suppressed my near anxiety and waited.

He said, "Sooner or later, it always comes down to the same question. What is the nature of the creator of all that exists?" Singer gave me a moment to ponder before continuing. "The academics say we're a collection of mass and energy—impossibly small atoms bound together by an invisible force they can't explain. To those folks who are educated beyond their capacity to comprehend, humanity is a meaningless speck on an endless canvas of the universe." He sighed. "What a shame it would be if they were correct."

The lesson apparently reached its intermission, but it was far from over. Singer's greatest talent was the use of time, and that talent was brilliantly on display that night.

After I'd stared into the heavens until everything around me melted away, the sniper pulled me back into his palm. He said, "I'm thankful they're wrong. Mankind isn't a speck. We're the reason everything else exists. It's all an endless gift from the God who loves us and asks for nothing more than adherence to a few simple desires He has."

"Commandments, right?"

His smile broadened. "That's a man-made term, my friend. Commands must be obeyed. Imagine Captain Sprayberry giving an order to the bridge crew and everyone around him ignoring the order."

I played along and tried imagining the chaos such insubordination would cause on the bridge.

Singer said, "There would be consequences, right?"

I chuckled. "I wouldn't want to be on the wrong end of those consequences."

He didn't laugh. Instead, he motioned toward the *Southern Cross*. "What if the captain came out on deck and yelled an order to the bridge crew on the other ship?"

I wasn't sure where we were headed, but I said, "They would ignore him because he's not their captain."

He let that weighted moment hang in the air until finally saying, "I guess that means we just have to remember which captain we serve and what He expects of those of us who rely on Him to be faithful to us . . . because loyalty requires trust."

I sat in silence as his words flowed like honey through my mind and across my soul.

Singer stood and laid a hand back on my shoulder. "Don't be distracted by shiny, temporary things around you. And most of all, don't forget that the captain you and I chose to serve is never short on loyalty . . . nor faithfulness."

Chapter 6
Reindeer Games

I sat alone in the dark, pondering Singer's wisdom, until the weight of my responsibility to those who rely on me for loyalty was too much to ignore.

My first stop was my cabin for a shower and a toothbrush, but sick bay was only minutes behind my ritual to rid myself of the Cuban smokey smell. When I stepped through the hatch, the bay was mostly dark. One nurse sat in front of a computer with her face aglow in the light from the monitor.

"How's Masha?" I asked.

The nurse glanced up. "She's awake and alert. She even ate some of her dinner. One of your guys is in there with her right now. I can't remember his name, but he's the pretty one with the guitar."

"That would be Shawn."

Her smile turned mischievous. "Yep, that's the one."

Not wanting to disturb their visit, I headed back for the corridor, but Masha's delicate voice stopped me in my tracks. "That's the bravest thing I've ever seen."

As I took a step closer to her curtain, I didn't feel good about eavesdropping, but I just had to hear Shawn's response.

"That's not bravery," he said. "Somebody had to help you, and I just happened to be in the right place at the right time."

"What do you mean it's not bravery?" she said. "You could've died trying to save me."

"I'd rather step into the light knowing I died trying to save a team-mate than spend the rest of my life living with the regret of not trying."

"That's pretty much the definition of bravery," she said.

"I've seen bravery, Masha, and what I did today doesn't qualify. I once watched a twenty-one-year-old, third-class petty officer stand be-tween a wounded SEAL who was dying on a rock in Afghanistan and hold off a dozen Talabani fighters while a corpsman fought to stabilize that shot-up SEAL behind him."

Despite my embarrassment of listening in, there was no chance I'd walk away without hearing the rest of that story.

He said, "When that steely-eyed frogman ran out of bullets, he turned the gunfight into a knife fight, and he died with sixteen bullet holes in his chest and nine dead jihadists on the ground all around him. The corpsman took out the other four with his sidearm in one hand while he kept working on the guy on the rock."

Masha gasped. "And you saw the whole thing? Why didn't you help them?"

Shawn cleared his throat. "Because . . . I was the SEAL on the rock with my guts hanging out of my body."

"Oh, my God," Masha cried. "I don't know what to say."

"Most people think bravery is not being afraid, but that's not it. Bravery is being afraid but still jumping into the fight because what you're fighting for is bigger than the coward that lives inside all of us."

I silently slipped away and lay in my bunk with Shawn's definition of bravery ringing in my head.

* * *

Morning came earlier than I wanted, and I skipped breakfast. My to-do list was longer and stronger than my hunger pangs, so I went to work.

The captain stuck a cup of coffee in my hand when I stepped onto the bridge. "Morning, Chase. What's the good word?"

I motioned through the porthole toward the *Southern Cross*. "I guess we don't need your buddy anymore."

The captain tilted his head. "What are you talking about?"

I took a sip. "Masha is stuck in sick bay for a while, convalescing from her ordeal in the water yesterday, so she won't need a ship for a while."

He checked his watch. "How long have you been awake?"

"Just a few minutes. Why?"

He laughed. "Your convalescing marine biologist is already aboard the *Southern Cross*, and the crew is headed over to install the infrastructure for our ROV."

"Did I miss a day or something? Dr. Shadrack said—"

Captain Sprayberry cut me off. "I don't know what happened to that girl overnight, but whatever it was, she's back on her feet and raring to go this morning. She looked like a brand-new woman when we carried her across in the tender just after sunup."

I said, "I guess Shawn planted a seed with his dissertation on bravery, and it looks like it found a little fertile ground."

"I don't know what you're talking about," Barry said, "but that's nothing new. We'll be ready to weigh anchor as soon as the brainiacs get the ROV up and running."

I checked the open expanse of water between us and the *Southern Cross*. "Do you think I could get a ride over with the technicians?"

The captain pulled his radio from his belt. "Tender One, Bridge."

The tender pilot's tinny voice crackled through the radio. "Go for Tender One."

"Stand by for one additional body. He'll be down in three minutes."

"Roger, Captain. Tender One is standing by."

Barry motioned toward the boat bobbing in the water beside us. "Go. You've got three minutes before they leave without you."

I stepped down into the tender, and we crossed the thousand yards separating the ships in no time. I climbed aboard and asked the deckhand if I could see the captain.

He called the bridge, and minutes later, I was shaking the captain's hand.

I said, "Chase Fulton. Pleasure to meet you, Captain. Thanks again for doing this for us."

He said, "No problem. We were sitting around twiddling our thumbs when Barry called, so we appreciate the work."

"Did anybody brief you on the mission?" I asked.

He said, "I've just come from a meeting with your Dr. Turner. She's impressive, and it doesn't hurt an old man's eyes to look at her, either."

"She's all business," I said. "So, I'd appreciate it if you'd keep your crew from gawking as much as possible."

He laughed. "I'll do my best, but we all have our limits."

"Thanks again," I said. "Would you mind if I went down to see her before we shove off?"

"Sure. I'll take you down there. It's easy to get lost on this old tub. I think Rube Goldberg must've designed the interior."

I followed him to the ROV control room several decks below the bridge, where I found Masha overseeing a collection of technicians.

I said, "Good morning. Ambitious much?"

She smiled up at me. "Don't be upset. I feel a lot better this morning, and I can't bear the thought of leaving the vaquita."

"I get it," I said. "How does Dr. Shadrack feel about you jumping ship?"

She looked sheepish. "I guess he didn't talk to you yet, huh?"

"No. Was he supposed to?"

"I think he was going to ask permission to jump with me."

"Is that so?" I asked.

"That's what he said."

I checked the time. "How do you feel about him staying with you?"

She shrugged. "I don't think it's necessary. They have a helicopter, so I could be in San Diego in two hours if I crash."

"In that case," I said, "I'll deny his request. But only on one condition."

"Name it."

"You have to report in at least once every twenty-four hours until Dr. Shadrack is satisfied you're back to full strength."

"I can do that," she said.

"In that case, I'll say farewell. Let me know if you need anything. I'll have an estimated timetable for the refit in a few days, so I'll keep you posted on the progress."

Moving gingerly, as if everything still hurt, she gave me a delicate hug. "Thank you for all of this. And I mean everything. You don't know what it means to me."

"You just figure out how to keep those vaquitas alive, and we'll take care of everything else."

* * *

When I climbed back to the weather deck, the *Lori Danielle* had moved to within feet of the starboard rail of the *Cross*, and the ROV was flying through the air, suspended below one of the L.D.'s deck cranes. The operator lowered the robotic rover onto the fitted cradle, and a pair of deckhands disconnected the rigging.

The next cycle of the crane delivered a crew basket, and I climbed aboard. The operator had a little fun, at my expense, when he let out ten feet of cable at full speed when I was halfway between the two ships. I jumped and grabbed two hands full of steel pipes that made up the basket frame.

When I finally touched down on the deck, I looked up to see Kodiak at the controls of the crane and yelled, "You'll pay for that one."

"The look on your face was worth it."

The professional crane operator standing a few feet away threw up both hands. "He threatened to shoot me in the ear if I didn't let him run the crane. I don't know him well enough to know if he was kidding."

I said, "Neither do I. You probably made the right call."

I dragged Kodiak from the crane's cab and onto the deck. "You're an idiot. You know that, right?"

He jabbed a finger through the air toward the other side of the ship. "Me? Look what they're doing."

I couldn't do anything except shake my head at the spectacle.

We crossed the deck to find the rest of our team throwing aspirin tablets into the air and shooting them with a BB gun.

Singer was on the deck a few feet away, so I said, "I guess you were right. We do need a mission. I'm proud of you for not letting them suck you into their reindeer games."

The sniper scoffed. "I don't know what you're talking about. I'm the reigning world champion with thirteen in a row. None of those jokers can even get close."

Gator held out the Red Rider in my direction. "Come on, boss. You know you want to."

I snatched it from his hand. "Where did you even get a BB gun?"

Mongo said, "From the armory. Where else?"

I ran six in a row after one miss and tossed the gun to Disco. "You're the resident elder. Can you please get your kindergarteners under control while I find something for us to do?"

He said, "Not my monkeys . . . not my circus."

I headed for the combat information center, where I could make a secure call to my handler in search of something for my monkeys to do.

To my surprise, he answered on the first ring. "Thanks for calling back. Make it the meat lover, large with thick crust, please."

"I'm not the pizza guy," I said, "but I am starting to feel like a ringmaster. Please tell me you have something for us to do."

He stammered. "Oh, hey, Chase. I was expecting somebody else."

"Yeah, I figured that. We're losing our minds out here. Can you scratch something up?"

"That's not really how this works," he said. "I don't have a honey-do list laying around."

"Lying," I said.

"No, I'm not. I'm telling the truth. Where are you anyway?"

I said, "We're about to head south out of the Sea of Cortez and through the canal. We'll literally take anything you've got. I admire what Hank's granddaughter is doing out here, but it's not our bag. We're itching for a fight."

"Let me see if I can shake some trees and see what falls out. I can't make any promises, but I know how dangerous bored operators can be."

"Thank you. You're a lifesaver. Would you believe they're skeet shooting with aspirin and BB guns?"

He asked, "Is Singer still on top with thirteen straight?"

"Just find us something to do, would you?"

Before he could come back with some witty retort, Skipper sucked in a sharp breath a few feet away.

"What is it?" I asked, rolling toward her.

"It's a distress signal from Hunter's sat-phone in the Amazon."

Chapter 7
The Land of Death

Stone W. Hunter came into my life at precisely the moment I needed him most, and from the instant we first shook hands, we shared a bond few people are ever fortunate enough to experience. He'd been an Air Force combat controller who'd been wounded so badly during a classified mission that the Air Force retired him and paid him a life-long pension. As a combat-wounded special operations veteran, he was quickly hired by the Naval Criminal Investigative Service as a civilian officer at the Kings Bay Naval Submarine Base, where he rose through the ranks in meteoric style.

I met him when I returned from one of the most agonizing missions of my career—a mission that changed my life forever. I pieced together a hodgepodge gang of the most unlikely characters to rescue what remained of a team of civilian operators who'd been abandoned at the top of the frozen Khyber Pass, on the border of Pakistan and Afghanistan, by a paramilitary contractor trying to save themselves the embarrassment of dealing with a failed mission. The men I pulled from that mountaintop—Clark, Mongo, and Singer—became the core of the team I'd lead and operate with on countless battlefields in every corner of the world.

Hunter hadn't been one of the operators left to die on that mountain halfway around the world, but he stepped directly into the only void my new team had. He knew more about the use of airborne assets on a battlefield than anyone I knew, but that was far from the limit of his tactical prowess. He was strong, fearless, and demanding of himself and those around him, and until I met Shawn the SEAL, he was the most capable underwater operator I could've imagined. The friendship Hunter and I forged was ironclad. I trusted him with my life more times than I could count, and he never faltered.

When an assassin's bullet tore into his neck and shoulder, Hunter survived when any other man would've given up the ghost. The horrific wound stole him from the carnal battlefield and deposited him into a war of eternal consequence. Believing that nothing short of God Himself could've kept him alive, he devoted his life to unwavering service to the Highest of Powers.

Only months before our operation involving the relocation of the vaquitas, Hunter joined a team of missionaries and trudged into the wilds of the Amazon to bring the gospel to tribes of men, women, and children who'd never seen a white man. I had offered him full access to our arsenal to build enough kits to train and arm his fellow believers so they could protect themselves from whatever the jungle could throw at them. He refused the offer and soldiered on behind the shield of the Cross instead of body armor and full-auto rifles.

If the distress call were authentic, my friend and brother was in more trouble than I was capable of understanding.

"Where is he?" I demanded.

Skipper was typing as quickly as her fingers could move and chewing through the barrel of an ink pen between her teeth. She hit a key and lifted both hands. "I can't tell you where *he* is, but his sat-phone is at five degrees, fifteen point nine minutes south, and sixty-two degrees, thirty-seven point nine minutes west."

I rolled close beside her. "Show me."

She plotted the position on a map of the Amazon Rainforest, and the coordinates fell just northwest of a place called Terra da Morte.

I said, "Does that mean what I think it means?"

"Yeah, it does. That's Portuguese for Land of Death."

A white-hot spear pierced my heart, and I fought back the rage boiling inside me. "I told him to take a kit. I practically begged him."

Skipper asked, "Do you want me to call the phone?"

"Yes! Call it."

She pulled on her headset and typed a series of numbers. Twenty seconds later, she said, "Nothing."

"How about satellites? Can you task one or a dozen to scour the area?"

She sighed. "Maybe, but that's the densest rainforest on the planet. All the satellites will show you is the treetop canopy."

"What about thermal or IR?"

She shook her head. "Same story. They simply can't see through the trees."

"Do we have any assets in the area?"

"That's a question for Clark."

That's when it occurred to me that I was still holding the phone in my other hand. "Clark? Are you still there?"

He said, "It sounds like you've got something to do now."

"How much did you hear?"

"Everything. Have Skipper shoot me the coordinates, and I'll see who we have in the area."

She sent the lat/long, and Clark said, "Give me twenty-four hours."

"Are you serious?" I barked. "Twenty-four hours? Hunter could be dead in twelve."

Clark's calm tone came back. "Hunter could be dead already. I'll do my best, but expect twenty-four hours."

I squeezed my fist until my knuckles turned white. "Are you authorizing the mission, or are we on our own?"

Clark said, "It depends on the assets in the area. If we have a team who can be there in hours instead of days, it's theirs."

"Fair enough," I said. "In the meantime, get us a charter out of San Diego or Yuma for St. Marys. We're gearing up to go get him."

He said, "I can't just snap my fingers and call up a charter flight across the country. I don't have that kind of authority."

"I do," I said, and turned to Skipper.

She nodded. "I've got a Hawker jet in Napa. They can be on the deck in San Diego in ninety minutes."

"Make it happen," I ordered, and I pressed the phone back to my face. "We're moving on this, Clark. If he's alive, we're getting him out of there, and if he's not, I'm making damned sure his body is buried in American soil."

He let out a long breath. "Bill the charter to the Board and keep your sat-phone turned on."

"That's more like it. Consider us operational. We'll answer the phone around the clock." I pressed the button to ring the navigation bridge.

"Bridge, First Officer."

"This is Chase in the CIC. We need authorization for air ops right now."

Without hesitation, the second-in-command said, "Air ops are approved. What else do you need?"

"That's it. Tell the captain to proceed as planned through the canal, but Sierra element won't be aboard."

"Roger. I'll pass the word. Whatever you're doing, Chase . . . Godspeed."

My next call was to Gun Bunny, and she was somehow even more reactive than the first officer. "Moving now, Chase. How many?"

"The whole team."

She said, "I'll call the captain to authorize—"

"It's already done. We'll meet you on the pad."

Skipper's hand was hovering over the 1MC, and I gave the nod.

She pressed the button, and her voice echoed through the ship. "Attention on deck. This is the combat information center. All Sierra elements move immediately to the helipad with passports. This is not a drill."

She secured her console and pulled a pair of Pelican cases from a locker, handing one to me. We weren't the first pair to the helipad, but we weren't the last. Disco and Gun Bunny were conducting the preflight inspection while the hangar crew maneuvered the five-thousand-pound flying machine from the hangar bay and onto the helipad.

By the time the Huey was unchained, every member of the team had already selected their perch for the two-hour flight. Skipper had her cases open and the mobile command center up and running before the rotors began their turn.

From the cockpit seats with Gun Bunny, Disco turned to peer into the cabin and held up a pair of fingers. "Two things. Where are we going, and are we ready?"

I would never ask my team for blind obedience in any situation. Every one of them was superior to me in a thousand ways, but the fact that they were aboard, strapped in, and ready to fly before knowing anything about our destination or mission spoke volumes about the trust they had in me. The weight of that trust was often more than I believed I could bear, but when the bullets flew in both directions, the devotion, respect, and faith we had in each other, and the team as a whole, combined to make us one of the world's finest small-unit fighting forces.

"San Diego International, and let's fly!"

As we climbed away from the *Lori Danielle*, I spoke into the mic of my headset. "Give me a thumbs-up if you can hear me."

Seven thumbs went into the air, and I started my briefing. "Less than twenty minutes ago, Skipper received an electronic distress signal from Hunter's sat-phone in the Amazon Rainforest. Attempts were made to contact him, but we were unable to establish comms. Even though he moved on to a higher calling, he's still one of us, and he always will be. We're going to get him."

I paused and glanced out the door toward the Sea of Cortez three thousand feet below. "Anyone who isn't in, you're welcome to step off the chopper now."

That got a muffled chuckle, but the steely eyes of my operators said they were in and that there would be no limit to the extent we would go to bring our brother home.

Skipper held up a finger from the back of the cabin.

I said, "Go, Skipper."

"I've prearranged customs and immigration clearance in San Diego."

"We never checked into Mexico, so we're still on American ground according to our passports."

She said, "That's what I mean. It's all taken care of. We can move immediately from the chopper to the Hawker. I'm tracking them now, and they should arrive forty minutes ahead of us."

"Just enough time to refuel for the quick turn," I said. "Any updates on the sat-phone?"

"The time between signals has increased to fifteen minutes. That means the phone is trying to preserve battery power. If it was fully charged when he set off the distress call, it's possible it could transmit for thirty-six hours, but that's a best-case scenario."

We flew in silence, and the looks on the faces inside the chopper said the coming mission was rolling inside each operator's head. We had no way to know what to expect, but there was only one acceptable outcome.

We came to a hover above the taxiway at San Diego and then taxied to the ramp beside the only Hawker jet in sight.

Gun Bunny curled a finger at me.

I stuck my head into the cockpit, and she asked, "If you'll give me the coordinates, I'll find a way to get there in the Huey."

"That's not a bad idea," I said. "Skipper will send you the coordinates, but stand by until the ship reaches Panama. We might be able to acquire air assets once we're in-country."

She nodded, and I turned to see an empty cabin behind me. My team was already headed up the stairs and into the Hawker.

When I climbed aboard, the team looked like square pegs in round holes. They did not look like the typical passengers aboard a luxury private jet.

One of the pilots climbed the stairs and gave us a once-over. "Which one of you is Elizabeth?"

Skipper raised a hand from the back. "That's me."

The pilot threaded his way down the aisle and took a seat beside our analyst. Although I couldn't hear their conversation, I had no doubt they were discussing the use of our private airport in St. Marys. Her answers apparently satisfied him, and he made his way back toward the cockpit.

His expression said he was a little concerned about our check bouncing, but he said, "We have a flight attendant who'll be here in ten minutes."

I cut him off. "We don't need a flight attendant. We need to be airborne. We're late for a board meeting."

He mouthed the words "board meeting," and I waved him toward the cockpit. "I've got the door. Get us rolling."

Chapter 8
Crazy Old Friends

Living in the world that is mine, I spend a great deal of time entirely alone—sometimes, even when I'm surrounded by people I love. The first hour of the eastbound flight was another such moment.

I spent the first half of the session trying to imagine the conditions Hunter had been living in prior to whatever happened that drove him to force his fingers onto the preassigned combination of buttons that would initiate the distress signal. He was the type of soldier who would ignore his own gaping wound to treat a bee sting on a teammate. *Selfless* is the only word in our language that comes remotely close to describing Stone W. Hunter.

I knew little about his mission, or as he referred to it, his calling. He told me about the remote locations in which he would serve alongside other missionaries who were devoted to the ultimate good of sharing the truest of love with people who would otherwise never encounter Christians. He mentioned building schools, providing rudimentary medical care, and sharing the gospel with primitive people who spoke no English and knew nothing about the world beyond their minuscule patch of the rainforest.

My parents performed such generosity throughout Central and South America, but theirs was laced with a thread of espionage. Hunter's service bore no intrusions from the concerns of geopolitical squabbles. Perhaps his work, combined with mine, is what my parents did, but I'll never know with certainty.

Of the possible scenarios that came to mind, the one that returned most often to the forefront of my supposition was a bit of mutiny in the jungle. Perhaps the indigenous people whose souls he was there to win turned on him and his brothers. Had they been slaughtered at the hands of those who couldn't understand why they were there? Had they crossed a line of belief the people couldn't accept?

Until I could put eyes on the situation or speak directly with him, there was no way for me to know the situation on the ground. Time and distance weren't the only barriers between my team and Hunter. The Amazon Rainforest consists of two and a half million square miles. If we could search a hundred square miles per day, it would take us nearly seventy years to cover the ground. Our only clue of where to begin was the electronic ping of a piece of delicate electronics in an agonizingly harsh environment.

The second half of the flight was spent in a far less speculative pursuit. I studied the maps Skipper provided and familiarized myself with the routes of the major rivers surrounding the location of Hunter's sat-phone signal. The region was vast and covered with vegetation that was as foreign to me as the dark side of the moon. What time I had logged in the jungle was limited to Central America, and the Amazon would be an entirely new area of operation.

It was time to count assets and liabilities. I fell solidly into the latter category, but I wasn't the only trigger-puller on our particular carnival ride.

I squeezed Mongo's arm. "How much jungle time do you have?"

He glanced back at me. "A year or so. Why?"

"I've got none."

"No worries," he said. "Just don't eat anything that looks edible, and assume that everything down there wants to eat you."

"That's encouraging."

"Talk to Kodiak. He was an instructor at the Jungle Warfare and Survival School for a while."

I slid into the seat beside the retired Green Beret. "I hear you've got a little experience underneath the canopy."

He wiped his face. "Yeah, I taught at the schoolhouse down there for a while."

I said, "I'm going to need a crash course. The jungle isn't my forte."

"Don't worry, boss. We'll take care of you. I've known some good ones, but Singer's the finest tracker I've ever met. They used to say he could track a falcon in the clouds."

"That little skill set might come in handy."

He asked, "Is Clark coming with us? He's got some good contacts down there, including some DEA guys. They know that place better than the natives."

"He's not coming, but I'll hit him up for some introductions."

Kodiak said, "If all else fails, I know a guy who burnt out down there and never came home. He was a SOG operator with the Special Activities Division for the Agency, but they say he lost it and walked away. I knew him when he was a green-suiter. We went through Ranger School together, and he was crazy even back then. I saw him chew a rattlesnake in half for biting him during the mountain phase."

"Sounds like my kind of guy," I said. "Do you know where he is now?"

Kodiak laughed. "*He* probably doesn't even know where he is, but I can put out some feelers."

"Do it. The plan may change, but right now, I'm looking at flying into Manaus. That's the closest big airport to Terra de Morte, and I'm hoping we can pick up some air assets there."

He said, "You're taking a sackful of American cash, right?"

"Never leave home without it."

Somewhere over Western Georgia, the pilots pulled the throttles back and began the descent. That was my cue to rattle Clark's cage.

"Hey, College Boy. I've got some good news."

"Let's hear it. I could use a healthy dose right now."

He said, "This is an officially funded rescue/recovery operation. The Board is behind you all the way, but there's a caveat."

"Let me guess. The U.S. Government will disavow any knowledge of our operation should we get busted."

"You're getting good at this gig," he said. "What do you need from me?"

"Do you want to come?"

He scoffed. "Not a chance. I'd just slow you down. What else do you need from me?"

"A big bag of cash would be nice, and we could use some local air assets if you can round them up."

Clark said, "Do you remember Leo, the crazy chopper pilot in Costa Rica?"

"How could I forget?"

He said, "I'll see if I can find him. I've got a couple other off-the-books contacts in that part of the world who might be able to get their hands on a flying machine. You're taking Disco, right?"

"Absolutely."

"Good. Between you and him, you should be able to fly anything I can dig up."

"I plan to hit the ground in Manaus. They've got plenty of concrete for the Gulfstream. How hard will it be to get a pallet of bullets and bangers into the country?"

He laughed. "Remember that bag of cash you requested?"

"That's what I thought."

"What's the timetable?" he asked.

"I plan to load out as soon as we get to Bonaventure and then get some sleep. It's a long flight, and I don't want Disco nodding off."

"Aren't there two pilots in the front seat of that Hawker you're on?"

"Yes. What about them?"

"Maybe they're type-rated in the G-Four. It never hurts to ask. They don't have to know what they're carrying. Get them to fly you down there, and then pay for a couple of first-class tickets back to the States. That'll cut eight hours off your trip. Besides, you're not going to sleep anyway."

"You've got a point. I'll throw some bait out there and see if they bite."

He said, "Great. Call me when you know more."

We touched down at our private field that had once been the municipal airport. It couldn't support itself financially, so we bought the airport and hired the manager. The property I inherited from my great-uncle abutted the airport, so we absorbed the real estate into Bonaventure and put our own padlocks on the fence.

The captain slithered from the cockpit and reached for the lavatory door.

I said, "We've got a real bathroom in the hangar with a good shower if you don't want to cram yourself into that phone booth."

He chuckled. "Thanks. I think I'll take you up on that."

I followed him down the stairs and unlocked the walk-through door into the hangar. As the lights came to life, bathing the pristine interior with a yellow glow, the pilot let out a low whistle. "That's a Grey Ghost. Is she yours?"

"She is, along with every other airplane on the property."

He said, "Nice. I used to fly the Ghost when I was in uniform."

"No kidding? Are you current?"

The captain nodded and pointed back toward the Hawker. "Patrick and I just went through recurrent training down in Savannah. We're type-rated on the whole Gulfstream line. The company's got a dozen or so, and we get to fly them occasionally."

I motioned toward the restroom. "The head's back there. Make yourself at home."

I lingered, waiting for him to come back, and when he did, I asked, "Do you have a gig after this one?"

He checked his watch. "I'll have to give the company a call, but I think we're off for the next four or five days. You never know what's going to pop up like your mission. I thought we were finished with the trip last night."

"Would you be interested in a little moonlighting?"

He cocked his head. "What kind of moonlighting?"

"I guess you figured out we're not really late for a board meeting."

He threw up his hands. "That's none of my business. As long as your credit card doesn't get declined, we don't ask any questions."

I motioned toward the *Grey Ghost*. "We need to be in Brazil in that airplane when the sun comes up. We've got a couple hours of work to do before we're ready to go, but the other pilot and I will need some sleep before we're fit to fly."

He lowered his chin. "You want to hire us to fly *your* Gulfstream to Brazil."

"That's right. What's your hourly rate?"

He clicked his tongue against his teeth a few times. "I'll tell you what we'll do. If you let us store the Hawker in your hangar while we're gone, we'll fly you down there for a grand a piece, plus an airline ticket home."

I stuck out my hand. "Do you take cash?"

He shook it. "Doesn't everybody?"

"I think we're going to get along just fine. I'm Chase Fulton, by the way."

"Name's Eric King, but call me Sky."

"Sky King . . . I dig it. I've got a couple nondisclosure agreements for you and Patrick, if you don't mind."

"NDAs, huh? This isn't illegal, is it?"

I waggled a hand. "Technically, maybe, but not for you. I'm the operator. You're just the contract drivers."

He narrowed his gaze. "No drugs. No human trafficking."

"Nothing like that, I assure you."

He still didn't appear convinced. "Guns?"

I drew my Secret Service credentials and opened the wallet for him.

He huffed. "Ah, that explains it. I think I underbid the contract."

"Don't worry, Sky. The federal government is an excellent tipper."

Chapter 9
Remember Benghazi

Don Maynard, our airport manager, showed up with the fuel truck. "Evening, Chase. You need to stop bringing home stray airplanes. We're running out of hangars."

"Hey, Don. Top off the Hawker, if you would, but we're not keeping her. She's just here for a conjugal visit. They'll be back to get her tomorrow night."

He climbed down from the truck. "Whatever you say, boss. Give the crew my number, and I'll meet them whenever they want."

Patrick and Sky caught a nap in the hangar office while my team and I loaded the Gulfstream for our excursion into the South American jungle. Kodiak managed the packing lists, and everyone was tired of hearing the phrase "mosquito netting" after the twelfth time he mentioned it.

"Go ahead and leave your net behind. You'll listen next time."

Needless to say, the nets went on the pallet. Unsure of our local transportation assets, we packed a range of gear from light infantry kits to air cavalry gear. Movement in the jungle would likely be on foot more than anything else, but leaving essential gear behind wasn't a mistake my team would make.

Sky came down the stairs just as Kodiak slipped the pallet through the cargo door of the *Ghost*. He said, "Should I look at that?"

I said, "You should not. The less you know, the better."

"Am I going to see you guys on the news?"

"Not if we do it right," I said. "Either way, you signed your life away, so you can't talk about it."

"The bigger the tip, the tighter my lip."

I slapped him on the back. "In that case, I'll make sure we sew them shut. Are you ready to fly?"

He studied the *Ghost* and then the Hawker he was responsible for. "We did agree on bringing her inside, right?"

"We did. Don will take care of that after we take off. In the meantime, I'll find Disco and get him to give you a cockpit orientation."

We towed the plane from the hangar and replaced it with the chartered Hawker. Disco took Sky and Patrick through the avionics and systems of the Gulfstream, and we loaded up.

Skipper called from the third-floor operation center at Bonaventure. "The op center is up and running. How's the loadout going?"

"We just sealed the doors, and we'll be airborne in ten minutes."

"Did you call Penny?"

"She's busy," I said.

"Too busy to tell her man she loves him before he runs off into the jungle for God knows how long? I'll call her."

"That's not necessary," I said. "I'll do it."

It rang five times, and I expected to hear her voicemail pick up, but it was Penny. "Hey, sorry . . . I was in the shower."

"So, you're out of the shower now and dripping wet, right?"

She giggled. "Wish you were here."

"Me too, but duty calls. Before we get to that, though, how was your studio thing?"

"Huh?"

"The studio thing you had to go to last night."

"Oh, that. It wasn't a big deal. What did you mean by 'duty calls'?"

"We got a distress call from Hunter in South America. He's in trouble, and we're going to get him."

She said, "What kind of trouble? Is he okay? What's going on down there? Where in South America?"

"Now, *that* sounds more like my wife. We don't know for sure. We can't get in touch with him. We just know he set off the distress signal on his sat-phone, and we're going to find him."

"That sounds serious. When are you leaving?"

"It is serious. Hunter wouldn't have hit that button if it hadn't been life and death. We're taxiing out now."

"Is the whole team going?"

"Yes, everybody except Clark."

"I guess that means Anya, too."

I grimaced. "Yes, she's going."

"I see. Okay, well, call me, okay?"

"I don't know what kind of comms we'll have on the ground, but I'll keep you posted when I can."

"You'll be able to talk with Skipper in the op center, won't you?"

"Hopefully. The jungle is pretty dense, so our sat-coms won't always have a clear sight of the sky."

"Do you have a plan?" she asked.

I never remembered her asking that question in the past. "You know how these things go. We don't always know what we're up against until we put our boots on the ground."

"But you're taking everything you need, right?"

"I believe so."

She hesitated a moment. "Why do you need Anya?"

I wanted the right answer to pop out of my mouth instantly, but it didn't happen. I didn't have the right answer. I didn't even have a decent answer. "Listen . . ."

"No, I get it. Be safe, okay?"

"I promise. Love you."

She whispered, "Yeah, I love you, too."

* * *

Disco sat in the cockpit jump seat during the taxi and takeoff, but five minutes after the wheels were in the wells, he ambled into the cabin. "They're going to be just fine up there. It's obvious they know what they're doing."

"That's reassuring," I said. "Maybe we can all get a couple of hours of sleep."

He said, "Listen. I know you're worried about Hunter, but look at it this way. If you were in that jungle and in trouble, who would you want coming to pull your butt out of the fire?"

I scanned the passenger cabin of the Gulfstream. "All of you."

"Exactly. Now, get some rest, and we'll hit the ground running. We're pretty good at this sort of thing."

* * *

We touched down six hours later at Manaus Airport, on the Amazon River, in the very heart of the Brazilian jungle. Although it was technically winter, just three degrees south of the equator, seasons meant very little. The air was heavy and seemed to cling to my flesh like a parasite desperately clawing to feed on my very existence until nothing remained.

Kodiak wiped a film of sweat from his brow just seconds after planting his boots on the tarmac. "Well, ain't this nice in the middle of the night? I can't wait for the sun to come up."

My sat-com chimed. "Go for Chase."

Skipper said, "I see you made it to Manaus. How is it?"

"Like a jungle paradise," I said. "We just hit the ground, so give us a few minutes to get our bearings, and we'll check in with you."

"Way ahead of you," she said. "Look for a black SUV."

"What are you talking about?"

"Just do what I tell you for once."

As my eyes adjusted to the limited light of the parking apron, a pair of headlights temporarily blinded me as a vehicle approached. I held up a hand to shield my face, and the driver dimmed the lights. The vehicle rolled to a stop, and the driver's window came down.

A bearded man wearing a backwards baseball cap leaned through the window. "Welcome to Brazil, boys. Need a lift?"

I turned away and asked Skipper, "Did you arrange a ride for us?"

She said, "You know I'm always going to take care of my boys. He's with the U.S. Consulate. Lock up the plane, get in the car, and listen when he talks."

I chuckled. "Aye-aye, Skipper."

Approaching the SUV, I stuck out a hand. "Thanks for showing up."

He ignored my hand and motioned to the back of the vehicle. "Throw your gear in the back and hop in."

"There's ten of us," I said.

He said, "So, leave off the gear and snuggle up. Are the pilots staying?"

I shook my head, and he said, "Good. That means there's only eight of you. There's a crew van that'll take them to the terminal. Your analyst already arranged a return flight for them."

I stood there wondering if I should ask to see some identification, and the driver said, "Ah, I almost forgot." He tossed a roll of something toward me. "Set your brakes and tape up the hatches."

I caught it and glanced down at the duct-tape-sized roll of bright-yellow tape. Once everyone was out of the *Ghost*, I climbed back aboard, set the parking brakes, and slid the red sign into the window, telling the linemen the plane couldn't be towed. Back on the stairs, I secured the hatch and taped all four seams. My Portuguese was weak, but even I could translate the heavy black marking against the yellow backing: "United States Diplomatic Vehicle – Do Not Disturb."

The Seal of the U.S. Department of State was a nice touch, and I tucked the roll into my rucksack.

Once inside the SUV, the man behind the wheel glanced up into the mirror. "Who's in charge?"

I said, "It looks like you are at the moment."

"Good answer," he said. "I'm Blimpy from the consulate. I'll get you guys inside the walls, and we'll talk about how we can help."

The remainder of the ride was spent in silence. Perhaps Blimpy was just a driver, or maybe he understood better than anyone how conversation outside the consulate walls made for flashing neon signs on the local grapevine.

We drove through a sallyport and beneath an awning.

Blimpy pointed to a door manned by a Marine with an M4 across his chest and business in his eyes. "Through there. Wait for me at the metal detector."

We dismounted, and the Marine studied me carefully. "Good morning, sir."

"Good morning. I didn't know we needed to guard the American Consulate in Brazil. These guys are our friends, aren't they?"

The Marine never changed expressions. "Remember Benghazi, sir?"

He held the door for us, and as instructed, my team and I waited for Blimpy at the metal detectors.

When he arrived, he waved us through, but no one moved. Blimpy hesitated and said, "Come on. Follow me." We looked up at the metal detectors, and he said, "They're not on. Let's go."

Had they been on, they would've sounded like an orchestra of electronic warning signals, but they remained silent as we passed through the scanners.

Blimpy led us down a corridor and pointed to the left. "Restrooms and snack machines are down there. If you have to go, do it now and meet me in the conference room at the end of the hall."

Everyone turned left, and we pushed our way into the men's room. Anya remained in the middle of the pack.

Shawn was first. "Is this cool, or are we about to be tossed out of the country?"

"It's good," I said. "Skipper set it up. We just need to make sure we know what to ask for."

Mongo said, "Do we want a local escort?"

"If he's solid, we do. Does anybody speak Portuguese?" Heads shook, and I said, "That alone is reason enough to request somebody with language skills."

Kodiak said, "They won't do it."

"They won't do what?" I asked.

"They won't give us any physical support. Remember what Clark said. If we get caught, nobody's coming to get us. If the consulate provides a translator, they're admitting we're sanctioned, and they're not going to do that."

"You're probably right," I said, "but let's see what we can get from this guy. Any ideas on who and what he is?"

Mongo said, "My guess would be a spook. Diplomats don't wear beards and backwards baseball caps."

We took turns making use of the facilities, and as directed, met Blimpy in the conference room.

He took the floor as soon as we were seated. "I'm missing a good night's sleep for this, so let's get down to business. You're here to find some missing missionaries, right?"

I nodded, and he said, "That would make you Chase, right?"

I continued nodding.

He said, "Right. Anyway, we haven't received any official requests from any organization indicating they've lost their missionaries. That isn't rare, though. A lot of times, we aren't notified when those guys show up in-country. If we don't know they're here, we can't be expected to get involved when they don't make their flights back to the States."

Singer spoke up. "The organization our friend works with is called the WORD Foundation."

Blimpy said, "Give me a minute."

He pulled out a tablet and typed something on the screen. "They're registered with us. If our records are up-to-date, they have twenty-four personnel in four operations in the country. Do you know which of the four ops your man is on?"

I said, "All we know is that he sent an electronic distress signal from these coordinates." I slid my tablet across the table to him, and he studied it carefully.

After several glances between his tablet and mine, he looked up. "And you're certain he's with the WORD Foundation?"

Singer said, "Absolutely certain. My church and I provide financial support for them. They're a solid organization."

Blimpy held up his hands. "Easy. I wasn't accusing anyone of anything. I just want to make sure I know as much as possible so I can give you the help you need. I'm familiar with WORD. They're one of the good ones. We get some real whackos down here sometimes."

Singer said, "I'm sure you do, but the Worldwide Organization of the Redeemer's Disciples isn't one of them."

Blimpy typed on his tablet again. "I didn't know it was an acronym. Thank you for that." Singer nodded, and Blimpy asked, "Has anyone notified WORD of this situation?"

It was my turn. "Our analyst has been on the phone with them. Can we get her on the line?"

Blimpy said, "Sure. Does it need to be a secure line?"

"Not for us," I said, "but if it'll make you more comfortable, we have that capability in the op center."

He laid his tablet on the table and slid mine back to me. "Analysts and op centers? You guys aren't missionaries, are you?"

Singer narrowed his gaze. "Everybody who's doing God's work is a missionary. We just happen to get most of our confessions at gunpoint rather than inside a wooden box with a priest."

Chapter 10
Old Rangers Never Die

Blimpy leaned back in his chair and ran his hand across his forehead and quickly receding hairline. "I picked the wrong week to extend my tour of duty."

We gave him the time he needed to gather himself, and he said, "Let's go off the record for a minute. Are you guys okay with that?"

I said, "I didn't know we were on the record."

"Good. We're not. Here's how I see this thing. Your buddy, the missionary, hasn't always been a missionary, has he?"

Singer and I shook our heads in stereo.

"Let me take another stab," Blimpy said. "You guys aren't officially with the WORD Foundation, are you?" Our headshaking continued, and he said, "You're going after him, and all you have is a lat and long where he set off the distress signal."

We stopped shaking our heads, and Blimpy took a long, deep breath. "We're back on the record, okay?"

We continued nodding, and I was growing more amused by our one-sided dialogue by the minute.

Blimpy said, "I've received no notification that the United States Department of State has any knowledge of the alleged missing man being in the country and working as a missionary or in any other capacity for any recognized organization. Therefore, the ambassador is unable to offer any official support for any operation concerning the alleged missing man. Is that understood?"

As more of an attempt to see how far we could stretch it, we continued nodding, but Blimpy shot us down. "I need you to answer that one out loud, fellas."

"We understand," I said.

With the apparent formalities complete, the man unbuttoned his cuffs and rolled up his sleeves, revealing a tattoo that read "Rangers Lead the Way."

He said, "In case you hadn't guessed, we're off the record again. Now, what do you boys need from an old shot-up door-kicker?"

The stars Singer mentioned aboard the *Lori Danielle* had just aligned for my team and me, and I wasn't going to waste the moment. "We need wheels, air assets, possibly a boat or two, and a number to call if we get out there and the sky falls on us."

"Take it easy," Blimpy said. "I'm not Santa Claus, but I've got a few friends. Please tell me you have sat-phones, because there's no cell service sixty seconds outside the city."

"We're good on comms," I said.

He pulled out a small pad and slid it across the table. "Write down these numbers, but if anyone from DC starts asking questions, you didn't get them from me."

He rattled off four names and six numbers, and I pocketed the small square of paper.

Blimpy stood. "For what it's worth, good luck out there. It's a big jungle, and everything goes bump in the night."

He led us back down the corridor to an exit door that didn't boast metal detectors. While holding the door for us, Blimpy took our sniper's arm as he passed. "You're Singer, aren't you?"

The Southern Baptist sniper said, "I am."

Blimpy almost smiled. "Thought so. We went through the high-angle sniper course together a lifetime ago. You're a legend, man. Don't get yourself dead out there, Ranger."

Singer gripped the man's hand. "Old Rangers never die. They just regroup and strike harder."

Blimpy pointed toward a heavy, six-wheeled truck with a canvas top resembling an old Deuce and a Half, but the vehicle wasn't American. "A few gold diggers got themselves crossed up with some bad boys out in the trees a couple months ago. That was their vehicle."

Singer asked, "Was it the bad boys' or the gold diggers'?"

"It belonged to the gold diggers. The bad boys have much better wheels. That thing isn't on anybody's books, so if you can get it started . . ."

Eavesdropping wasn't an exercise I took pleasure in, but the information I gleaned from their exchange gave me a little hope that we weren't as alone as I believed a few minutes earlier.

Getting the old truck started wasn't a challenge for my team. Fifteen minutes after obtaining permission from a U.S. State Department official, we drove away in our newly requisitioned, jungle-ready, six-wheel-drive behemoth. The vehicle's canvas cover made the job of unloading the *Grey Ghost* privately a simple exercise in bucket-brigade operations.

"How much do you think this monster weighs?" I asked.

Mongo was first to offer an educated guess. "We pulled around fifteen hundred from our pallet, and we go about fourteen hundred as a team. The truck is a little bigger than a Deuce and a Half, so I figure around fifteen to sixteen thousand pounds. With a little padding for safety, that puts us just under twenty thousand pounds. You're worried about the ferry, aren't you?"

I chuckled. "What's it like carrying that big brain of yours around all day? It has to get heavy, right?"

He leaned against the side of the truck. "You know how muscle weighs more than fat? It's kind of like that."

I said, "Let's go see if we can sink a ferry boat with our muscled-up brains and ten tons of party favors."

Before leaving the airport, I called the op center back at Bonaventure to update Skipper.

She sounded groggy. "Hey, Chase. Sorry, I forwarded the phone and took a little nap."

"Everybody needs sleep," I said. "I'll keep it brief. We're in-country and already making friends. We acquired a heavy truck, and the gear's out of the airplane. Did you happen to book us a place to sleep tonight?"

She yawned. "No. I didn't know if you'd hit the ground running."

"No worries. We'll take care of it. I'll check in tomorrow."

Her yawning continued. "You mean later today, right?"

"I guess so. Sleep well."

Rather than parking our beast of a truck in some hotel parking lot, we camped out in the hangar with the *Grey Ghost*. It wasn't luxurious by any means, but it was dry and mostly devoid of mosquitos.

My team and I were up with the sun and headed for the river. Disco drove, because that's what he does—be it a truck he's never seen or an airplane he knows like the back of his hand.

After arriving at the ferry terminal, we took our place in line. We were far from the largest machine in the queue, so my concerns about *weight* were replaced by concerns about our *wait*. The line was long, and it appeared that only one ferry was operating.

As I studied the map against the terrain and waterways in front of us, I was intrigued by the convergence of the black water of the Rio Negro and the brown, muddy Solimões. The two didn't blend well and seemed to cling to their own identities and distinctive colors as they slowly merged to form the mighty Amazon.

We waited through two cycles of the ferry before a second boat finally joined the first and doubled the capacity of the only means of crossing the river. It cost fifty American dollars for us to cross to Ponto da Banana, and I couldn't quash the feeling that we'd been dramatically overcharged.

The relatively bustling city behind us vanished, and our world became a narrow dirt road lined on each side by pure jungle. The map called it Road 319, but calling it "a road" at all was a stretch. If there were a legal speed limit on the dirt trail, it wasn't posted, but it wouldn't matter. Our high-speed, low-drag machine seemed to be capable of nothing greater than fifty kilometers per hour.

The first several miles of the adventure involved being passed by every manner of vehicle, from motorcycles through semis and everything in between, but as we traveled farther southwest, we quickly found ourselves alone. From a security perspective, seeing no one else made us easy to locate and identify, but aside from the consulate and a pair of charter pilots, no one outside the team had any reason to expect us to be in South America. What I couldn't predict, though, was the aftermath of a run-in with the very people who never expected to see us.

We made a stop at what seemed to qualify as a gas station in the middle of the Amazon and squeezed every drop of fuel we could into the truck.

I prayed my Spanish was close enough to Portuguese to get my point across when I asked the man who was mostly asleep if I could buy fuel cans.

He stretched and furrowed his brow. "*Galão de gasolina?*"

I smiled. "*Sí!*"

"*Quantos?*"

The language barrier cracked a little more every time one of us recognized a word, and I said, "*Toda.*"

I hoped the feminine Spanish for *all* was good enough, but our first roadblock popped up. Confusion covered his sun-worn face. "*¿Todos?*"

That's close enough, I thought, so I nodded, and he waved a hand for me to follow him.

I obeyed, and we stepped through an opening in the back of the structure that could roughly be described as a door. He pointed to a stack of at least two hundred gas cans, and even though we didn't share a language, we laughed.

I held up two fingers from my left hand and made a zero with my right. "*Veinte.*"

He continued laughing. "*Sim, vinte.*"

After some sort of complex exchange-rate calculation, I paid six hundred eighty-four dollars for two tanks and twenty cans of fuel I hoped wasn't contaminated.

Back on the so-called road, the truck smoked no more than it had before refueling, so my contamination concerns were at least temporarily assuaged.

Four more hours into the drive, Disco let out a sigh that could mean nothing other than exhaustion, so I stepped up. "I'll drive a while if you want."

"Oh, believe me when I say that I definitely want." He rolled the truck to a stop without concerning himself with leaving the single traffic lane.

Gator flipped aside the canvas flap separating the cab from the bed. "Is everything okay?"

I said, "We're trading seats. The old man needs his afternoon nap."

The entire team dismounted and stretched while trying to work out the knots in their backs from riding in the back of our ultra-modern conveyance. As if we'd planned the stop, we planted ourselves on the edge of the road and sliced into our heavy plastic MRE pouches. Negotiations ensued, and soon, most of us had a meal we could live with. Cramming calories into our bodies was essential, but MREs would never qualify as a quality dining experience.

Gator studied a lump of something pink in his hand. "What do you think a ham loaf really is?"

That got a hearty chuckle from the rest of the team, who'd worn our country's uniform and eaten ham loaves all over the world.

Mongo said, "If you're not going to eat it, toss it over here. That's one of my favorites."

Gator gave the lump a toss, but it slipped from his fingertips and landed in the roadside canal of black water a few feet in front of us. Before Mongo could scold our youngster for a pitiful toss, something exploded from beneath the obsidian surface of the water and devoured the ham loaf.

The team retreated as one, and someone yelled, "Was that an alligator?"

Mongo dusted off his pants. "No, it was probably a black caiman.

There aren't any gators in the Amazon River basin except for the one we brought with us, and he has an unnatural hatred of the beloved ham loaf."

Anya spun, staring into the vegetation on the opposite side of the road. "Quiet!" Everyone turned in her direction, and she said, "Something is not right. We should take cover or maybe leave."

"What do you think it is?" Kodiak asked.

Anya eased backward toward the truck. "Is people trying to be quiet. We should go."

I headed for the driver's door, but Kodiak planted a palm in my chest. "No, sir. You're the VC, and the VC doesn't drive."

I rounded the front of the truck, making my way to the appointed vehicle commander's seat while the remainder of the team headed for the back. The instant my boot hit the fuel tank step, rifle fire cut through the skin and canvas of the truck.

I dived for the steep embankment leading down to the caiman's watery realm, but I wasn't alone. Four other bodies slid from the road, digging their boots into the loose dirt of the bank. Everyone stopped before reaching the water, and I searched for the remaining two souls with whom I'd just eaten lunch.

Chapter 11

New Sheriff

I found Kodiak and Singer tucked behind the truck's tires. Nobody seemed to be leaking blood, but a quick scan of my team's posture told me that each of us made the same critical mistake when we climbed from the truck for lunch. Everyone was holding a pistol, but there wasn't a rifle in sight. We had just put ourselves in a position that was impossible to defend with whatever an alligator is called in South America at our backs, and at least a pair of rifles advancing from our twelve o'clock.

We weren't wearing our sat-coms or body armor, but regardless of our liabilities, we had no authority over the decision to fight. We were *in* the fight. All that remained was determining how much pain we were going to inflict on our attackers.

Glancing down the line of commandos to my left, I found Anya at the opposite end. I gave the signal to flank and advance, and she moved like a cat while I stumbled like something far less graceful. We put a hundred yards between each of us and the truck before sprinting across the road and disappearing into the dense vegetation.

I kicked myself a dozen more times for working without comms and especially for abandoning our rifles in the vehicle. If I survived the coming minutes, I would never make those mistakes again.

Believing Anya knew the tactics I wanted to employ, I made the ninety-degree turn and slowly crept toward her. She should've been doing exactly the same some two hundred yards away. If we could close on our aggressor's flanks, regardless of their firepower, our likelihood of winning the fight would increase exponentially.

After every step, I froze and listened.

The jungle is not a serene, quiet environment. It's full of life most people will never see, and most of that life makes a lot of noise. When the jungle goes quiet, something has gone terribly wrong, and in that moment, the world around me was silent.

As the sound of my heart pounded in my ears, I begged for a breaking twig or a sliding foot, but silence remained until two 9mm rounds from a hundred yards ahead pierced the air. The pair of shots set off a cacophony of rifle fire directed toward the north. Anya had either fired on the aggressors or fired simply to draw their fire. From my position, there was no way to know which was true, but I took full advantage of the noise to increase my pace and close the distance between me and the shooters.

Two more pistol rounds sounded, and I aimed into the ground and squeezed off two of my own. At the very least, the apparent crossfire would confuse our enemy enough to cause them to make a mistake—a mistake on which we would capitalize.

As the rifle fire continued, the sound of our truck coming to life joined the orchestra. I could almost see the black smoke pouring from the exhaust pipes as the engine roared at maximum RPM. The sound of the tires leaving the road turned to the beautiful noise of trees being crushed, brush being ripped from the jungle floor, and mud flying in every direction.

To my great delight, I recognized the reports of extremely familiar rifles sending 5.56mm full metal jackets through the air at 2900 feet per second, and I retreated to leave the lane of fire wide open for the rest of my team.

The rifles quieted, the engine noise fell to idle, and a pair of commanding voices replaced the previous chorus. "Get down! Get on your face! Down! Down! Down!"

I learned long ago that commands given at sufficient volume tend to leap the language barrier. It was likely the aggressors turned victims were surrendering in perfect form.

I yelled, "Moving from the south!"

Anya answered with, "Moving from north."

Singer's perfect baritone echoed through the trees. "All secure. Advance at will."

Stomping my way through the brush until the heavy truck came into sight, I grinned like a kid at Christmas. I don't know who'd been driving, but the rest of the team had decorated the tailgate with body armor and assaulted the unknown force with a homemade Bradley fighting vehicle advancing backward. Four men lay on the ground with fingers laced behind their heads, and my team stood over them like conquistadores, but without the funny helmets.

I rolled the first man onto his back with my boot and knelt beside him with the muzzle of my pistol pressed perfectly into his right eye. "Why were you shooting at us?"

I wasn't expecting the language in which he answered me. "It was an accident, man. We thought you were somebody else. Seriously, dude. It was a mistake."

American, I thought. *Interesting*.

I pressed harder. "It was no accident nor mistake. It was the worst decision of your life. Now, who did you think we were?"

He trembled. "It was just a mistake, that's all."

I yanked the pistol from his eye and sent a round into the dirt an inch from his ear. He bucked and yelled like a terrified child.

"The next one goes through your skull. *Who* did you think we were?"

One of the men a few feet to my right said, "We thought you were the prospectors. You're in their truck."

I forced my victim back onto his stomach and stuck a knee in the new talker's back. "What prospectors?"

He said, "Ever since that show came on, everybody thinks they're going to come down here, do some digging in the dirt, and make a fortune in gold."

"So, you thought we were gold diggers?" He sighed, so I pressed my muzzle to the back of his head, forcing his face deeper into the mud. "I've run out of all the warning shots I brought with me, so I recommend you answer me when I ask you a question."

He mumbled something, but with his mouth an inch deep in jungle mud, I couldn't understand a word.

I grabbed a handful of hair and yanked his face clear. "So, you think it's okay to shoot at prospectors?"

"We weren't trying to kill you. That's why we shot at your truck and not you. We were just trying to scare you away."

"That must make you the local sheriff. Is that right?"

He thrashed in a wasted effort to free his hair from my grip. "No, we ain't no sheriff, but we've got a claim, bought and paid for. Down here, you have to defend your claim or else . . ."

I leaned close. "Or else you end up facedown in the mud answering questions from people like me?"

"I told you we didn't know it was you. We thought—"

I slammed his face back into the ground. "No, hotshot. That's the problem. You *didn't* think. Where's your vehicle?"

A third man spoke up. "You're not taking our vehicle."

I looked up at him, but Anya raised a finger. "I will take care of this one."

She unlaced his hands from behind his head and said, "You are right-handed, yes?" He jerked away from her, so she slipped the blade of a fighting knife beneath his eye. "Hold still and tell to me which is strong hand."

"Okay, I'm right-handed."

"In this case, I will be kind and only destroy left hand."

She pinned the man's left wrist to the ground under her knee and pressed the tip of her blade between the second and third bones on the back of his hand. "You will now tell to me where is vehicle or I will make you one-handed man."

"Take it easy. Look, we clearly made a terrible mistake."

The next sound out of his mouth was not a word in any language I'd ever heard. As Anya's knife pierced the man's hand, his brain exploded with pain he was incapable of comprehending.

The Russian patted the back of his head as if he were a frightened child. "Shh . . . Quiet now. Is okay. Is almost over."

He raged, and the last member of the trigger-happy foursome leapt to his feet and sprinted from the small clearing and to the east.

Our all-American free safety from K-State laughed. "I'll catch him. You guys go ahead and have some fun. I'll be back before you know it."

The kid was fast, and every day, he became a little more dangerous to anyone who raised a fist in front of him.

The man with the newly pierced left hand convulsed on the ground, and our favorite Russian continued consoling him. "It does not hurt that bad. Is fear confusing your brain. Tell to me where is truck, and maybe I will kill you quickly. If you do not tell, I will have so much fun with you."

"You can have the truck. You can have whatever you want. It's a quarter mile behind us. Just let us go . . . please."

Anya withdrew the knife from the man's hand and rolled him onto his back, slicing a long ribbon of his shirt as he turned. She wrapped his bloody hand in the cloth and said, "You should have doctor look at hand. Is more than just flesh wound. And thank you for truck." She kissed him on his forehead as if sincerely thanking him for the vehicle.

I can only imagine the gesture was meant to further confuse the man, and it appeared to work.

He clasped his wounded left hand with his right and groaned, "Who are you people?"

Anya gently patted his cheek. "We are new sheriff in town."

The sound of a diesel engine whistling through the trees made me believe Gator's runner was heading for home, but I was wrong. The massive vehicle thundered through the trees until coming to a stop with its tailgate only inches from ours. The man who'd wasted an attempt at escaping was tied to the driver's mirror with 550 cord bound around his wrists.

Gator hopped down from the truck. "I found him. Oh, and their truck, too. He just wanted to get a little exercise, so we went for a run and did a little light sparring."

"It looks like you won," I said.

He shrugged. "I don't remember the last time I lost."

Anya had a little fun tormenting the four men while the rest of us moved our gear from the old shot-up truck and into the shiny new one.

When the reloading job was done, Mongo cleaned and sutured the man's wounded hand. "That'll do in case you don't have time to see your family doctor right away."

I dusted off my hands. "Well, I guess that's goodbye, guys. It was nice to meet you."

"Wait a minute," one of them said. "You can't just leave us out here."

I said, "Yes, we can. You've heard the phrase 'To the victor go the spoils,' haven't you? You started this fight, and we won. That means we're the victors, and your truck is the spoil. There is one last thing I'd like to know before we go. That is, if you don't mind. I wouldn't want to inconvenience you guys."

"What? What do you want to know?"

I stepped in front of the apparent former leader of the pack. "Before I let Miss Moscow over there gut you like pigs, I'd like to know if you've seen any missionaries running around out here in the jungle."

Chapter 12
Key Man

The man stared up at me with absolute confusion all over his face. "Missionaries? What are you talking about?"

"We've played this game already," I said. "Your buddy over there is deaf in one ear because he wanted to dance instead of answer my questions. The other idiot with a hole in his hand made the same bad choice. Surely you're smart enough to learn from their mistakes."

He blinked several times in rapid succession. "What missionaries? I don't know what you're talking about."

I grabbed a fistful of his hair, yanked his head backward, and shoved my pistol beneath his chin. In a low, menacing voice, I said, "If the next words out of your mouth aren't information about the missionaries I'm looking for, I'm going to paint the sky with the contents of your skull and give your buddies a chance to answer."

"Okay, okay. There aren't any tribal villages southeast of the road."

I pressed the muzzle another inch farther into his flesh and a mile further into his psyche. Suddenly, he was compliant and full of useful information.

"All the missionaries are northwest of the road. They're all on that side, not over here."

"And where are these bought-and-paid-for gold claims you say are yours?"

He stretched onto the tips of his toes from the pressure of my muzzle beneath his chin. "We've got three. One over here, and two on the other side."

I relaxed a little pressure and let him settle back to his feet. "And whose name are the claims registered in?"

"South-Wind Ventures. Tommy Southard and Gary Windham."

"And are you either of those people?"

He groaned. "No, they're both in Arizona at corporate."

"Do they know you're shooting at people in South America?"

He didn't answer, so I sent him back onto his toes. His ability to speak made a miraculous return. "No . . . I mean, I don't know."

My team and I had suppressed the assault, gained overwhelming control over the enemy, assessed and treated the wounded, and progressed to the inquisition phase, yet I was still unable to draw a picture of the organization we were up against. I needed a little time and a lot more information to put it together.

I kept my position of power but turned to Singer. "Collect IDs and get your Ranger buddy on the phone."

The man balancing on the muzzle of my Glock protested. "Wait a minute. We don't need to involve anybody else. We can work this out."

I laughed. "I don't think you understand how things *work out* after you shoot at us. You've probably figured out by now that we're not a soft target like your gold-digging friends, but it's clear you're not fully grasping the gravity of your situation."

Gator, Kodiak, and Mongo searched each of our prisoners and collected everything they had in their pockets, including their IDs.

Singer stood with his sat-phone poised to make the call to the consulate.

I said, "Wait sixty seconds."

Singer nodded, but he didn't drop the phone.

I threw a knee shot into my new friend's most delicate target, and he buckled. With a little encouragement from my left hand, he continued to his knees, and I said, "You've got forty-five seconds to tell me everything you know. Don't waste it."

He caught his breath. "All I know is my company has millions of dollars invested in mining gold in this godforsaken jungle, and they pay us to keep that operation moving. We deal with anybody who gets in our way. That's our job. We're just doing our job."

"You've still got twenty seconds. Are you sure there's nothing else you want to tell me? A story about some missionaries, perhaps?"

"I don't know anything about any missionaries. I swear."

"Okay. Now you have a choice. Do you want to deal with the American authorities, the Brazilian authorities, or us?"

He pleaded, "Don't do this to us, please."

I laughed again. "Not doing this is off the table. You took care of that when you fired your rifles at us. You sealed your fate with that first trigger pull, so pick one. Americans, Brazilians, or us?"

"What are you going to do to us?"

"I'm going to tie you to a tree and feed you pieces of your rifles until you bleed out. Then, you can be a nice meaty buffet for all the hungry wildlife, like those black caiman on the other side of the road."

"You can't do this, man."

I scanned the area. "Let's see. There are eight of us and four of you. We've got all the guns, and your hands are zip-tied behind your backs. Remind me one more time what it is I *can't* do."

"Look, man. Our company, South-Wind, they'll pay a ransom. We're valuable to them. Call them. You'll see. I'll give you the number."

I pulled my sat-phone from a cargo pocket. "Let's have it."

He rattled off an Arizona number while I dialed.

Several seconds later, a pleasant-sounding lady answered. "Good morning. South-Wind Ventures."

I pressed the speaker button so our new best friends could hear the conversation. "Connect me to Tommy Southard or Gary Windham."

"I'm sorry, sir. Mr. Southard and Mr. Windham are both in a meeting. May I take a message?"

"You may," I said. "You may walk into their meeting right now and tell them you have a man on the telephone who needs to talk with them about the murders of four of their employees in Brazil."

She gasped. "Oh, my God. You can't be serious."

"Tommy Southard or Gary Windham, now!"

The woman shrieked. "Get Mr. Southard, immediately."

A few seconds passed before a confident voice blasted from the speaker. "This is Tommy Southard. Who are you?"

"Well, hello there, Tommy. I'm the guy your men tried to kill about half an hour ago. Thankfully, they failed. Let me read you their names."

Mongo held each ID in front of my face, and I read off the full names and addresses for each of the four men. "Are these your guys?"

"Who are you? Did you say murders?"

I said, "Listen to me, Tommy. I need to know if these four men work for you. Yes or no?"

"Yes, they work for our company. Did you say they've been murdered?"

"Their murders are currently in pending status, but rest assured that I will not hesitate to upgrade that status to active in a heartbeat. These guys seem to think you'll pay a ransom for them. If they're as important as they think they are, you've probably got a key man policy on them. What's the max payout on that policy, Tommy?"

"Slow down," he said.

I cut him off. "You seem to be just as ignorant as your guys on the ground. I'm the guy with all the guns and all the cards. How much are your four invaluable employees worth?"

"You listen to me—"

"That's not going to happen, Tommy. You'll do the listening, and you'll speak only when I ask you a direct question. Got it? That's a direct question, Tommy."

"Fine. I've got it. What do you want?"

"I want a number. All four men are alive and well, for now. What's that worth to South-Wind Ventures?"

"How do I know you're not going to kill them anyway?"

"Oh, my. That sounded like a question from you, and I already established the rules, Tommy."

I motioned for Mongo to shove one of the men to the ground, and I held the sat-phone beside my pistol. The bullet left the muzzle at supersonic speed and quickly buried itself harmlessly in the soft earth.

Tommy yelled, "No!"

"Calm down," I said. "We have to learn to obey the rules. Now you have three men remaining. How much are they worth?"

"How much do you want?"

I lowered the phone beside my pistol and squeezed off another round. "We're down to two. I need a number, Tommy."

He said, "We don't have a policy on them."

"Was that supposed to be a number? It didn't sound like a number. Maybe I misheard you. Was it a number, Tommy?"

"Look, we can work something out."

I fired a third shot from within inches of the sat-phone. "They already tried the work-something-out strategy. You've got one man remaining, and I'm dialing his family right now so they can hear you murder him."

"Stop this! In thirty-six hours, I'll have two teams of commandos scouring every inch of that country for you, and you'll be dead before the sun goes down tomorrow night."

"What a shame," I said. "Go ahead and send them, but make sure they bring their own body bags. I'm running low, and I don't want to have to ship them back to Arizona in fifty-five-gallon drums. Say goodbye to the last man standing, Tommy."

I pulled the trigger a fourth time and ended the call.

Three of the four men on the ground at my feet were crying, and the fourth wore the look of a man standing on the edge of the abyss.

I holstered my pistol and said, "Boys, your company just sold you down the river. All four of you. It would appear that your bargaining chip just vanished into thin air. I'm not an unreasonable man. I'm really not. And I'm going to prove it to you."

I had their attention, so I motioned for Singer to step up. He did, and I laid a hand on his shoulder. "I want you to talk with these men about their relationship with God and what happens when they leave this world. Would you do that for them and for me?"

The sniper said, "Yes, sir."

"Good. The rest of us will be over there sitting on the tailgate. If anybody tries something stupid, we'll consider that an express ticket to the afterlife."

I led the remainder of the team away and held a powwow beside the trucks while our guru ministered to the damned.

I spoke softly. "Tell me what you think. What's going on here?"

To my surprise, Anya was first to speak. "You are really going to kill them, yes?"

"No, I'm not going to kill them, but they're probably in for a fate almost as bad. I plan to turn them over to the consulate. I assume the Brazilian authorities will handle it from there, but we need to get as much as possible out of them before we surrender them."

"Agreed," Mongo said. "It's pretty clear we've wandered into the Old West down here, and those guys are the James Gang. They may not be the ones who made Hunter disappear, but I'd bet dollars to dimes they know something about it."

Kodiak nodded. "Agreed. I think we can call off the threat posture. You've convinced them they're going to die, and Singer's driving that point home. There's no reason to keep pushing it. I say we separate and question all four of them. When we've got four stories, we'll compare notes and see what passes the smell test."

"I like it," I said. "Let's work in teams of two. Singer and Gator, Kodiak and Anya, Mongo and Disco, and I'll take Shawn."

"Good cop, bad cop?" Shawn asked.

I said, "No, I agree with Kodiak. There's no reason for a bad cop. In fact, I think we should dangle a deal in front of them if it looks like they're on the verge of giving up something good."

Anya took the floor again. "What is plan when we are finished with them if you are not going to kill them?"

I said, "When Singer is finished, we'll have him call the consulate and arrange for us to surrender these guys. He's got the in with the Ranger, so I think we should nurture that relationship."

I posted Gator and Kodiak to hover over the detainees while I pulled Singer from the prayer meeting. "How'd it go?"

Singer said, "We've got three believers and one atheist."

"In that case," I said, "I want the atheist."

"Yeah. Me, too."

"Give your Ranger buddy a call and tell him where he can find his truck with four attempted murderers tied up inside."

He dialed the phone, and we broke off into four little interrogation circles.

Chapter 13
Integrity

Shawn and I collected our nonbeliever and walked him out of earshot from the three other South-Wind Ventures employees.

Before we could begin the conversation, the man said, "I tried to tell them."

Shawn winked at me, and we shared the celebration in silence.

"What did you try to tell them?" Shawn asked.

He said, "I told them this cowboy crap was going to get us killed, but they're idiots. I told them we weren't the only ones with guns down here."

I drew my knife, and the man flinched. I said, "Relax. You're obviously the brains of the operation. I'm not going to stab you. I'm cutting your hands free."

He froze until the zip ties fell from his wrists and I pocketed the knife. He rubbed his wrists and hung his head.

"Don't stop talking now," Shawn said.

Without looking up, he mumbled, "You're really going to kill us, aren't you? Why else would you cut the cuffs?"

I glanced down at the man's ID and called Bonaventure.

Skipper answered. "Op center."

Without preamble, I said, "I need to know everything you can dig up on South-Wind Ventures out of Flagstaff, Arizona. I also need everything on their two primaries, Tommy Southard and Gary Windham."

"I'm on it," she said. "What else?"

"Run a quick BGC on a Cleveland Michael Perry of Waycross, Georgia."

"Stand by."

After a rapid-fire attack on her keyboard, she said, "Cleveland Michael Perry, twenty-nine years old, honorable discharge from the Eighty-Second Airborne. He was an Eleven Charlie with two combat deployments. He did five years and got out as an E-five sergeant. Married once. She is Carmella, also twenty-nine. They've got a daughter, six, and her name is Madeline. Pays his bills, seven forty credit score. No priors. He's worked for that company you named since he got out of the Army. That looks like six years. Do you need me to go deeper?"

"That'll do. Nice work. I'll call you back within an hour with a sitrep."

She said, "Op center, out."

I stowed the sat-phone and cocked my head. "All right, Cleveland."

"It's Mike," he said.

"I'd go by Mike, as well. So, Mike, our chaplain says you think we're alone in this universe. That's on you, but what it means for me is that I have to assume your sense of morality is based on something other than accountability to a Creator."

He clenched his jaw, and I said, "If you cooperate with us, I won't be forced to take a path neither of us will enjoy. Do you understand?"

"Yes. I just heard you ask for my background check, so yeah, I understand. Can you do one thing for me before you put a bullet in my head?"

I stared back at him in silence, and he said, "At least tell me who you guys work for. It's obvious you're not missionaries or gold miners."

I answered without hesitation. "We don't work for anybody. Our purpose for existence this week is to find a missing friend of ours somewhere in this jungle, and it looks like your buddies threw you right into the middle of our search."

"So, you're not DEA?"

I shook my head, and he said, "I'm not buying it. What do you have to lose by telling me who you are? You're going to kill all of us anyway."

"We're not DEA or any other alphabet soup agency. That's all you need to know, and from here on out, we ask the questions."

His look said he wasn't satisfied with my answer, but satisfying Cleveland Michael Perry wasn't high on my list of priorities.

Shawn said, "Tell us about these idiots on your team."

The man huffed. "What do you want to know? They're cowboys with no combat experience who think they know everything."

"And you've got real combat experience?" Shawn asked.

"Two deployments," he said. "I was a mortar sergeant in the Eighty-Second, but something tells me you already knew that."

Shawn said, "You're pretty sharp. Why aren't you in charge of the idiots?"

"I'm low man on this squad. They've all been with the company longer."

"Why are you talking to us?" I asked.

He took a long breath and let it out. "I've been to SERE school, and I'm trying to do the S."

I said, "Do the S?"

"Yeah, survive. I figure there's no Geneva Convention in place here, so my only chance is to show some integrity."

Shawn asked, "What do you mean?"

Mike looked disappointed. "You don't have to pretend. It's obvious you guys are former military, and by the way you handle yourselves, you weren't regular Army."

Shawn said, "Not bad. I was a SEAL, and most of the rest of the guys were SF."

"Thought so. That means you already know what integrity is. It's doing what's right when it's the hardest thing to do. Shooting at you guys wasn't right, no matter who you are, and what we did in that village last week wasn't right either, but I'm stuck. It's not like I can just walk away. I'm three thousand miles from home, and I've got bills to pay."

"And a wife and daughter to feed," I said.

He huffed. "I guess whoever you called is pretty good at rapid background checks."

"Yep. Now, tell me what happened in the village last week."

He continued rubbing his wrists. "It's a long, complex story."

"Give us the CliffsNotes version," I said.

"The company bought a claim. You know what that is, right?"

"Go ahead and tell us," I said.

"It's the right to mine a certain area of the jungle. It's usually a thousand to ten thousand acres. That's what my company does. They buy up claims, prospect, and then mine if it looks like there's enough gold or other minerals to make it profitable. I started out as labor on a mining operation in Alaska, but I moved up pretty quick."

I said, "Stay on track. Tell us about the village."

He spat on the ground beside his foot and licked his lips, so Shawn tossed him a half-empty bottle of water. He caught it, twisted off the cap, and drank half of it before offering it back to the SEAL.

Shawn held up a hand. "It's yours."

Mike swallowed the rest. "Thanks." He crushed the bottle, recapped it, and stuck it in his pocket.

I was starting to like him. He didn't drink the last of the water without offering it to Shawn, and he didn't throw the plastic bottle on the ground. For a man who believed he was minutes or hours away from dying, his integrity seemed to prevail.

He said, "Anyway. They bought a claim, and one of our jobs down here is to scout the claim. It's not like prospecting. We're not looking for gold. We're looking for anything that might stand in the way of getting to the gold if there were any in the ground. We look for access into and out of the site, hostiles, and indicators, like flowing water from high ground. I don't know what you know about mining, but water tends to wash gold and other minerals into the low points in rivers and creeks."

"What do you mean by hostiles?" I asked.

"In the case of the village, hostiles were about a hundred naked natives and a few Americans."

I opened my sat-phone, pulled up a picture, and held it in front of him. "Was this guy one of the Americans?"

He leaned forward and studied the picture of Hunter on the small screen. Ten seconds into his gazing, he grabbed my wrist, yanked me forward onto my knees, and threw a thundering side kick toward Shawn.

I reached out and swept his planted foot from beneath him, sending him onto his back with Shawn standing over him with his right foot twisted unnaturally inward.

Shawn glanced down at me. "You good, chief?"

"I'm good. You?"

He nodded. "Nice try, kid, but you've now failed at the R—resistance—but it was a noble effort. Since you were probably planning to follow it up with the E—escape—we have to cuff you again."

Shawn cinched a second pair of flex-cuffs onto Mike's wrists and sat him back upright.

I made my way back to my perch and pulled the sat-phone from the dirt. "Where were we? Oh, yeah . . . The photo lineup."

I held the phone in front of him again. "Was this guy there?"

Mike squirmed. "Does he have a screwed-up shoulder and arm?"

"Was he there?" I demanded.

"Yeah, he was there. He's your guy, isn't he?"

"He's on our list."

Mike chewed his lip, and I tried to slow my breathing and heart rate. "I told you, neither of us wants to go down this road, but you need to understand how violent I'm willing to become to find my friend, and that violence doesn't exclude Carmella and little Madeline."

He raged against his restraints, and Shawn planted a boot in front of him. "Don't."

I leaned in again. "The integrity you seem to hold dear works both ways. To me, it means not making threats I'm not willing to commit. You cooperate, and your family will never know we exist."

He growled. "If you hurt my family—"

Shawn struck him in the throat with an abbreviated shot that left him gagging. "If we hurt your family, it will be *your* doing. Give us what we want, and you don't have to worry about what we'll do."

He coughed, gagged, and finally regathered his breath. "Look. I already told you I don't feel good about what we did. I'm going to tell you whatever you want to know, but I'll retaliate every time you so much as hint at hurting my family."

With every passing minute, I became a bigger Cleveland Michael Perry fan, but I had to continue the interrogation. "Tell us what you did to the village."

"We burned the building."

"What building?"

"I don't know, but it was something the Americans built, I'm sure. Everything else in the village was teepees and grass huts. This thing was stick-built using commercial lumber."

"Why did you burn it?" I asked.

"You've got to understand these natives. Most of them have never seen a white man. They can't speak any language other than that grunting and popping crap they do. They're more superstitious than anybody in the world. If you can convince them that some god or the universe or whatever is telling them to leave, that's the easiest way to get them out. That's what we were trying to do."

"Did it work?" Shawn asked.

"No, and the Americans are to blame for that. They're down here preaching religion and telling the natives there's only one god. They've got these poor guys so confused that they start believing the Americans are gods, too. I'm sure your buddy told them it wasn't the will of the gods or the God for the tribe to move, so they didn't. I'm telling you. The whole place is grass huts, firepits, and naked people with their faces painted up. It's the most screwed-up thing I've ever seen."

"Keep it together," I said. "They didn't move, so what did you do next?"

He looked away and shook his head.

I snapped my fingers. "Right here. Eyes on me. What did you do?"

"It wasn't me, okay? I didn't do it. It was Bobby and Smith. It wasn't me."

"Okay, it wasn't you. What did Bobby and Smith do?"

"They killed one of them."

I thought my heart was going to beat itself out of my chest. "One of the Americans?"

"No, one of the native children."

"A child?" I roared.

He couldn't look me in the eye. "Yeah, a little kid. They said that's the one thing that will make them move for sure, but they were wrong about that, too."

I couldn't keep my seat any longer, so I leapt to my feet, trying to keep my composure. "If you're telling the truth, everything about this mission just changed, and the rest of your life did, too."

"What do you mean?" Mike asked.

I stared down at him. "Look me in the eye and swear on your daughter's life you're telling the truth."

He didn't blink. "If you swear to keep your hands off my daughter and get me out of here, I'll testify under oath, but there's more to the story. Do you want to hear it or not?"

"Make it quick."

He cleared his throat. "Killing that kid didn't scare them off. It turned them into Amazon jungle warriors or something. I know you won't believe it, but they had spears, hatchets, and bows and arrows. It was like something out of the movies."

I wanted every detail, but time and Hunter's life lay in the balance, so I drew my pistol.

Mike flinched, and I pressed a finger to my lips. I squeezed off two rapid shots into the ground and walked away, leaving Shawn and Mike alone. At least one of them had to be wondering what the insane leader of the crazy band of Americans was about to do next. I wasn't certain what I was going to do, but I knew without a doubt it would be done with integrity.

Chapter 14
Jungle Warfare

With Mike Perry's version of events plowing its way through my skull, I collected Singer, Kodiak, and Mongo, leaving the remaining three to have a little fun with their detainees. I felt a little pity for Anya's man, but if Mike was telling the truth, Anya's subject deserved whatever the Russian did to him.

When we were far enough away from everyone else, I said, "Let's have it."

Singer shook his head. "I couldn't get anything out of him. We tried everything we know."

Kodiak said, "We did a little better than that. Anya's a bit scary when she gets spooled up. Our guy claimed they got attacked on the other side of the road by some—and I quote—'out of control natives.' He said they were forced to defend themselves."

I said, "How about you, Mongo?"

The big man said, "We got a similar story. Our guy played the victim card, but we weren't buying it."

I spent the next two minutes retelling Mike Perry's story, and an idea came to me. When I finished, I said, "What do you think about putting your three together and asking about the fire and the murder of the baby?"

Mongo said, "It might be more effective if we kept them separated and started offering deals."

I considered both options and settled on Mongo's plan. "Let's see if we can get them to turn on each other. My money's on them turning into vipers."

We broke up, and I followed Mongo back to his man, Bobby, whose restraints had been upgraded.

Disco said, "He got frisky, so we encouraged him to hold still."

I took a knee in front of the well-restrained prisoner. "Tell me about the fire you set."

He pursed his lips to spit in my face, but Mongo's enormous left jab changed his plan.

I pulled him back onto his knees and repeated, "Tell me about the fire."

He glared back at me, and I called an audible. "Smith said the fire was your idea . . . and the baby, too."

"That son of a bitch. None of this was my idea. He's in charge. He's responsible. I just did what I was told."

I moved to within an inch of his nose. "Do you always do what you're told when it comes to killing babies?"

His face burned red, but he didn't say another word.

I walked away and joined Kodiak and Anya with Smith. Unlike Bobby, Smith wasn't flex-cuffed. He was trussed up like a rodeo calf with 550 cord and knots only Russians can tie.

"You look comfortable," I said. "Enjoying the Eastern European hospitality?"

He growled. "Whoever you people are, you better pray you kill us before we get our hands on you."

I raised my eyebrows. "Nice. You sound like a man in charge. Are you the boss, Mr. Smith?"

He huffed, but nothing coming out of his mouth sounded like English words.

Anya twisted one of his fingers until I thought it would separate at the knuckle. "You will answer when asked question, or I will do to you terrible things, and I will do them very slowly."

He bellowed like a wounded animal. "I've got rights! You can't—"

The knuckle gave way, and a wave of nausea rolled across his face.

I slapped him several times and directed his attention toward me. "No, no, no. Don't you dare pass out. Stay with me. We're just getting started, and you'll need to learn to tolerate some pain if you plan on being stubborn."

He panted like a dog, and I said, "Good. Catch your breath and tell me about the fire you ordered."

He spoke from somewhere deep in his gut. "Nobody was supposed to get hurt."

"So, you just go around burning buildings and expect nothing bad to happen afterwards?"

He grunted, and I continued. "Why did you murder the child?"

"They attacked us. The kid was a casualty of war."

"Oh," I said. "War. That's what this is. Sorry, I didn't know you had the authority to declare war on anybody, but since you've educated me, now I understand."

The fire inside the man was nearing the surface, and he was on the verge of exploding. That's exactly where I wanted him.

"Since you made this a war, you can consider me an ally of those natives, and you know what they say about the enemy of my enemy, right?" I gave him another minute to continue roasting before I said, "I find it interesting that the others tell a very different story from yours. They all agree that you made the call to burn the structure and to murder that innocent child. That sounds a lot like a mutiny to me, Captain."

"They're lying."

"If that's true, they're all telling the same lie independently."

"It's that new kid, isn't it? He's the one running his mouth."

I backed away, giving him a little space to breathe. "Are you talking about Perry, the only one of you who's ever actually been to war against a real enemy? Is that who you're calling the new kid?" I glanced up at Singer, then back at Smith. "When our chaplain spoke with you, he came away with the impression that there were three believers and one atheist. So far, the odd man out is the only one showing any remorse for what you did and what you ordered the rest of the team to do."

"Cut me loose, and I'll teach you about remorse."

I patted him on the head with as much condescension as I could pour out. "Is that what you really want? A schoolyard brawl to settle this?" I rolled the dice and said, "Since you set the rules, I've got a better idea. How about I burn down your house and slaughter your baby? After all, that seems to be what you believe is fair." I shoved him onto his back and walked away.

Vinny was my last stop, and he told the same story as Bobby without the necessity of broken fingers or thundering fists from Mongo.

Back in front of Mike, I said, "It's time to cut a deal, Mr. Perry."

He rolled his shoulders as the strain of his arms being cuffed behind his back took its toll. "What kind of deal?"

"Cut him loose," I said.

Shawn sliced the flex-cuffs.

"You're going to make a sworn statement to the U.S. Consulate, and then you're coming with us."

"Coming with you where?"

"That's exactly *why* you're coming with us."

"No, I asked *where*," he said.

"You're going to take us to the village where your team burned the building and killed the baby. You can find your way back there, right?"

"Yeah, I can find it again, but does that mean . . ."

Anticipating his question, I said, "If we were going to kill any of you, we would've done it when we had you flanked two hours ago."

It didn't look exactly like relief, but something in his expression changed, and he said, "What about what we did?"

I said, "Your statement to the consulate and any subsequent required testimony will take care of that. It's obvious you're not responsible for any of it."

"Yeah, sure, I'll testify, but I still need a job. I can't afford to—"

I cut him off. "We'll pay you a daily rate for taking us to the village, and then we'll fly you back to Georgia. We've got a lot of friends in the security business who can use a former paratrooper. And don't worry about finding work. Worry about making things right. The work will take care of itself."

"What are you going to do with the rest of the guys?"

"We're turning them over to the U.S. Government, but I suspect they'll be tried for their crimes here in Brazil."

"So, you guys *are* government operators."

"No, I was telling the truth. We don't work for anybody on this one. We're strictly on our own."

He held up both hands. "Okay, I won't ask again. When are we headed to Manaus? That's where the consulate is, right?"

I offered him a hand and helped him to his feet. "We've got a little diversion we need to play before going anywhere. We're going to give you a tranquilizer injection. It's short-term, and you'll be awake and fine in fifteen minutes."

"I don't like the sound of that."

I said, "You're getting the injection regardless of your cooperation, but it'll be a lot more pleasant if you trust us on this one."

"It sounds like I don't have much choice, so let's have it."

Shawn stuck him with the tranquilizer, and he took a knee. The effects came on quickly, and Shawn helped him gently to the ground.

"Go get 'em, one at a time," I said.

Shawn trotted off into the jungle, and in the next ten minutes, we had all four men unconscious. Three of them were tied together with several of Anya's special Soviet knots and shoved into the bed of our original truck. Mike Perry was nestled like a sleeping child in our newly acquired, all-purpose, all-terrain vehicle, courtesy of South-Wind Ventures.

After our exciting encounter with the wannabe commandos, it was time for a sitrep, and just as I expected, Skipper picked up on the first ring. "Op center."

"Hey, Skipper. I've got a situation report for you."

"It's about time," she said. "Is everybody all right?"

"We're all fine, and we've picked up a stray."

I spent five minutes bringing her up to speed on what we'd learned and how our plan to move ahead changed with Mike Perry's involvement.

"And you trust this guy?" she asked.

I said, "I'm not sure *trust* is exactly the right term, but he has enormous incentive to keep his word. Have you done any more digging on him and South-Wind?"

"Yeah, I've got a full background on him, and I'll shoot the intel on South-Wind to your tablets. They're a big company, financially, but they don't have many employees. Most seem to be contractors. The bulk of their operations are in Alaska and Canada, but they've steadily increased their presence in South America the past four years."

"Did you find anything interesting on the primaries Southard and Windham?"

"They're well connected, politically," she said. "They make the right campaign contributions, and they've got a lot of pull. If you're planning to take them down, you're in for a fight."

"I don't necessarily want to take them down. I just want to know if they're dirty. I get the feeling a guy named Smith was on a power trip down here, and he's the real bad egg, but if he was getting orders from Flagstaff, this thing may stink all the way to the top."

"It'll all come out in the wash," she said. "So, Hunter was definitely with the tribe they were after?"

"It looks like it. We're getting closer by the hour, so we'll have more for you soon."

The next call was made by Singer on speakerphone, and Blimpy answered with a mouthful of something. "Consulate."

Singer said, "Swallow whatever you're eating and listen up."

The man made a few animal noises and asked, "Who is this?"

"The guys who borrowed your gold-digger truck. We had a little accident and thought you might want to come take a look at the damage."

"What are you talking about? I told you that thing is off the books."

"Not anymore it's not," Singer said. "Just wait until you hear this story."

Shawn and Mongo had Mike Perry awake and alert and ready to spill his guts.

Singer asked, "Do you have the ability to record calls?"

"We record all the calls, just like the embassy."

The sniper said, "Good, because you'll want a transcript of this one."

We put Mike on the phone, and he laid out the story as if he'd taken meticulous notes at every step along the way.

When Blimpy was finished asking questions, Singer took the phone. "We've bundled up Smith, Vinny, and Bobby, and you'll find them in the back of the truck you let us borrow at these coordinates. They'll have some rope burns and hangovers, but they should be alive when you get here."

Blimpy said, "I knew you guys were going to be trouble when you walked in, but I didn't expect you to start a jungle warfare campaign in my backyard."

Chapter 15
I'll Fly Away

With Mike Perry closely held under seven sets of watchful eyes and the same number of skeptical hearts, we backed away from the gold-digger's truck, where Smith, Bobby, and Vinny lay bound, gagged, and tethered to each other. Ensuring those three made it into the hands of the U.S. Consulate before freeing themselves and escaping, we positioned ourselves at a sufficient distance from the truck to avoid detection. When the team arrived to collect the three bad guys, I wanted to watch it happen, but I wasn't interested in being involved.

Mongo unrolled a topo map on the ground and placed stones at each corner. He nudged Mike and pointed toward the chart. "Show me where we are and where we're going."

Mike took a knee, pulled a compass from his kit, and laid it on the map. After aligning the grid with the compass, he made a ball of black mud about the size of a pea and placed it on the chart within a kilometer of our position. "We're here, give or take a klick. It's hard to pinpoint on a map of this scale."

Mongo said, "Close enough. Where are we headed?"

Mike traced a finger across the paper chart and tapped a remote spot that appeared to be nothing more than dense jungle. "Here. This is where we're going."

He pinched another ball of mud from the ground, but Mongo waved him off.

"I've got it." He drew a pen from his pocket and circled the spot Mike indicated. "And you're a hundred percent on this?"

Our guest said, "Absolutely, but it's several days on the ground. We've got two rivers to cross and no ferries."

I joined the conversation. "How many days?"

"I don't know. I could probably do it solo in four or five, but I've never moved with your unit. I can't say for sure, though. I've never done it on the ground."

"What are you talking about?" I asked.

"We had a chopper, but even with the helo, it's still at least a day's walk from the nearest suitable landing zone."

I considered his statement. "Let me get this straight. You landed a chopper a day's walk from the village, hiked in, burned the building, and hiked back out?"

"No. We dropped an incendiary grenade from the chopper."

"What about the baby?" I asked. "Your story conflicts pretty badly with the other guys' "

He didn't hesitate. "We hiked in that time. That's how we got in the fight."

"Explain that in a little more detail."

He dropped his head. "It's not easy to talk about."

I straightened. "It's also not easy to talk about my friend being out there in that jungle and in need of my help while I'm babysitting a team of murderers and arsons. Talk."

"I get it," he said. "Like I said, it's a day's hike into the village from the closest LZ. When the tribe didn't pack up and leave after the fire, Smith made the call to take the next step."

"And by next step, you mean murdering the child."

He nodded, and I groaned and said, "I'm still having some heartburn over that decision. Why didn't you walk away when you knew Smith was going to kill the baby?"

"Because I didn't know right away. At first, the plan was just to snatch the child—or at least that's what Smith told us. It was me and

Bobby who snuck into the village and took the child in the middle of the night."

"And you were okay with that?" I asked.

"No, not really, but what was I supposed to do? It's not like I could just hike out and catch a bus home. I was stuck with these guys, and financially, I couldn't just quit. I've got responsibilities."

I brushed off his attempt at defense. "So, you kidnapped the baby in the middle of the night. Then what?"

He set his jaw. "I don't want to talk about that."

I lowered my chin. "What you want or don't want isn't particularly important to me. Right now, you're my best hope of finding my friend. You need to get it through your head that you're not one of the good guys. You just seem to be the least bad of the bad guys at the moment."

"At least let me skip the details of what they did to that child."

I surrendered. "Fine. What happened after they murdered the child?"

"Bobby took her body back into the village, and as far as I know, he put her back where we got her."

"But you didn't go with him?"

"I couldn't. It was too much for me."

I wanted to believe him, but his need to separate himself from what was done left me skeptical. I asked, "How were the people in the village supposed to know the child had been killed and that she hadn't simply died in her sleep?"

He bit the flesh inside his jaw so violently, blood left the corner of his mouth, and his body trembled. "There was no way to mistake what they did to that little girl. It was . . ."

The weight of the memory seemed to crush him, and I allowed him the moment to collect himself before asking, "What happened then?"

"Bobby got caught before he made it out of the camp. That's when the whole thing exploded into absolute chaos. Have you ever heard those natives yell?"

In that instant, I was transformed back to my days as an innocent child too young to know my age or which continent I was on. My missionary parents—or so I believed them to be—took both my sister and me to the remotest reaches of Central and South America until they were murdered in Panama. One such posting rang in my head as if I'd never left that distant hole in the jungle as the midnight lightning struck so close it both felt and sounded as if the world were collapsing on us. The driving rain and howling wind seemed to cry out like imprisoned souls begging for release from their torment, but the rage of the sky dissolved into nothing as the screams of the natives pierced the inky darkness. The blast of lightning and gushing wind sent a massive tree collapsing onto a row of huts that were little more than woven reeds and leaves, killing everybody inside each of the modest homes. The loss of the ones they loved must've driven daggers through the hearts of the remaining tribesmen until their ache escaped their mouths as spears of sorrow and hammers of fury. As frightened as I'd been by the storm that night so long ago, those screams bore through me even now in dreams I can't escape on nights when nature's fury seems at war with peace itself.

"Yeah, I've heard the screams," I admitted.

"Then you know," Mike said. "It's not like a normal scream. It's primal."

I fought to force down the memory throbbing inside my head. "Did they attack?"

He nodded as if reliving the scene. "They attacked Bobby. We couldn't let them kill him, so we moved in and did what we had to do."

"How many?" I asked.

"How many people were in the village?"

"No. How many did you kill?"

"I don't know . . . A lot."

"What about my friend? The one in the picture."

"I don't know, but I remember his face. He fought just as hard as the tribesmen. It was like he was one of them."

"How did you escape?"

He licked his lips. "We retreated as soon as we got to Bobby. He was cut and beaten but alive, so we hauled him out of there and split up into two teams. Bobby stayed with Smith and moved slowly back toward the LZ while Vinny and I stayed in the fight, trying to lead the natives away from them."

"How long?" I asked.

"I don't know for sure, but it was around three in the morning when it started—maybe a little earlier—and it lasted well into the next night. It had to be more than twelve hours."

I tried to imagine how it must've felt to be pursued by a village of furious tribesmen ready for war. "Was there more gunfire?"

Mike said, "Yeah, we didn't have a choice. They were faster than us, and they knew the jungle way better than we did. If we hadn't fired on them, they would've never stopped coming, and we would've never escaped."

As if on cue, the sound of an approaching helicopter froze us in place, and I said, "Is that your helo?"

Mike listened to the air. "I don't think so. Ours sounds deeper. That's something small."

When the helicopter touched down on the road, my view of the airframe wasn't good enough to identify it, but I was surprised to see only one man step to the ground. Pressing the binoculars to my face, I watched for at least one more set of boots to hit the ground, but they didn't come. Instead, the single man waded from the road and into the jungle. Even cuffed, it would take more than one man to wrangle all three men from the truck and back aboard the chopper.

Repositioning to get a better angle on the helicopter, I searched the skin, trying to find a U.S. government seal of any kind, but the plain brown paint job bore no such markings.

I handed the glasses to Mongo. "I don't like it. Does that look like a consulate bird to you?"

He peered through the binoculars. "It does not. That's a Bell Triple Two or a Two Thirty. I don't think the feds run either of those."

"Could it be Brazilian military or police?" I asked.

"Could be, but I'd think they'd have some kind of official markings."

I shoved the binos toward Mike. "Take a close look. Is that yours?"

It took him only seconds to say, "Definitely not. Ours is a Bell Four Twenty-nine, and it's blue. I don't know what that thing is."

"This isn't good," I said without realizing I was talking out loud.

Mike said, "That's not the feds, is it?"

"I don't think so, but I can't be sure."

He pressed the glasses back to his face. "That guy's walking them back out."

I grabbed the binos. The man who stepped from the chopper had apparently cut the three South-Wind commandos loose, and the whole scene looked a lot more like a rescue than an apprehension.

Singer must've sensed my unease. "I can ground that chopper with one shot."

I had an instant to make a decision that could dramatically alter the remainder of our lives. If I gave Singer the green light to pull the trigger, it would likely result in a war with South-Wind, a company with both political clout and coffers full of cash to spend. If I let them fly away, even if the helo were friendly to South-Wind, I'd have a block of time to put distance between us and our pursuers and hopefully move ten strides closer to Hunter.

Singer lay at my feet and extended the bipod below his rifle. As his breathing slowed, the soft humming began, and I was once again transported to a simpler time on the pew of an old Baptist church nestled on the rocky bank of a beautiful creek. His melodious tone pulled words from the first verse of the old gospel standard from my lips, and I said, "Let them fly away."

Chapter 16
Avoiding the White Man

With the binoculars still pressed to my face, I watched the rotor of the unmarked helicopter spool up to full speed. A few seconds later, the skids left the brown surface of the road, and the machine climbed above the trees, banked to the east, and disappeared.

Singer flipped the safety back into place, folded his bipod, and shouldered the rifle. "Good call, boss."

I wasn't certain I agreed with his assessment, but I wasn't going to waste another second. In that moment, nothing mattered more than closing the distance between Hunter and me.

We mounted the new truck, and I put Mike Perry behind the wheel. I wasn't ready to trust him, but making him the driver limited his ability to escape. Mongo's move to force Mike to pinpoint the position of the village on the chart was brilliant. If he strayed from the path that would ultimately take us to the scene of the fight, I would notice.

As the wheels began rolling, I second-guessed my decision to let the chopper escape, but the damage was done, and moving forward was our only option. Had I allowed Singer to take out the rotor, we would've been tied to that location for hours cleaning up the mess. I wanted that behind me. Nothing in the rearview mirror was an immediate threat, and it certainly wasn't going to lead me to Hunter.

After another hour headed southwest on the dirt road, Mike pulled to the side. "Let me see that map again."

I pulled it from the dash and handed it to him. Mike unrolled it and folded it until our position appeared in the center of the panel. He studied it and tucked it under his right leg. "We'll leave the road in another five miles or so."

I leaned to catch a glimpse of the map, and he pulled it from beneath his leg. "Here."

I took it and looked for an intersecting road in the next five miles. Nothing resembling a road appeared on the chart, but I held my tongue. A few minutes later, we turned onto a path that made our previous dirt road look like an interstate highway.

"Well, this looks like fun," I said.

"It's either this or hike," Mike said.

"How far will this take us?"

"It'll take us close to where you said the emergency signal came from."

"How do you know where the signal came from?"

He motioned toward the chart. "Somebody wrote it on the map. I assumed that's where you wanted to go first."

"That's a good assumption. Is this as bad as the trail gets?"

He laughed. "Not hardly. It's this good for maybe a couple of miles, then it turns into pure jungle. We'll still be able to drive until we get close to the river, but after that, it's all on foot. Unless you've got a helicopter in your pocket . . ."

I pulled out my sat-phone and held it to the windshield.

Mike laughed again. "Good luck with that."

"When we get to a clearing, I need to make a call."

He smiled. "You haven't spent much time in the jungle, have you?"

"Some."

"Clearings in the jungle happen for one of two reasons. Either a river runs through it, or a lot of men chopped down a lot of trees. Natural clearings don't exist."

"In that case, if we don't find a clearing, we'll start chopping."

We bounced and slid our way farther into the largest rainforest on

Earth. The progress was slow, but we were averaging well over four times the speed we could make on foot. I would stay with the vehicle as long as it could outpace a forced march. We weren't burning calories, risking injury, or being exposed to the elements, but once we put our boots to work, all of that would change.

A look back at the map showed our direction was at least forty-five degrees away from Hunter's signal, and Mike seemed to notice my concern.

He said, "The natives will never use a trail. There's too much chance of encountering a white man, and they don't have any interest in having our worlds collide. That's part of the problem with people like your buddy Hunter."

I said, "What's Hunter doing to hurt the natives?"

"They just want to be left alone and live their lives. All your guy is doing is patting his holy ego on the back. These people have lived in this jungle since long before Christianity or any other religion showed up, and they'll probably still be here when the rest of us are dead and gone."

"So, you think we should just leave them alone and let them live the way they've lived for thousands of years?"

"Exactly."

I gave him a nod. "In that case, I'll take your advice and make this pledge to the natives all over the world. I vow to never drop an incendiary grenade—or any grenade for that matter—on their village. And I swear I'll never slaughter one of their children. Your turn, Mr. Holy Ego."

He gripped the wheel with both hands and made no offer to continue the conversation.

Ninety minutes into the bush, we rolled to a stop on a narrow ridge, and Mike shut down the truck. Although he hadn't spoken a word in over an hour, he said, "Hey, can I have two minutes to tell you a story?"

I checked my watch as the rest of the team dismounted the vehicle. "Go."

He took a long inhale as if planning to tell the whole story without taking a second breath. "About twenty years ago, there was a ten-year-old boy with parents who were probably a lot like yours."

I huffed. "Don't assume that you know anything about my parents. They're off-limits. Got it?"

"Sorry. I was just saying your parents were probably Christians like you."

He waited for a reaction from me, but I didn't give him the satisfaction.

He continued. "Anyway, this boy's parents were Christians . . . the hardcore type. They sent him off to summer camp with a bunch of other kids from the church. It was way out in the woods. They swam, canoed, shot bows and arrows, and had Bible classes every day. Maybe you've been to a camp like that."

I sat motionless and silent, and he finally took another breath. "So, about a week into this camp, one of the guys who taught the classes started inviting some of the boys into private sessions, one at a time, and the boy I'm telling you about was one of the ones who got invited. Are you getting the picture yet?"

I softened my expression, and he kept talking.

"This boy who'd been taught to be respectful to adults, especially adults in the church, was getting raped in the woods by a piece of garbage who claimed to be a man of God." He groaned. "Here's the best part. When that boy told his parents what happened, they didn't believe him. They called him a liar, beat him, grounded him, and took away everything in his room except a bed, a lamp, and a Bible."

He paused, stared out the window for a moment, and continued. "About a year later, a bunch of kids came forward accusing that guy of the same stuff he did to that boy, and the guy hung himself in his garage. Do you want to know what that boy's parents said when that happened? They said, 'See what a bunch of lies can do? You ungrateful kids making up stories about a good man made him kill himself. You're no better than a murderer, and God's going to punish you and all your little heathen friends for what you did to that good man. At least we know he's in Heaven, where he won't have to deal with rotten liars like you ever again.'"

After a moment of utter silence, he said, "I'm that boy. So, next time your sniper back there tries to tell me how much his God loves me, he can choke on it because I know the truth." He spat out the window and turned back to face me. "Oh, and by the way . . . Those men you let escape on that helicopter—those three men who sliced open a baby and turned her inside out—all three of them claim to be Christians, just like you."

I'm ashamed to admit that I had no idea what to say. I was utterly and completely speechless at that moment.

Before I could piece together anything to spit out of my mouth, Mike said, "This is where your distress signal originated, so have fun looking for a sat-phone the size of your wallet."

I should've stayed in the truck and told him the truth about men of true faith who lived to serve a loving, benevolent God, but the words wouldn't come. Finally, I leaned across the cab, pulled the key from the ignition, and stepped from the vehicle.

As far as I could see in every direction, there was nothing but lower ground, especially to the north, where a long, narrow lake spread out for miles and slight breaks in the foliage shone like beacons of light into the darkened world under the treetops. Singer paced back and forth, staring at the ground as if searching for his lost car keys, and Anya stared upward into the trees. The rest of the team fell somewhere between the two extremes in their search techniques.

I stepped beside Singer. "What do you see?"

He brushed his boot against a fern. "There were people here. There's no question about that. But they weren't wearing boots like Hunter's."

"Do you mean you can tell what kind of boots they were wearing?"

He looked up at me. "They weren't wearing boots of any kind. Every depression I've found has toes."

"Did you find any boot tracks at all?"

"Not yet, but if this is where Hunter set off his sat-phone, he had to be here. There's no way the natives would've known how to work the phone."

"Could they have been carrying him?"

He shrugged. "Who knows?"

"How fresh are the tracks?"

"It's impossible to know. The ground is so soft, and I don't know when it rained last."

I ran back to the truck and stuck my head inside. "When was the last time it rained?"

Mike said, "It rains all the time. I don't know."

"I need you to remember the last time it rained hard enough to wash away footprints."

He laughed. "Are you trying to figure out how long ago somebody was here?"

I pounded my fist on the dash. "How long has it been?"

He closed his eyes. "Maybe three or four days ago. It's been dryer than usual."

"And when did you hit that village?"

"Maybe nine or ten days ago. Time runs together down here."

I let the timetable spread out on the screen inside my head, and I thought out loud. "We received Hunter's distress signal four days ago, so that puts the attack five or six days before that. How long would it take natives to get from the village to this ridge with and without an injured man?"

"I don't know the terrain between here and there well enough to say, but it doesn't make any sense why they'd cross two rivers and come this far south, especially if they were carrying a wounded man."

I grabbed the map and spread it out on the hood, then I traced a line from our position to the circle where the village was supposed to be. Nothing about the route looked easy. It was exactly the kind of route no sensible person would take—unless that person was doing everything in his power to avoid the white man.

"Get out here," I demanded, and Mike obeyed.

I held one finger on the village and one on our position. "If the natives traveled between these two spots, where were they going?"

"Are you serious, man? Do you really expect me to be able to guess what they were thinking? They paint themselves with berry juice and throw spears. My brain can't wrap itself around that kind of thinking."

I shoved my finger toward his chest. "When you were in the Eighty-Second Airborne, you painted your face green and jumped out of perfectly good airplanes with guns and knives and shelter halves. There's so little difference between that and what these natives are doing that you may be the only American in this jungle who *can* wrap his head around what they're doing. So, make your best guess."

He took a step closer and pored over the map, but before he could produce a guess, Anya's Russian accent rang through the trees. "I found telephone!"

Chapter 17

Tribesmen and Russian Gymnasts

With Anya's voice still ringing in the air, I turned to find her, but she was nowhere to be seen. My eyes finally settled on Mongo, who was shaking his head and pointing skyward. I followed his outstretched arm until everyone's favorite Russian came into view some forty feet above the jungle floor. She was clinging to the narrow trunk of a palm tree and waving Hunter's black sat-phone in the air.

I had a thousand questions, but the one that popped out of my mouth was, "How did you get up there?"

Although I couldn't see her eyes from that distance, I'm confident she rolled them. "Silly boy. Catch!"

I panicked, but to my great relief, she didn't jump. She merely dropped the phone, and I made the catch with ease.

Her descent was impressive, and she landed on the ground only a second or two behind the phone. "I have maybe theory. Yes, *theory* is correct word."

"We'll get back to your theory," I said. "First, I have to know what made you look in the top of that tree for the phone."

"This is all part of theory," she said. "We have tried many times to make satellite telephone call, but we cannot because of trees. We are on top of mountain. Okay, maybe not mountain, but at least hill, and telephone still does not work. This means if phone was here, it had to be on top of tree to see satellites."

"How did you know it was that particular tree?"

"I did not. I climbed several trees and finally saw glimpse of phone from that tree over there." She pointed to a second tree even taller than the one in which she found the phone.

"How many trees were you going to climb before you gave up?"

She cocked her head. "Why would I give up? We are coming to find Hunter. Giving up is not what we do."

I tossed Hunter's phone to Mongo. "Get this thing charging. With any luck, he tried to send a message, and we may be able to retrieve it."

Anya stepped beside me. "You did not hear rest of theory, and is important."

I had a hundred thoughts running through my mind, and my heart raced with anticipation at what Mongo might find on that phone once it sucked up enough juice to light the screen. I didn't need one of Anya's crazy ideas rolling around in my head, but the shortest direction between to the two points that interested me seemed to be directly through her, so I let her talk. "Let's hear it."

She glanced up the tree she'd descended only minutes before, and the sun filtering through the canopy danced across the tiny crow's feet that one of the best cosmetic surgeons had ignored when he put her back together. She was still beautiful—and always would be—but she wasn't the twenty-five-year-old goddess I met a lifetime before. She was something less, and somehow, so much more.

She asked, "Do you believe Hunter climbed tree?"

My eyes followed hers back to the top of the palm. "Hunter's got a mechanical shoulder and part of an arm. He couldn't have climbed that tree *before* he got shot, let alone last week."

Her theory suddenly became far more important than I believed possible, and I called to Kodiak, "Can you climb that tree?"

"Nope. I wouldn't even try."

"How about you, Mongo?"

The big man laughed. "Not hardly."

Shawn and Gator exchanged stares, and the former Division 1 free safety said, "I'll bet you a hundred I can get farther up that tree than you, old man."

The SEAL grinned. "Make it five hundred, and you're on."

Gator said, "Done," and darted toward the tree like a kid toward an ice cream truck. He wrapped his hands around the trunk and climbed like a highline electrician headed up a pole. That effort survived about eight feet, and he collapsed toward the tree, wrapping the trunk in a bear hug. His progress didn't stop, but it slowed until he moved upward like a three-toed sloth. His boots bit into the rough bark of the tree, but only long enough for that bark to crumble, forcing him to replant every stride. When his upward momentum turned to holding on for dear life, he was less than a dozen feet up the tree. Wrapping both legs around the trunk, he drew his knife and stuck it in the wood as far as he could reach above his head. His descent was far from graceful, but he landed on his feet . . . mostly.

Without ceremony, Shawn broke into a sprint and ran the first three and a half strides up the tree until gravity won the battle, and that's when he revealed his secret weapon. With one quick motion, he whipped his nylon belt around the tree and caught the free end in his left hand. Like a lumberjack, he continued up the tree until his boots met the same fate as Gator's. By the time the boots failed, he had already planted his left one on top of Gator's blade. He looked down, saluted the up-looking throng, and kicked the knife from the trunk. Down he came even less gracefully than the kid, but he landed with one hand extended. "That'll be five hundred, youngster."

I grabbed his shoulder. "Could you have gone farther?"

He shook his head. "I was out of gas. If his knife hadn't been there, I would've been done three or four feet lower."

I turned back to the Russian, and she said, "I told to you theory was important. The two most fit men on team could not climb tree. This means missionary people could not either. Only tribesmen and Russian gymnasts can do this."

THE CALLING CHASE · 123

"That means Hunter was with the natives when they were in this spot," I said.

"This is not all it means. It means also they were working together and communicating. Is not easy to tell someone to put telephone in top of tree with only hand signals and grunting."

I leaned back against the front bumper of the truck. "That means Hunter was alive and right here four days ago." Spinning back to Mike, I pounded on the chart still spread out on the hood. "Figure it out. Make your best guess where they were going and how far they could travel in four days."

"I've been working on it while you guys were having field day, and I've got an idea. This is going to sound crazy, but stay with me."

The team formed a semicircle around the truck as Mike slid a finger across the chart. "There's a place called Belo Monte. It's right about here."

Everyone leaned in to stare at the spot beneath his finger. To me, it looked like every other spot for five hundred miles in every direction.

Mike said, "Remember, you forced me to make a guess, and that's the best one I can come up with."

"Why would they go to Belo Monte?" I asked.

"There are about a billion folklore stories in the jungle, so it's impossible to know what's true and what's superstition, but from the stories I've heard, the village at Belo Monte has two things these particular natives need. First is a medicine man, or whatever they call their doctors or healers—whatever they are. At least some of them are hurt, and your friend could be one of them."

The thought of Hunter having another bullet hole in him, especially from Americans pulling triggers over a gold mining claim, sickened me, but I swallowed the bile in my throat and asked, "What's the second thing they need?"

Mike closed his eyes. "This one sounds pretty stupid, but there's some kind of shaman or spirit guide or some BS in Belo Monte. That's part of the reason Smith and the others chopped that girl up so badly."

I fought back the ire and said, "I'm not following."

"Don't try to make sense of it. It's all a bunch of hocus-pocus garbage, but Smith said they would take the body to this spirit guy because the tribesmen would believe the girl was attacked by an evil spirit. He had a name for all of it, but I was too disgusted by the whole thing to even listen."

The more I thought about what they'd done to that innocent child, the more I wanted to get my hands around their throats, but rage wasn't going to accomplish anything. I collected myself and asked, "What about a route?"

He sighed. "I'm not trying to be difficult, but I honestly don't have a clue. They would likely stay away from common trails and especially any roads, but beyond that, I'm not the expert."

I bored holes through the map as I tried to imagine the terrain under the carpet of leaves. That's when Kodiak's profession of confidence in Singer as a tracker finally clicked inside my skull.

I looked up to pick him out of the gathered team, but his was the only missing face. "Where's Singer?"

Mongo pointed to the northwest. "He's in the trees over there. I guess nature called."

I tapped the map with a fingertip. "Keep studying, and find me a logical route to Belo Monte."

Mongo gripped my arm. "A logical route for us or for the tribe?"

"Both."

It took ten minutes, but I finally found the sniper walking a zigzag course through the trees and staring at the ground. Instead of interrupting whatever he was doing, I watched for several minutes. When my curiosity reached critical mass, I said, "Did you lose something?"

He glanced over his shoulder. "Just my brother."

"That's why we're here," I said. "Are you still looking for footprints?"

"Not just prints. I'm looking for any signs that humans may have been through here, and I'm finding a few."

"Show me."

He motioned me toward him and pointed to a downed tree lying on the ground in front of him. "Take a look at that sliver of shiny bark. You have to move your head back and forth until the light hits it just right. See it?"

I looked where he was pointing and bobbed like a boxer in the ring, but nothing shiny popped out at me. "I don't see it."

He formed a triangle with his hands and laid it on the tree. "Look between my fingers, and lean left very slowly."

I followed his instructions and said, "Nope. Still not seeing it."

Singer stood. "That's all right. You've got me for tracking." He pointed to the west. "That's a brush of a boot sole moving in that direction."

"A boot?"

"Exactly. And natives don't wear boots. I haven't found their arrival path yet, but they definitely left in this direction."

"Forgive my ignorance," I said, "but if there's a barely visible boot scuff on that log, why aren't there boot tracks in the soil?"

He pointed to the ground behind me. "Are you leaving any boot prints?"

I visually followed the path I'd walked. "I see some minor depressions, but there's no tread marks."

He stepped in front of me, and as if he were a horse being shod, lifted a foot to show the sole of his boot. "What do you see?"

"Mud."

He lowered his foot. "It takes about ten minutes of walking in this environment to completely fill the treads with soil, moss, and vegetation. It's not exactly mud, but you get the picture. Once the tread is packed full, it's a large, flat surface area, so the weight is spread out and it leaves an even smaller impression than the bare feet of the natives."

"How'd you learn all of that?"

He took a seat on the log. "I've read every book there is about tracking, especially the ones from the frontier West. Did you know Buffalo

Bill Cody could look at a horse's hoof print and tell you the name of the farrier who smithed the shoe?"

"Why would I know something like that?"

He blew off the question. "Besides all the reading, I've chased targets all over the world, an inch at a time. Do that long enough, and signs like that boot scuff start to jump off the ground like neon lights."

"Why didn't you ever mention this skill set?"

He said, "We've never needed it until now."

"Do you have any more hidden talents I don't know about?"

"I can stick out my tongue and touch my nose."

I threw up a hand. "I don't think I want to see that one."

He looked disappointed, yet still determined. "Come on. You'd like it, I promise."

Singer had three modes: kill, teach, and sleep. I couldn't determine which was coming, but I gave in.

"Okay. Let's see it."

He grabbed his chin and worked his jaw back and forth several times as if stretching for an Olympic event. Finally, he said, "Ready?"

"Can't wait."

He stuck his tongue out as far as humanly possible. It looked painful, but the pain—at least for me—was yet to come. Instead of curling his tongue toward the tip of his nose, he left it fully extended and on display. Then, in grand fashion, he touched the tip of his nose with his left index finger and laughed as if the universe demanded it.

I stood, shaking my head, and he threw an arm around my shoulders. "I told you I was going to stick out my tongue and touch my nose. I did both, exactly as I said I would, but you expected something different. When that paratrooper of yours opens up, listen to what he *means* instead of what he *says*."

Ah, it was teaching mode.

From somewhere beneath Anya's favorite tree came Mongo's booming voice. "Chase! Get over here! Hunter's phone is alive."

Chapter 18
Extra Socks

Anticipation has little to do with reality, and expectation is most often far more powerful than realization. Understanding what happens inside the human brain in extreme moments is often more agonizing than beneficial. A decade of education on the abnormalities of the mind should've given me the ability to casually walk to the truck and hold out my hand for Hunter's phone, but like everything else in my life that I should be capable of handling with ease, I turned this one into an exercise in gymnastics.

The vegetation and soil—that I called mud—in my boot treads robbed the footwear of their ability to bite the terrain into submission. Instead, they became rudimentary ice skates, and I turned into Bambi, the baby deer. The display should've been a source of enormous amusement for the team, but no one offered so much as a smile. When I finally reached the truck, Mongo laid Hunter's phone in my hand.

8 D. 5 CW. 5 WW. 3-5 Att MedFP. ODT SW.

After reading the cryptic message on the tiny screen, I looked up, and Mongo stared back with pain in his eyes. He said, "Can you decode it?"

I nodded, and the rest of the team, including Mike Perry, leaned in. "Eight dead, five critically wounded, five walking wounded, three to five attackers with medium firepower, our direction of travel southwest." I grabbed Mike and stepped to the front of the truck. "Show me where Belo Monte is again."

He touched a spot lying due southwest.

I sighed. "It's still not a democracy, but does anyone disagree with Belo Monte as a likely destination?"

Heads shook, but no one spoke.

I folded the map and said, "Southwest it is. We'll go as far as the truck will take us and then strike out on foot with enough gear to keep us alive."

Mongo laid a hand on the map. "Wait a minute. We're on the highest ground in any direction, with the ability to get a phone above the canopy. Why aren't we taking advantage of that?"

"What do you have in mind?"

He climbed into the back of the truck and came out with a pair of radios and a sat-phone. "We've got line-of-sight open-channel comms and a sat-phone. We send Anya back up that tree, and thirty seconds later, we'll be talking to Skipper."

I planted a palm on his chest. "That's why we're happy to pay the huge bill to keep you fed, big man. It's that big brain of yours."

He ignored me and handed the radio and phone to Anya. "Feel like making one more ascent?"

She pocketed the devices. "Catch me if I fall?"

"You know it."

She curled her feet around the trunk and began the slow climb, each movement as precise as a surgeon's scalpel. After watching Gator and Shawn fail, seeing Anya climb with relative ease was impressive. It took her several minutes to reach the top, but she made the climb look easy.

The radio in Mongo's palm crackled to life. "Is Anya. You can hear me, yes?"

The moment was as serious as any we'd experienced since we stepped foot into the jungle, but hearing her identify herself made me chuckle, so I lifted the radio. "Is Chase. How do we know it's really you?"

A fighting knife flew within inches of my face and stuck in the soft ground less than a foot from the boot on my only remaining real foot.

She said, "Believe me now?"

Our petty game was over. "Has the sat-phone found a satellite yet?"

"Yes, two of them, according to screen."

"Excellent. Press and hold the number one. It should connect to the op center at Bonaventure in a few seconds. Hold the radio about six inches in front of the phone so it doesn't squeal."

Anya said, "Screen is filling with messages."

"Don't worry about that," I said. "Just make the call."

A few seconds passed, and Skipper's beautiful voice floated from the radio. "Chase? Is that you?"

"It's me, but indirectly," I said. "How do you hear?"

"There's a little static, but you're clear. Have you found Hunter?"

"Not yet, but we found his sat-phone."

I gave her the report we discovered on the phone, and she gasped. "How many of them are the missionaries?"

"We don't know, and it doesn't matter at this point. We believe they're moving to a place called Belo Monte, where there's a medicine man."

"How do you know?"

"We were going on Mike Perry's hunch until we found Hunter's message. Everything points that way. Can you give us some route guidance?"

"Give me a minute."

I said, "Good. While you're figuring out a route, I want to list the things I need to cover in this call in case we get cut off. We need a route, a helicopter, and medical supplies."

"We can work on all of that," she said, "but I think your best bet is the city of Tapauá at the confluence of the Ipixuna Purus rivers. It's a town of about fifteen thousand people. Portuguese is the language, but you should be able to get by with Spanish. Until I can get you a chopper, you can probably buy a . . ."

The transmission crackled and cut out, and I said, "Skipper? Are you there?"

Anya said, "I am sorry. Is my fault. I will fix."

"What happened?"

"I almost fell from tree, but is fine now."

She dialed again, and we were reconnected. "Chase?"

"Yeah. Sorry. We had a technical difficulty, but it's under control now."

Anya said, "I am technical difficulty. I am sorry. Is not easy holding to tree and also radio and phone. Is long way down."

Skipper said, "What?"

I tried to head off the long conversation. "Anya is at the top of a tree with my sat-phone and a radio. I'm talking to you through the radio relayed through the sat-phone."

"Anya's in a tree?"

"Don't worry about that. Tell me about Tapauá."

She said, "I don't know how much you heard, but it's a town on the river that leads to Belo Monte. You can probably pick up a boat there. The river is crazy crooked, but it's better than walking a hundred and thirty miles through the jungle."

"That sounds good, but I want you to plot a reasonable course through the jungle that the natives and Hunter might've taken. They'll do everything possible to avoid contact with any outsiders, so Tapauá definitely wouldn't be on their path."

"Got it," she said. "How do you want me to send it to you?"

"I don't know. That's your specialty."

"I'll send it to your sat-phone, and you can download it to your tablet from there. You know how to do that, right?"

I shot a glance at Mongo, and he nodded.

"Yes, we can do that. How far is Tapauá?"

She said, "It's thirty-five miles, straight-line distance, but it looks like solid jungle. How long will that take you?"

"Hopefully, we can make some of it in the vehicle at ten miles an hour or better, but we'll only be able to make fifteen miles per day in thick jungle."

"So, worst-case, that's two days." She paused as if she were thinking and then said, "Oh! Look at that. Tapauá has an airport."

"You've got to be kidding."

"Not kidding. It's not much of an airport, but it looks like they've got fuel and a partially paved runway."

"How long will it take the Huey to get there?" I asked.

"Hang on. I'll get Barbie on the line. If we can get the chopper to you, we can deliver the medical supplies."

I said, "If you happen to have a Portuguese to Spanish dictionary, that would be handy, too."

She chuckled. "I don't think I do, but I can print off a bunch of common phrases for you."

"Make it happen," I said.

"Hang on a minute. I've got Barbie on the line, and she's looking at the chart."

I could barely hear them talking, and I couldn't make out what they were saying until Barbie said, "It won't be easy, but I can do it. It's fifteen hundred miles. I'll stack as many barrels of fuel as I can on the Huey and be there in twenty-four hours, maybe a little more. Solo night flying over the jungle is a death wish. I should beat you to Tapauá, though."

I said, "It looks like things are finally coming together."

The team around me groaned. Superstition didn't run rampant in my team, but optimism like that had proven to be a curse more than once.

I tried to ignore the groaning. "Bring Ronda."

Barbie said, "Ronda? Why?"

"Just as a precaution," I said. "I don't anticipate a fight, but I want her on that Minigun if things fall apart down here."

"You got it, boss. She'll be handy in the cockpit, anyway. We'll be airborne as soon as the crew can stack the fuel drums."

"There's one more thing," I said.

"Shoot."

"Bring some good boots, several pairs of socks, water, and MREs. I hope it doesn't come to this, but if this thing turns into a soup sandwich, we may have to hike out of there, and I don't want to have to carry you."

"Sounds like fun," she said. "See ya soon."

Skipper said, "It's me again. What else do you need?"

I scanned the faces around me, but no one had any suggestions. An instant away from hanging up, I saw a beam of sunlight filter through an opening in the trees. "Throw a couple of good stout drones on the chopper. I've got an idea."

With the call complete, I waved for our little Russian Zacchaeus to come down from the tree, and for once, she did as I asked.

Mike slammed a palm onto the map spread across the hood of our truck. "Found it."

That captured everyone's attention, and I said, "Share with the class, Little Johnny."

He didn't look up and instead bent even closer to the map. "Take a look at this. There's a natural vein running from the north side of this clearing. I don't know what it is or was, but there's a topo feature that looks like a winding road to the river valley to the northwest."

I said, "We don't want to go northwest. Our objective is southwest."

He held up a finger. "I agree with you if you're measuring the route in distance, but not if you're measuring it in time."

If he had our attention before that moment, we were suddenly eating from his hand. "If this break is real and not some kind of error in the map, we might be able to take the truck almost all the way to the river. I'm no expert, but every time I've come to a river in this country, the terrain has been practically flat. I don't see any reason why this river would be any different."

I slapped him on the back. "And walking flat ground alongside a river is always easier than fighting slopes in the hills."

He held up his hands. "Remember that I've never been where we're going, so I could be totally wrong about all of it, but if I were making the decision, that's the route I would take."

"What about the natives?"

"I wish I knew. They don't think like us, so anything I said would be a pure guess based on nothing. Why do you want to know their route so badly?"

I pointed toward the ground. "Because we know Hunter was with them right here, so it's likely he's still with them. If we can intercept them, we can get our man out of here without waiting for them to get to Belo Monte."

Mike folded the map. "There's something you're not considering."

"What's that?"

He drummed his fingertips against his leg. "If we intercept those guys, they're going to fight. They're going to throw rocks and spears, and they're going to shoot at us with arrows six or seven feet long. When they do it, they'll either be completely silent or they'll scream like wild animals, and trust me, you don't want either of those things to happen. So, you'd better come up with a plan to snatch your guy without starting a fight."

I said, "I don't think you understand. We're not the ones who burned their village and murdered a child."

"Maybe not, but to those savages, you look and sound just like the ones who did."

Chapter 19
You Don't Have a Soul

Mike Perry's terrain feature wasn't as prominent as I'd hoped, but the course wasn't impassable. The first mile was far more vertical than the map implied, but we kept the truck's tires mostly on the ground during the descent. We were still making a slightly better pace than walking, so abandoning the vehicle wasn't in the immediate cards.

I was on the verge of opening my mouth and demonstrating the weakness of my world geography knowledge. "The Purus River flows northeast, right?"

Mike chuckled. "Yeah. Every drop of water east of the Andes flows to the Atlantic."

"That makes the whole trip upstream until we recover our man. How fast does that river flow?"

"I don't know, but the topo map doesn't show any dramatic slope. I would guess it's pretty lazy."

I said, "Even if it is slow, it's still an avenue of egress if things get weird, and they always get weird."

As the slope decreased, the vegetation increased, slowing us even further. The flatter the ground became, the more I believed our mud-packed boots would be a faster conveyance than the heavy vehicle.

When our turns became ninety degrees or greater to avoid stands of massive trees and impenetrable undergrowth, I called an audible. "Shut it down, Mike. It's time to use our feet."

He brought the vehicle to a stop and killed the engine. "I thought you were going to call it. The closer we get to the river, the more water and nutrients the trees get, so they tend to take over."

He pushed open his door, and I said, "Sit tight for a minute. I'll be right back."

He left the door standing open and propped his foot in the V formed by the leading edge of the door and the side of the windshield.

I slid from the seat and rounded the tailgate. "We're ground pounding from here. Somebody figure out roughly where we are, and Singer, come with me."

The sniper leapt from the truck as if he were eighteen again and landed on the ground like a cat. "What's up?"

I motioned for him to follow me into the brush. "Let's take a walk."

He fell in step beside me, and we put a few dozen yards between us and the rest of the team before planting ourselves on a fallen log. As we sat, his eyes remained focused on something in the trees.

"What are you looking at?"

He pointed over my shoulder, and I turned to see a massive snake, above and behind me, with at least three feet of his length dangling from the limb. I leapt from the log and built some separation while I drew my pistol.

Singer raised a hand. "Take it easy. It's just an emerald boa. He eats rodents and bats, so you're not on the menu. He's just trying to figure out what we are and if we're a threat."

"Oh, I'm a threat all right."

Singer laughed. "As long as you don't corner him, you've got nothing to worry about."

"That may be true, but I'm not turning my back on him again."

He continued chuckling. "Trade spots with me. I'm good with having him behind me."

"I think I'd rather find another place to talk."

He stood. "Suit yourself, but just because you can't see them doesn't mean they're not there."

"I'll take my chances."

We found a second log even larger and more comfortable than the first, and as far as I could tell, there were no serpents dangling overhead.

"Feel better?" he asked.

"Much."

Before I could begin our conversation, Singer said, "You're thinking about cutting him loose, aren't you?"

"How'd you know?"

He said, "We've been together long enough to start predicting each other's actions, haven't we?"

"I suppose so, but I'm wrestling with this decision a little."

"Tell me what you're thinking," he said.

"If I cut him loose to take the truck back to civilization, there's no way to predict what he'll do. He might run back to Smith and his original team. He knows where we're headed, and he's seen our tools. He can deliver a pretty strong report if he runs back with malice on his mind."

Singer cocked his head. "Is that really what you think he'll do?"

Conversations with Singer sometimes felt like counseling sessions, although he often let me do both the asking and answering. I'd never stop believing he was a much better psychologist than I'd ever be.

I said, "No, I don't expect him to do that, but he's mentioned several times that he doesn't have many options, and guys who run out of exit routes sometimes take the path of least resistance."

"What would he have to gain by doing that?"

I scratched my chin. "Familiarity and proof of allegiance."

Singer said, "Okay, I'll buy that. So, what can we do to keep that from happening?"

"We can hold onto him until this thing is over."

"We could do that, but if he's an unwilling participant, he'll slow us down on foot, and we don't need that."

"What's the advantage of keeping him?"

Singer said, "I don't know. We know where we're going, and he's only slightly more experienced in this particular jungle than we are."

"So, you think I should let him go?"

He scooted a few inches closer and lowered his tone. "This isn't a conversation about letting Mike go, is it?"

"How do you always know what's going on inside my head?"

He smiled. "We covered that already. We've been together a long time, and I pay attention. Tell me what this is really about."

I dug at the soft ground with the toe of my boot. "I want you to talk to him."

"About what?"

I sighed. "About what happened to him as a child."

Singer placed a palm at the center of his chest. "You want *me* to have a talk with him when you've spent the last two days getting to know him? You've watched him make decisions, weigh options, and soldier on, and you did all of that while I was in the back of the truck not having any interaction with him. In spite of all that, you think I'm the best choice to have that talk with him?"

"It's time for a confession," I said.

"It always is."

I dug a piece of bark from my seat with a fingernail. "Here's the truth. I don't know what to say to him. That's your world."

He looked up, and I jerked to check over my head for another demon snake.

Singer seemed amused by my anxiety over the serpent, but he didn't prod. Instead, he pointed upward. "That's not my world, Chase. It's His. Just tell Mike what you know to be true from your own experience."

"What if I get it wrong?"

"Do you think he'll believe even less if you can't come up with the right thing to say? He's already a nonbeliever. It's not like you're going to make it worse, but I do have a little advice for you if you want it."

I said, "I always want your advice."

"Don't quote a bunch of Scripture. You'll never convert a nonbeliever by hitting him in the face with something he believes is a lie."

That wasn't the advice I expected, but perhaps it was exactly what I
needed to hear.

He asked, "Would it make you feel better if I listen and promise to
jump in if you get too far off track?"

"Oh, yeah. That would help a bunch."

He patted the log. "This is a pretty good talking bench. Why don't
you bring the kid back here? You won't see me when you get back, but
I'll be exactly where you need me. We snipers are pretty good at being
places nobody expects us to be."

I slapped his shoulder. "Thank you. I'd be lost without you."

I made my way back to the truck, and I grew more uncomfortable
with every step. The only relief I felt was knowing that Singer would
be waiting to pounce when I screwed up.

"Hey, Mike," I said.

"Yeah?"

"Come with me."

He climbed down from the truck and trotted toward me. "Let's go
for a little walk."

He stopped in his tracks. "Look, man. If you're going to kill me,
just do it right here. I've been up front with you, so I think you owe
me that much."

I waved him closer. "I'm not going to kill you. I just want to talk to
you without a bunch of prying ears listening in."

He hesitated but finally stepped toward me, and I led him back to
Singer's log.

I straddled the downed tree and said, "Have a seat."

"What's this about?"

I patted the tree. "It's about you."

He situated himself on the log. "Okay, let's have it."

I took in the long breath I'd need to get through my opening shot.
"Tell me about your daughter."

In a flash, he jumped to his feet. "Take off that body armor and gun belt, and let's settle this, you son of a—"

I raised both hands. "We're not going to fight, and I'm not threatening your daughter. That's not what this is about."

The Army had clearly taught him to fight. His feet were positioned perfectly, and both hands were up and guarding his face. He was focused, and he was leaning forward on the balls of his feet. I was in a nearly defenseless situation, and any upward move I made would be met with severe aggression, but knowing Singer was likely only feet away reassured me that Mike wouldn't get more than one punch landed before the sniper sprang into action.

I slowly lowered my hands. "I'm not threatening you or anyone in your family. That's not what this is about."

I twisted my body to the left, exposing my holstered Glock. "I'll put my hands anywhere you want them, and you can draw my pistol. It's yours. If you want to put a bullet in me, do it."

Whether it was my calm demeanor or my willingness to surrender my weapon that softened him, I'll never know, but he lowered his guard. "Why would you give me your gun?"

"Because I don't need it for this conversation. I'm serious. Take my weapon. It's yours now."

He made no effort to step toward me, and a look of confusion overtook his face. "You're crazy, man. You know that, right?"

"Yeah, we all are. Every one of us who straps on a gun belt and goes off to fight somebody else's battle is crazy, and you're one of us."

He couldn't take his eyes from my Glock, so I tucked both hands into the front of my pants behind my belt, making it impossible for me to react quickly enough to prevent him from taking the pistol. "Go ahead. Take it. I mean it."

He stared at my wrists, where they disappeared behind the front of my belt, and he took a stutter step forward. With his right hand raised between our faces to block a potential headbutt, he reached with his left and released the retention catch on my holster. The pistol slid from its confinement, and he took a retreating step. By the time my hands were back out of my pants, Mike was four or five feet away with the Glock expertly gripped in both hands.

He said, "I could kill you right now, you know that."

"Yes, you could, but I don't think you will."

"What makes you so sure?"

"Because you're not a murderer. You're a good man, Mike."

He hesitated and lowered the pistol. "You don't know what I am."

"You'd be surprised. Although I've not lived your life, I once had the same doubts as you."

The muzzle fell another inch . . . and then another.

"What are you talking about?" he asked.

"The story you told me in the truck. I didn't live through that, and you shouldn't have, either. It's an unthinkable travesty and exactly why Hell exists."

After another few inches, the muzzle was no longer pointed at anything attached to my body—not even my prosthetic.

"We're both soldiers," I said. "We've seen things civilized men should never have to witness, but it doesn't end there. We've both done things that should've never been required of us."

His shoulders softened, and his weight left the balls of his feet and settled on his heels. "You were Special Forces, right?"

"No, I never wore the uniform."

"Then that makes you CIA."

"Not exactly. I carry federal law enforcement credentials, but that's to keep me out of the back seats of local police cars when I get caught doing things civilians aren't allowed to do."

He moved a step closer to the log. "So, you're a fed, but not really?"

"It's both more complicated than you'd ever believe, and also far simpler. Have a seat."

He leaned against the tree, but he clearly wasn't ready to sit down again. "What do you mean you had the same doubts as me? Mine isn't doubt. It's firsthand knowledge."

I wanted him to talk, but he wasn't ready, so I prodded a little more. "When I'm not somewhere carrying a gun and wearing body armor, I'm a psychologist. I have a clinical practice in St. Marys, Georgia, not too far from where you live in Waycross. I treat former and current operators with PTSD and other ghosts they carry around in their head lockers."

He cut in, and I was pleased to hear him open his mouth. "Is that what this is? Some kind of psychobabble, woe-is-me crap? I don't have PTSD, and I sleep just fine. I don't need a psychiatrist or psychologist to tell me to work through my feelings or take this pill or that one. I'm fine."

"Very few of us are fine, Mike, but I completely understand what you're saying. I've looked men in the eye and put bullets up their noses all over the world. Like you, I don't lie awake at night haunted by their faces. I get it, but that's not what I want to talk about."

He huffed. "Then what else is there to talk about? Are we going to get your friend or what?"

We'd reached a precipice, and I wasn't turning back. If I screwed it up, Singer was there to catch me and clean up my mess.

I said, "What happened to you at the camp and the ordeal your parents put you through afterwards was horrible. It can never be undone. There's a mile-long list of clinical terms to describe what happened in your head back then, and even now, but right now, right here in this jungle, none of those terms change anything. I forced you to bring us this far. I threatened you and your family, and I shouldn't have done that, but I can justify it because I'm doing what is necessary to find my friend, Hunter. And you need to know that I won't lose any sleep over any of this unless we fail."

He sat in silence, staring back at me, and I said, "You could've walked away back there on that hilltop where we found the sat-phone, and you know it. Nobody pointed a gun at you, and nobody tied you to the truck. You brought us down the side of that mountain because you wanted to. You made the decision to make this mission at least partially yours. You may not realize that's the decision you made, and it may not have been conscious, but look at yourself. You're the one holding the gun. I've got a knife, but essentially, I'm at your mercy, and you didn't run. You know you're not in danger. At least subconsciously you know it. Otherwise, you would've put two in my skull and run for your life. Why didn't you?"

He looked down at the gun. "Because it's not the right thing to do."

I relaxed, even if only a little. "Because it's not the right thing to do. Who gets to make that decision, Mike? Who gets to say what's right and wrong?"

He looked up. "Me. I get to make it. We all get to make that decision a million times in our life, and it's always us who gets to do it."

I said, "What happens when two people have a difference of opinion on what's right? Is one of them always wrong?"

He held the pistol loosely in his left hand and tapped on the tree with his right. "No, but there's a definitive right and wrong, and we all know that. What that bastard did to me and those other boys is wrong by anybody's definition."

"I agree, and that's part of the reason I know there's a God, and a Heaven, and a very real Hell. I let you take my pistol not because I had a death wish, but because I knew you felt that innate sense of right and wrong."

He shook his head, but he didn't speak, so I pulled off my body armor. "Let's start over. You've got the gun, and I'm a soft target now. So, tell me about your daughter."

The ire rising in him was almost visible, and he raised the pistol again. I didn't duck or turn away. I let him point it straight at my unprotected chest, and I prayed that Singer wouldn't strike from above like the emerald boa.

I asked, "Were you there when she was born?"

The gun didn't move. "Yeah, I was there."

"Think about that day, Mike. How many other babies were born in that same hospital that day?"

He squinted and shook his head. "Why does that matter?"

"Did you see other babies that day?"

He continued squinting. "Sure I did. It was a labor and delivery ward. There were babies everywhere."

"Tell me how you felt when the nurse handed you that gorgeous baby girl of yours."

He swallowed hard and lowered the pistol. A tear rolled from the corner of one eye, and he turned just far enough to hide it from me. "I fell in love with her as soon as I saw her. You've probably got kids, so you know."

"I don't have children. I can't. I was injured on a mountain in Afghanistan, and I'm not capable of fathering a child, but I don't have to have children to know how magical that moment must've been for you. She was perfect, and in that moment, you would've died for her without hesitation, wouldn't you have?"

"Still would," he said.

"What about those other babies in the hospital that day? Did you feel exactly the same about each of them?"

"No, that's stupid."

"What makes it stupid, Mike? They're exactly the same as your daughter. They were only minutes or maybe hours old. They were completely dependent on everyone around them to feed them, bathe them, keep them warm, and keep them alive. They were all the same, so if we're all just some grand cosmic accident, why didn't you feel the same love and need to protect every one of those babies?"

"Because she was mine," he said.

"Did you consciously make that decision?"

"What decision?"

"The decision to love her unconditionally."

He frowned. "You're not making any sense. Of course I didn't consciously make that decision. I'm her father."

"Indeed, you are, and no matter how hard they try, science can't explain that connection and that love. That's why I know there's a God

—because nothing short of Him could make you love that little girl the way you do. You were ready to kill me simply because I asked you to tell me about her. That's exactly how God loves us, except a billion times more."

"Then why does this God of yours let people like Smith, Bobby, and Vinny slice up an innocent little girl, all because there might be some gold in the ground underneath that village?"

I said, "I wish I had a brilliant answer for that question, but I don't. I don't understand everything I believe, and that's okay. Look at it this way. You and I have both seen evil . . . pure evil. You saw it when Smith murdered that child outside the village, and I've seen it all over the world. You agree with that, right?"

He nodded, and I continued. "We all have, but is that evil really a thing, or is it the absence of ultimate good? Is it the absence of God, just like cold is merely the absence of heat?"

"I don't really understand what that means."

"Neither do I, but we don't have to understand it for it to be true. Maybe God gave us the free will to choose Him or to turn from Him. Maybe the unthinkable things that happen in the world are temporary, even though they're horrific to us."

He asked, "Is this what you brought me out here to discuss?"

I didn't have a real answer for that question, so I redirected. "Do you believe you have a soul, Mike?"

"Who knows?"

I was about to unleash a timeless truth I learned from the writing of C. S. Lewis, and I prayed it would hit the mark. "Here's what I believe. You don't have a soul, and neither do I."

He screwed up his face. "What are you talking about? I thought having a soul is what the whole thing is about. I thought people like you believed they knew all about the soul and all that, but now you're telling me I don't even have one?"

I smiled. "That's exactly what I'm telling you. You don't *have* a soul. You *are* a soul. You are that spirit that loves and adores your baby girl. You are that invisible energy that inherently knows what Smith and the others did is wrong. You don't have a soul, Mike, because you *are* a soul. You *have* a body. And that body will fail and die one day, but you—the real you, that soul inside your temporary body—will live on, either being rewarded for accepting the love of God and believing He sent His son to die and pay the price we could never pay, or you'll spend all eternity separated from that loving God, your beautiful little girl, and everything that's good."

He and I sat in utter silence for what felt like an eternity before I said, "You don't have to believe right now. I get it. I've been there. But for the sake of your soul and for Madeline's, just be open to the possibility and remember how you felt the very first time you ever held her."

He pretended to wipe sweat from his face, but the moisture came from his eyes and not his brow. "This is the weirdest conversation I've ever had, man."

"It's about to get weirder," I said. "You're free to go. You can take the truck and backtrack your way to whatever you left behind back there. Take all the food and water you think you'll need. And you can take my pistol. If you want, I'll even give you a rifle. It's up to you. But as for me, I'm not going back to where I've been. I'm going to find my friend, my brother, and I'm going to take him home."

He spun the Glock in his palm and offered it back to me, butt-first. "What if I want to go with you? What if I've got more questions?"

I took the pistol and slid it back into its holster. "I'll never have all the answers, but I promise to help you find them."

Chapter 20

Forever Young and Bulletproof

Mike and I walked from the trees and back to the truck, where the rest of the team stood by the tailgate with the map splayed out across the surface. To my disbelief, Singer stood beside Shawn while whistling an old familiar tune, but I couldn't quite place it.

I locked eyes with the sniper and pointed behind me. "I thought you were . . ."

He gave me a wink. "I told you I'd be right where you needed me, and that's where I am. Is everything cool?"

I should've known the whole episode was another teaching moment, but I wasn't certain what lesson I was supposed to learn. "Very cool. Put a kit together for Mike. He's going all the way with us."

Kodiak climbed into the truck and tossed out a vest and pistol belt identical to the ones we were wearing. Mike adjusted both and strapped them on as if he'd done it a few thousand times. Next from the truck came four 9mm magazines and eight 5.56mm rifle mags. Before tossing them to Mike, though, Kodiak eyed me as if asking permission, and I nodded. The paratrooper positioned the spare mags and reached up for the next set of tools. Kodiak handed him an M4 and a Glock 17, each with a fresh magazine. Mike loaded both weapons, flipped the rifle on safe, and slung it across his shoulder.

"Who wants point?" I asked. "I'll take it," came at least four replies, and I said, "Kodiak, you're up front for the first couple of hours. And Mongo, you're the caboose."

The big man's size made him all but worthless anywhere in the stack other than at the tail. He was impossible to see around, through, or over, so he was accustomed to relegation to rear guard.

"Did we get a resection spot?" I asked.

Shawn slid the map toward me. "We're within half a klick of this spot." His fingertip landed on a position that looked exactly like every other position on the map, with the exception of a dramatic looping bend in the river.

"Did you spot the river?" I asked.

"We did. It's eight hundred meters that way, and the topography checks."

I measured off the remaining distance to the town of Tapauá. "It looks like thirty-two klicks. What's that, about twenty miles?"

Kodiak said, "That's what I scaled, as well. If we follow the bends of the river, it'll take three days, but if we take a more direct route and nobody gets hurt, we can make it inside twenty-four hours."

Based on the vegetation where we were standing, I didn't have the same confidence in our pace, but no one else seemed to disagree, so I didn't question the call.

I patted the tailgate of the truck. "Pull the battery, bag it, and bury it someplace we can find it. That'll keep the vehicle here in case we need it for exfil."

Gator pulled a tool bag from the bed. "I'm on it."

I said, "There's one more thing we need to discuss before we move out." Gator froze, the rest of the team leaned in, and I said, "We're moving to the objective, but it's possible we'll make contact. I believe Smith, Vinny, and Bobby were rescued instead of being apprehended by the two men in the chopper. If I'm right, they're likely coming after us."

Mike nodded silently, and I pointed at him. "You know them better than any of us. Are they likely to hit us?"

"It's hard to say. If Smith is still in charge, I'd say yes. He's not good at letting stuff go. The problem for them is knowing where we are.

There's no chance they could guess we hit that mountain and then trucked down here to the river. If they're guessing, they'll probably pick Belo Monte. It wouldn't surprise me if they chose to hit us there."

The word *us* didn't sit well with me. Mike wasn't one of *us*, but he seemed to think differently. I swallowed the sour taste and moved on. "That means if we make contact between here and Tapauá, they're not likely to be hostiles. We look like DEA, so if we stumble across a cartel, we're in for a serious fight."

Mongo asked, "ROE?"

"Rules of engagement are simple. Stay alive. We don't want to leave a trail of bodies through the jungle, but we have to do whatever it takes to recover Hunter. Any questions?"

Heads shook, and Gator went to work on the battery.

I studied each kit. "Check water, chow, and ammo. Is everybody good?"

The team checked each other's gear, and Gator returned from his battery burial.

I shook Kodiak's ruck. "Get us out of here."

As if on cue, every member of the team press-checked their weapons and fell in line behind the point man. I positioned myself at the number-four spot so I could always see every member of the team unless the vegetation became thick enough to prevent me from doing so.

As we moved out, Kodiak set a pace that felt like two miles per hour, but we wouldn't be able to sustain that speed. As we grew tired, we would naturally slow, but the greatest hurdle would be darkness. Even though we had some of the best night-vision equipment available, it still relied on at least some natural light to function well. We could project infrared floods from our weapon-mounted lights that would be visible through our nods, but using a rifle as a flashlight for hours at a time becomes not only cumbersome, but also detrimental to battery life. If we could maintain the two-mph pace until dark, we could enjoy the luxury of a few hours of sleep, but there were a great many ifs between us and sunset.

The natural noise of the jungle is beautiful, but it's also one of the best intelligence networks in existence. Animals of every description yelled, screamed, barked, or chirped as we approached. I could only assume they were warning their buddies that a loud, clumsy squad of Americans was on its way.

Two hours into the march, I jogged my way to the front to check on the point man. "You doing all right up here?"

Kodiak danced a few steps for show. "Just great. How's the pace?"

"We can pick it up a tick if you feel good about it."

He checked over his shoulder. "How's the big man in the back?"

I keyed my line-of-sight UHF radio. "Sierra Six, Sierra One. How are you holding up back there?"

"I'm good to go. Let's step it up a little. From back here, everybody looks strong."

I asked, "Is anybody opposed to increasing the pace ten to fifteen percent?"

A chorus of approval was my answer, and Kodiak lengthened his stride. When I made it back to my number-four position and fell back into the pace of the march, it felt good to move a little faster. Every mile we could put behind us before darkness consumed the rainforest would be one fewer for the next day.

Four hours into the trek, I keyed my mic. "Let's take five."

The column collapsed, and we circled up with cautious focus in every direction. Pulling guard was the natural posture of my team, and Mike fell in as if he'd trained with us for years.

I conducted a visual check on the team and asked, "Are everyone's feet okay? Change your socks if necessary."

Mongo shucked off his boots one at a time and replaced his soaked socks with a fresh, dry pair. Everyone else seemed to be ready to continue.

A glance at my watch told a story I didn't want to be true. "We've got about ninety minutes until it's too dark to move. Let's press hard if everybody's good. Disco, you doing all right?"

The old man on the team wiped his brow. "I'm solid, boss."

I took a step toward him. "Don't overdo it. If you're dragging, we'll slow down."

"I know. I'm good for now, but I'll let you know if it's too much."

"We need you healthy."

He twisted, stretching his back. "What we need is Hunter back, safe and sound."

There wasn't a single member of our team who'd slow down as long as we knew Hunter was still out there in the jungle somewhere and possibly hurt.

I gave the order. "Two more minutes."

Anya slithered toward me as I leaned against a tree and retied my boots. "You are checking for everyone else. Who is checking for you?"

"I'm fine."

She said, "I am watching you, and you are dragging right leg. This is not what person who is fine does."

I knocked on my prosthetic. "I only have half of a right leg. Dragging is what I do."

"We should make slower pace."

"No, we should not. If you were lost out there, we wouldn't slow down."

She closed her eyes and seemed to breathe in the statement. "Do you really mean this?"

"Anya, you're one of us. Just because you don't have a Y chromosome doesn't mean you're not one of our brothers."

"This has never been true for me. When I was SVR officer, I was always alone, and no one would come for me if I were lost."

"You're not SVR anymore. You're an American girl."

Anya slid a hand into her pocket and produced the tiny, plastic American flag she always carried. She spun it between her fingers. "Is exactly what I want to be. Well, not all I want, but mostly."

"We're not taking this any further," I said. "It's time to move."

I hopped to my feet . . . foot. "Let's move out. Gator, I want you on point. Singer, you back him up and teach the kid how to lead a column."

Gator's youth showed its face, and he set at least a four-mile-per-hour pace.

My prosthetic and I couldn't keep up, and I felt Anya's hand on my hip. "This is too fast."

Disco's voice sounded in my ear almost simultaneously. "Slow it down for an old man."

Singer said, "I'll break one of the kid's toes. That should slow him down."

Soon, we were back to Kodiak's original pace, and the relentless crawl of darkness encompassed the boundless jungle, minute by minute.

An hour later, Gator called it. "Bring it in."

We collapsed on him, and he said, "Sorry about the pace. I got a little excited."

Disco tossed a moss-covered rock and struck our point man in the center of his chest. "Just wait, youngster. You'll get old one day if you're lucky."

"Not me," he said. "I'll always be twenty-four and bulletproof."

I brought the shenanigans to a halt. "Nice choice for the stop. Who's got the spot?"

Singer raised a finger, so I asked, "How'd we do?"

He said, "Galloping Gator over there tried to kill us, but we made eighteen klicks. That's twelve miles for you non-infantry types. I think he did a fine job picking a spot to pass out."

"I agree," I said. "I'll take first watch."

I was pleased to hear Anya say, "I will take also first watch."

She and I positioned ourselves at opposite ends of the site while the rest of the team settled in for the night. Our two-hour rotations were standard practice, leaving no need for us to discuss the arrangement.

Within forty-five minutes, the team was asleep, and I was learning to commune with the rainforest. The sounds lessened but didn't completely fall away. I wondered what manner of creature could create such sounds, and simultaneously, I wondered what Anya was thinking on the other side of the encampment. She was likely planning to slice the entrails from any intruder who dared show his face in the dark, while I was more concerned with learning to meld with the jungle.

A time check told me we were only minutes away from being relieved by the next shift, but the clock isn't what had my attention. The sudden silence had me scanning everything until the absence of sound was pierced by the snap of a bowstring and the whistle of a handmade arrow piercing the wind only inches from my face. The dull thud of the arrow burying itself into the tree beside me echoed like thunder inside both my head and my quivering soul.

Chapter 21
West?

The arrow vibrated in harmonic oscillations and rang like a tuning fork to the electronic hearing aids inside my ears. The sound was peaceful and somehow reassuring in its tone, although likely inaudible to the natural ear. I was mesmerized by the hum and temporarily incapable of the only sensible call I could make.

After an instant or perhaps a lifetime, I yelled, "Contact west!"

Every member of the team was instantly on their feet with night-vision nods in place and rifles at the ready, but I was still frozen in place. The arrow's hypnotic ring had faded, but the call that had exploded from my mouth rang logically untrue.

West? Why would anyone attack from the west with the river at their back?

There was nothing tactically sound about that maneuver. Regardless of the size of the force, my team and I were only seconds away from pinning them down between us and that river, with no hope of escape.

A powerful hand grasped my shoulder and propelled me forward. "Get down, boss! What are you doing?"

Suddenly shaken from my stupor, I followed Shawn's command and hit the deck with my rifle raised in front of me.

He landed on the soft earth beside me. "Are you hit?"

I whispered, "No, I'm good. It was an arrow."

"An arrow?"

The disbelief in his voice echoed my own. "Affirmative, an arrow. A seven-foot-long arrow."

He shook his head as the mystery drove its way into his skull. "Natives?"

"Or somebody pretending to be natives."

The tactical side of his SEAL brain forced the oddity aside. "Gator and Kodiak are flanking. Everyone else is advancing ahead. We don't have comms with Anya."

The tiny envelope inside my brain, where I store the lessons on chivalry my father doled out in my youth, bucked as if yearning to force its way to the surface, and everything inside my chest wanted to sprint to Anya's last known position. Doing so, however, would've no doubt left me with a second arrow singing its vibrato from deep within my spine.

Forcing myself to focus ahead, I advanced alongside Shawn while listening intently for any sound of movement that wasn't my team.

No rounds had been fired from our side, and that was but one of the many oddities of the assault.

Mongo's voice came quietly through the bone conduction device cemented to my mandible. "Go to open-channel comms."

That feature of our radio system allowed us to speak without the need to press a button. It was as if we were standing side by side in conversation. The system was a power hog, but under fire, it was a tactical necessity.

Shawn raised himself onto his elbows and slowly scanned the area in front of us. When he lowered himself back to the ground, he whispered, "There's nobody out there."

I ordered, "Flanks report."

Kodiak said, "No contact."

Gator said, "Same on the southern flank. Nothing."

Was the single arrow only a warning and not an attack?

I said, "Press to the river, hold the flanks, and report all contact."

We continued our snail's-pace advance, hyperaware of every movement around us. Although my natural hearing was practically nonexistent, the amplification my implanted hearing devices provided gave me the ability to pick out barely audible sounds.

A scampering sound came from ahead and right.

"Do you hear that?"

Shawn shook his head, and I paused my advance to listen without rustling.

It was definitely scampering, but my nods couldn't amplify the minuscule natural light well enough to give me a view to match the sound.

I said, "Shawn, flood the area ahead and right."

He switched on his infrared light mounted above the barrel of his rifle, and the jungle came alive. The scampering continued, and I searched every inch of the ground in hopes of catching sight of any movement. Finally, it came, but it was little more than a flash.

I fanned my rifle to the right and brought my own IR to life. The motion was gone, but the sound was not. The scampering moved to my right, and I rolled onto my side to direct both my light and rifle toward the sound I still couldn't identify.

A flash appeared, and I flipped my selector from safe to full auto and prepped my trigger.

"Careful," Shawn whispered. "Kodiak's over there on that flank."

My thumb found the selector and flipped it back to semi. Spraying a fan of full-auto fire blindly into the jungle wasn't going to happen, no matter what was scampering in the night.

As my eyes followed my ears, I desperately peered into the undergrowth, yearning to see what was moving.

Shawn laid a hand on my back. "Whatever you hear, it's not human."

I rolled back to my belly and pressed on toward the river until the slowly flowing water was both in sight and well within audible range. Nothing human appeared between us and the water, and I said, "Close the flanks on the water."

Kodiak and Gator answered in unison. "Moving."

I glance toward Shawn on my left. "What's going on, SEAL?"

The next sound was unlike anything I'd ever heard from a human. It sounded like physical contact, in conjunction with disbelief and confusion, rolled into an audible grunt no one should ever make.

I called, "Who was that? Report!"

Kodiak said, "Something just attacked my helmet and nods."

"What was it?" I demanded.

"I've got no idea."

"Did you kill it?"

"No, it was too fast."

"Was it human?"

He said, "I don't know, but it was small."

Laughter came across the radio, and it soon morphed into Mongo's voice. "It was a spider monkey."

I crushed the brevity of the moment. "Report human contact."

Shawn raised himself back onto his elbows. "Nobody's out there, boss. It's just an empty riverbank."

"Monkeys don't shoot seven-foot-long arrows," I said. With the threat obviously gone, I let radio discipline dissolve. "Anya, report!"

Nothing.

"Siera-Eight, Sierra One, report."

Nothing.

I said, "Kodiak and Gator, hold the river. Everyone else, close on Anya's last position."

Shawn hopped to his knees and rescanned the area with his IR light and nods. "Clear."

A cascading echo of the same call came from everyone except Anya, and I leapt to my feet. The instant I stood upright, a spear at least ten feet long landed in the three-foot space between the SEAL and me.

"They're in the trees!" I called as Shawn and I moved to the concealment of the underbrush to our right.

Our eyes flew to the canopy overhead, but the treetops were just as empty as the riverbank.

As a team, we'd faced thousands of enemies all over the globe, but we'd never encountered a truly invisible foe. No matter how hard we looked, no one appeared.

Disco spoke for the first time. "I just caught an arrow an inch from my skull."

Singer said, "I got one, as well."

"Mine is a spear way too close for comfort," came Mongo's call.

I closed my eyes for an instant and digested everything in the environment as two more calls reported arrows or spears dangerously close.

"Retreat!" I ordered, and we fell back toward our bivouac site.

With seven-eighths of my team, I said, "They're obviously not trying to kill us. They had more than ample opportunity and are clearly trying to keep us away from Anya's position."

"Do you think they killed her?" Gator asked.

"There's no way to know, but we're outclassed. Whoever these people are, they're practically invisible in the jungle." I turned to Mike. "Is your team capable of something like this?"

"They're not my team," he said. "I'm with you now, but no, none of those guys could do any of this. It has to be the natives. You can't imagine what they're capable of."

I said, "Singer, can you get eyes on Anya's position?"

"Sure. Can I take Gator?"

I motioned for the student to follow his teacher, and they vanished into the jungle.

"Kodiak, you've got more time down here than anyone else. What's happening?"

He drew in a long breath and slowly let it escape. "It's one of two things. Mike, they may have taken her as retaliation for what was done to the baby girl you and your team took."

The paratrooper said, "I told you they're not my team."

"They were when you took the baby," he said.

Mike lowered his head, and Kodiak continued. "The other possibility is they're holding her as a bargaining chip. If that's the case, it means this isn't the tribe from the burned village."

"What makes you say that?" I asked.

"I get the feeling they're working together. I think whoever's shooting arrows and throwing spears at us is another community covering the tracks of the tribe Hunter's with."

"That's an interesting theory," I said, "but why aren't they killing us? It's obvious they could. There's no way that seven near misses are accidents."

"That's what makes me believe it's not the same tribe. If it were the same folks, they would likely tear us to pieces to get back at us for the fire and murder."

"Us?" I said. "We didn't do it."

"Yeah, *we* know that, but they probably don't. We're white men from another world, so to them, we're likely all the same."

"I don't like it," I said, "but I'm not willing to start a gunfight with them. That would make us no better than Smith and his team. We've got no beef with these guys. We just want to recover Hunter."

Kodiak grimaced. "Again, we know that, but they don't."

Singer said, "Hey, Mike. Did you have any encounters with a tribe who understood English?"

"No, if they understood us, they pretended not to, so I don't think they have any idea what we're saying."

I asked, "How do the missionaries communicate with them?"

Singer said, "I've heard stories about using picture cards, but I've never seen them."

I felt the tension rising in my spine. "We have to make a choice. Do we go after Anya or Hunter first?"

Mongo said, "Anya's trail is warmer. I say we do what we can to get her back. Leaving her behind ain't the way we do business."

As if right on schedule, our sniper team reported. "We've got eyes on Anya's position, but she's not there."

Singer's ominous words sent chills running down my back.

"Can you move in?" I couldn't force myself to ask the real question, but Singer knew without me having to ask.

"There's no sign of blood, but there was a struggle."

"Did they leave a trail?" I asked.

"They left more than that. Her radio is pinned to a tree with a pair of her fighting knives stuck through it."

My heart sank, and my ire soared. "They took her. That makes this a fight. Move in on Singer and Gator. The rules of engagement just changed. We're getting our Russian back, even if we have to put them down to do it."

Chapter 22

Oh, Bring Back My Boondy to Me

Singer pulled Anya's knives from the trunk of the tree and tossed what remained of her radio to Gator. He pocketed the device that was likely too far gone, even for Dr. Mankiller to repair.

I took one of the knives from the sniper's hand and slid it into my pack. I'll never know why I wanted it, but for some reason, I couldn't resist tucking it away. "Can you track them in the dark?"

Singer adjusted his nods. "I already have. There were four sets of distinguishable footprints. One appeared to be a hundred pounds heavier than the other three."

I sighed. "He was carrying Anya."

"That's the only reasonable answer."

"So, where did they go?"

He nodded toward the mud bank of the lazy river driving its way to the northeast.

"Boats?" I asked.

"No sign of anything except bare feet."

I turned to Mike. "How deep is that river?"

He handed me his radio and nods and shucked off his body armor. "I don't know, but I'll find out."

A few seconds later, Mike slid down the bank and into the river. When he stood, the water hit him just above his belt, but as he moved farther from dry ground, his shoulders were soon submerged. Abandoning the idea of walking, he swam until he could stand again on the opposite side. The current had taken him only a dozen feet down-stream, so I was relieved to know the downstream flow wasn't strong enough to make the river a challenge in either direction.

He drew his flashlight from his kit and shined it along the bank, ap-parently searching for prints where the natives had climbed from the river.

Singer watched closely. "The kid's got good instincts."

"Sometimes," I admitted, "but I still don't trust him."

"You gave him a rifle."

"That's not the kind of trust I'm talking about."

Mike stopped his search and found footing on the sloping bank of mud a hundred feet away. He cupped his mouth in his hands and yelled, "I've got some tracks."

"Into or out of the water?" Singer asked.

The next sound from Mike's mouth was anything but an answer to Singer's question. Instead, it was the growl of a wounded animal as he fell forward into the water with a massive arrow protruding from his shoulder.

I didn't hesitate. "Mongo and Shawn, you go after Mike. Every-body else, on me. Rally point is right here if this thing falls apart. Keep the comms open."

The seven of us hit the water and split into two teams immediately. Mongo and Shawn stroked downstream in a desperate attempt to get to Mike before he drowned or bled out, while the rest of us swam the width of the river and clawed our way up the bank. The weight of our gear and body armor tugged at our thrashing bodies as the burden tried to pin us to the muddy bottom, but our will and utter determi-nation won out.

With our feet back on solid ground and our rifles drained of river water, we patrolled with the M4s at low ready and our nods trained on the jungle before us. We moved with driven purpose, our thoughts on nothing short of recovering Anya alive. Our pace wasn't a sprint, but we wasted no time advancing deeper into the bush.

Mongo's voice thundered in my ear. "We got him!"

"Alive?"

"For now."

Before I could give the order to return Mike to the rally point, Gator called, "Movement ten o'clock!"

We turned slightly left and pressed toward Gator's contact.

I leaned forward as if doing so would give me some ability to see farther and clearer, and to my amazement, it seemed to work. The bare back of a small man running westward with a bow strung around his shoulders and a quiver of arrows tied around his waist appeared in my optic. I raised my rifle and centered the EOTECH red dot between his shoulders as I pressed the slack from my trigger.

Any shot anywhere on his body would ultimately be a kill shot. Some would be instant and painless, while others could result in a wound that would never heal in that environment until infection took him and he slowly succumbed to the trauma.

Would a bullet through his spine deliver Anya back into our hands? Would I survive the aftermath of killing him, or would the memory fester inside me just as the bullet wound would destroy him in time?

In an instant, I pressed through the trigger break twice and watched the back-to-back muzzle flashes inside my nods. I couldn't see the supersonic rounds searing their way through the humid night air, but the result of the full metal jacketed projectiles was unmistakable. The fleeing man collapsed to the ground with both arms spread, and he lay motionless as I continued my advance.

When I reached his side, I took a knee and placed a hand on his back, ensuring he would stay down as my team formed a security perimeter around me. With the assurance that none of the remaining tribesmen would attack as I dealt with my target, I rolled him onto his back and stared down into his terrified face. Bark and debris filled his hair from the damage my rounds had done to the tree trunk just above his head.

With my helmet and night-vision device in front of my eyes, I must have appeared to be an alien from a world beyond his comprehension. The mysterious glow of the nods probably gave me an ominous glow and confused him even further. I lifted the nods and loosened the chin strap of the helmet. As I pulled the gear from my head, his expression softened, but only slightly. The white light emitted by my flashlight was likely something he had never experienced, so I placed the light in his palm and waited.

He shone it against the ground around us and then into the trees above our heads. His terror seemed to melt into curiosity, and that was exactly what I was hoping to accomplish. I showed him the switch to turn the light on and off, and he smiled at the revelation, clicking the switch several times. He covered the light with his hand and frowned when it didn't burn his palm, and then he sniffed the light and finally turned it on me.

I squinted, but I didn't resist. Having him afraid of me would accomplish nothing, but having him curious about me worked to my limitless advantage. It was time to turn up the fascination to a level he could never comprehend.

While he held my light on me, I raised both hands and patted the air in a gesture intended to have him relax. Then, I lifted my helmet and gently placed it on his head. The man shied away from the weight of the gear for a moment until I lowered the night-vision devices into place in front of his eyes. He let out an audible gasp and ducked away as if trying to escape the nods.

I patted the air again and positioned myself in front of him while covering the light with my hand. He flinched when my features grew vivid and clear only inches in front of him, despite the obsidian darkness beneath the cover of trees.

I took his hand in mine and placed it on the nods, showing him how to raise and lower the device. He repeated the movement several times in utter fascination, and after several minutes of the night-vision game, he placed a hand on my chest and said, "*Tu-Tu Non Cataan.*"

I held his hand against me. "No. I am Chase."

"*Tu-Tu Non Cataan.*"

I lifted his hand and patted my chest with it several times. "Chase."

"*Tu-Tu Non Cataan.*"

We were getting nowhere, so I changed tactics. I slowly pulled my phone from my pocket and positioned his hand and my flashlight toward my face. I snapped a picture of my face and turned the screen toward him.

He raised the nods and gently touched the screen, sliding his fingertips across the smooth glass. Then, he reached for my face and ran his fingers across my flesh before returning his touch to the screen.

I moved his hand, still holding my light, until his face was illuminated by the glow. After capturing what was surely the first photo ever taken of the native, I turned the screen back to him. Probably for the first time in his life, he saw his own reflection. Time after time, he touched the screen and then his face. The recognition slowly became obvious, and that was the hurdle I most needed to overcome.

I turned my phone and flipped through the pictures, hoping against hope that I had the one I needed. The closest thing I could find was a picture of Anya's passport, so I brought it up and zoomed into the photo of her face. It wasn't a great picture, but it was unmistakably her. I spun the screen back to face him, and he focused on Anya's picture.

After staring at the screen for a long moment, he nodded ever so slightly and said, "*Boondy.*"

I tapped the screen with the tip of my index finger and then pressed my hand to my chest. He looked between me and the screen. "*Tu-Tu Non Cataan boondy.*"

Technically, communication consists of three distinct elements: sender, receiver, and message. We nailed the sender and receiver part, but the message was still a little cloudy for my new friend and me.

I took our game one step further by flipping to Hunter's picture and turning the screen to face him again.

The man leaned toward the screen and squinted before whispering, "*Boo natta.*" He pointed toward the southwest.

I said, "*Boo natta*," and motioned in the same direction he was pointing.

Something resembling a smile crossed his lips. I flipped back to Anya's picture, showed him, and then squeezed the phone to my chest.

He said, "*Boondy*," and I repeated the word.

I pointed through the air in every direction in grand sweeping motions and said, "*Boondy?*"

At first, he cocked his head, but after a moment, he touched Anya's face on the screen and then touched my chest over my heart.

I nodded and motioned with my hands to bring her back. The man seemed to understand, but I couldn't be certain. He formed a horn around his mouth with both hands and yelled into the night. Nothing he said sounded anything like an English word, but it was loud.

After a few seconds, a distant cry sounded through the air. "*Bin bin!*"

He yelled, "*Bin bin nee Tu-Tu Non Cataan.*"

For all I knew, we could've been singing "My Bonny Lies Over the Ocean" in some ancient tribal language, but I wanted to believe his fellow tribesmen were bringing my Russian back.

Singer said, "Movement, two o'clock."

Disco said, "Movement, ten o'clock."

I wanted to believe the danger was over, but it was beginning to look like we were on the verge of being flanked with our backs to the river that time.

"Answer aggression with extreme violence," I said. "We can't lose anyone else."

The native sitting before me called into the air again with an entirely new message, and his call was answered by an even more complex sentence from his brothers closing on us. Then, he did something that was beautifully understandable in every language. He pulled his bow from across his shoulders and laid it on the ground in front of me.

I dropped the magazine from my M4 and pulled the charging handle to eject the round in the battery. Just as he'd lain his weapon at my feet, I laid mine at his.

Another call left his mouth that I would never understand, but it seemed to draw his fellow tribesmen from the trees. I didn't count them, but there were easily a dozen or more. One of them held Anya cradled in his arms.

My man motioned toward the native holding Anya and said, "*Boondy Tu-Tu Non Cataan boondy poon poon.*"

The man holding Anya slowly approached, looking between me and his brother at my feet. None of us moved as the man approached, but my team kept a watchful eye on the band of natives surrounding us.

After an agonizingly slow approach, the tribesman laid Anya on the ground in front of me and said, "*Poon poon boondy.*"

The idiot who lived inside my head couldn't wait to call Anya "Poon Poon Boondy" when she woke up, but the soldier in me wanted to know that she was still alive. I pressed two fingers to her neck and felt her bounding pulse, then I raised each eyelid and felt the breath leaving her nose.

The man who'd placed her before me pointed to a spot on her neck and held up a feathered dart in one hand. He dropped the dart into a long bamboo shaft and pressed his lips to the end. An instant later, the dart was sticking into the root of a tree near my foot.

Of all the weapons I had encountered in every corner of the world, I never thought I'd face a blowgun.

Singer took a knee beside Anya's limp form and pulled a capsule of smelling salt from his kit. After he snapped it open and held it below her nostrils, she squirmed, and her eyelids fluttered open.

Whatever poison the dart had carried apparently erased her ability to speak English, and the Russian that melted from her drowsy tongue sounded more like the language of the tribesmen than that of the tzars.

Chapter 23

Learn the Language

I believed we had recovered Anya, but I wasn't certain the tribesmen would let us leave without a fight. They seemed to understand the concept of give-and-take based on the mutual surrender of our weapons, so I needed to present an offering.

I tried to let the primitive part of my brain do the thinking in that moment.

What would I want from the giant American if I were the native staring up at Tu-Tu Non Cataan?

The answer came in an instant, and I shot my hand into my pocket. I produced a flint and steel and shook them dry, then I gathered a few shards of the bark I'd shot from the tree and formed a small pile of kin- dling. It took four attempts, but the tool finally produced enough spark to ignite the splinters.

The universal gasp from the tribesmen told me I was on the right track, so I let the fire burn for a few seconds before stepping on it and handing the flint and steel to the tribesman. He examined it closely and awkwardly rubbed the two pieces together with no results, so I patted the air between us again in a reassuring, calming gesture and took his hands in mine. I squeezed his fingers until he was gripping the tools firmly enough to create a spark, then I moved his hands to the tinder and struck the flint until the splinters ignited once again.

After stepping on the fire again, I pointed to the bark. He played with the flint and steel until he repeated my success and started the first fire of his life with a modern tool.

He grinned as if I'd given him the keys to the universe and said, "*Tu-Tu Non Cataan ooga, Tu-Tu Non Cataan.*"

I wanted so badly to understand, but he was as much a mystery to me as I was to him. He offered the fire starter back to me, but I waved him off and gestured for him to keep it. His expression said he couldn't understand why I would give him such a powerful tool, but I hoped he put enough value on the flint to leave Anya with us.

He clearly had other ideas when he muttered something to the man who'd been carrying Anya and produced a piece of smooth wood with carving cut into its surface. It appeared to be a picture of the treetops with light shining through them.

He pressed the piece of art into my hands and repeated, "*Tu-Tu Non Cataan.*"

When I slipped the carving into my pocket, the man took Anya's hand in his. I was intrigued but concerned, and I wouldn't let him carry her back into the trees, even if the next round I fired had to find his center mass.

Instead of leading her away, he placed her hand in mine and squeezed my fingers around hers. "*Tu-Tu Non Cataan boondy.*"

Anya was apparently my boondy again.

Mongo called through the radio. "I don't know what kind of party you're having out there, but Mike needs some serious help. We've got to get him out of here."

I asked, "Where are you?"

"We're on the west side of the river, about a hundred meters down-stream from our original crossing."

"Hold your position," I said. "We're coming to you, and we're bringing some friends."

I lifted the crude bow from the ground and returned it to its rightful owner. He accepted it and lifted my rifle from the dirt, so I took it and motioned for them to follow me. They did, but their movement made it clear they didn't trust us any more than we trusted them.

We found Mongo, Shawn, and Mike exactly where I expected, but Shawn's reaction told me I should've been clearer about the guests I was bringing to the party. He leapt to his feet and raised his rifle, but I stepped in front of him.

"Easy. They're no threat."

He lowered his rifle, but his scowl persisted. "Tell that to Mike."

Mongo was by far the most well-trained and experienced medic on the team, but caring for an arrow wound in the middle of the jungle was outside even his expertise. He said, "I broke the arrow shaft, but I didn't try to remove the head. It's a pressure dressing, but he lost a lot of blood before we could get to him."

I took a knee beside Mike and examined the dressing on the back of his shoulder and the protruding arrow shaft. "How you doing, paratrooper?"

"I've had better days," he mumbled.

I looked up over my shoulder. "Do we have morphine?"

Mike grabbed my leg. "No morphine. I'm allergic. I'll quit breathing ten seconds after you stick me."

"Can you walk?" I asked.

"Maybe for a while, but I don't know what the arrowhead inside my shoulder is going to do if I start moving around."

I looked up at Mongo. "If we pull it out, can you stitch it up?"

"Maybe, but without morphine, the pain might kill him. I'd like to know what the arrowhead looks like."

I pointed toward the quiver strung around the native's waist and made a gesture to hopefully get him to surrender an arrow.

He frowned but pulled two arrows from the quiver and handed both of them to me. One was sharpened like a pencil and terminated in an extremely sharp wooden point. If the arrow in Mike's shoulder looked like that one, removing it would be a simple matter of applying pressure around the entry wound and sliding the arrow straight out in exactly the opposite direction it went in.

The second arrow told a different story. It was tipped with a sharpened stone laced to the arrow with some sort of sinew. The arrowhead resembled some of the Native American relics I'd seen, but the stonework was far more crude. If that's what was inside Mike, he likely wouldn't survive the removal.

It was time for round two of learn-to-speak-their-language. I held up both arrows beside Mike's wound and pointed to each in turn and then toward the broken shaft protruding from Mike's back. I hoped my gesture made it clear that I wanted to know which kind of arrow they'd used to shoot Mike.

I thought it was working until the man shook his head and turned away.

I glanced at the team. "Does anybody have any suggestions on how to get this point across?"

Instead of my team offering ideas, one of the tribesmen held up an arrow that looked more like a spear. It was at least six feet tall and topped with an even larger stone tip. He pointed toward the arrow and then to the bloody shaft in Mike's back.

I said, "Well, this isn't good."

Mongo grimaced. "If we try to back that thing out, it'll rip him apart."

I settled onto the ground beside Mike. "It's time to make some decisions. You're in bad shape. There's no way to sugarcoat it. You need a real doctor in a real hospital. Before you pass out, I want to know what you want me to do."

He said, "Move out of the way for a minute."

I feared he was about to draw his pistol and open up on the tribe, and I couldn't let that happen. "You can't shoot them."

"I'm not going to shoot them. I'm going to ask for their help."

I stood and moved away while Mike motioned toward the wound and then made a gesture as if pulling out the arrow.

The man I almost shot in the back took Mike's hand in his and nodded. A second tribesman rolled several leaves into a ball and handed it to the first man, who offered it to Mike.

He took the ball and held it between his fingers. The tribesman moved Mike's hand toward his mouth, pressing the ball to his lips.

Mike recoiled. "You're crazy. I'm not eating that. You already tried to kill me once. Are you trying to poison me now?"

The native took the ball of leaves from Mike's hand and put it in his own mouth. He chewed and pointed toward his throat simultaneously. While making gestures down his neck and into his stomach, he shook his head violently left and right. Then, he pulled the ball from his mouth and offered it back to Mike, who made no effort to accept it.

I said, "I think it's some sort of natural medicine—maybe like an antibiotic."

"I don't trust them," he said.

"Maybe not, but the other option is us carrying you out of here with a razor-sharp rock stuck in your shoulder."

I took the ball of leaves from the tribesman and stuck it into my mouth, then I chewed several times but didn't swallow. The taste was bitter and unpleasant, though I didn't stop breathing. Seconds later, I felt a lot like I was in a dentist's chair with my mouth completely numb.

"It's anesthetic," I said as I drooled from the corner of my mouth.

"Are you sure?" Mike asked.

I pinched my lips and jaws several times. "Nothing. Whatever it is, it's good stuff."

Mike surrendered and held out his hand. I placed the twice-chewed ball into his palm, and he made a face. The native laid a fresh ball of the same leaves into Mike's hand and relieved him of the wet one.

Mike timidly bit the poultice between his teeth and chewed lightly. The native nodded and began the work of removing the pressure bandage Mongo had applied to the wound.

Our giant stepped forward. "That's not a good idea. He'll bleed out."

I held up a hand. "Let's see what he does. We can always dress the wound again."

Mike mumbled through the numbness. "Does anybody care if I'm okay with this?"

We ignored him as the native pulled the bloody bandages from the wound. After unrolling the first ball of leaves, he pressed them around the arrow shaft as Mike roared in pain. He held out a hand in front of Mike's mouth, and the paratrooper spit out the leaves. The tribesman continued unrolling and pressing the sodden foliage around the wound. A third ball of leaves went into Mike's mouth, and he was soon swaying his head back and forth until his eyelids fell closed.

The native plucked the plants from Mike's mouth and took a long breath. A second tribesman knelt in front of Mike and applied pressure to the front of his shoulder.

I had no idea what was about to happen, but I was eternally grateful I wasn't in Mike's shoes.

The first native placed a palm across the broken butt of the arrow protruding from Mike's shoulder and glanced at his brother. They nodded in unison, and an instant later, the arrowhead emerged from Mike's chest. The man grasped the arrowhead and pulled the broken shaft through the wound. Blood followed, and the tribesman pressed the ball of leaves into the exit wound. Then, using the pressure dressing Mongo had applied earlier, the man created two new dressings and pressed them to both sides of the wound.

Mongo took over and taped the dressings in place. He said, "Other than having the arrow out of his chest, I'm not sure he's in any better condition than he was a few minutes ago."

I said, "At least we can move him without risking further internal damage."

"I guess, but it's sure going to slow us down."

"We don't have a choice," I said.

With the wounds dressed and taped, Mongo used his size to intimidate two of the tribesmen into surrendering their spears. We used the long shafts as spars and constructed a litter with a pair of wet-weather jackets.

Getting Mike back across the river wasn't going to be fun, but with a little luck, he'd stay alive long enough for us to make it to Tapauá.

The natives produced several more balls of leaves and pressed them into my palm. Then, as if they'd been apparitions, they vanished into the darkened jungle without a sound.

Chapter 24
Kill, Then Heal

"Chto proiskhodit?"

Anya's slurred question was exactly the same as mine, and my only answer was, "I have no idea what's happening."

She rubbed her neck and scratched the tiny wound where the dart had pierced her flesh. "I am . . . uh, I do not know word. *Smushchen-nyy*."

"The word is *confused*," I said. "A lot happened in the last half hour. I'll catch you up when you're a little sharper. For now, stay with me so we can cross the river without losing you again."

"YA vsegda budu s toboy, Chasechka."

Her pledge to never leave me didn't deserve a response, so I grabbed her gun belt and dragged her down the muddy riverbank and into the water.

Shawn, Gator, and Mongo managed the litter carrying Mike. Everything about the operation was dangerous, awkward, and painfully slow. Manhandling a drowsy Russian assassin across the river was far from a walk in the park, but all of us made it relatively unscathed.

When everyone was safely on the eastern bank, we grounded the litter and took a knee to catch our breath and walk through a welfare check.

Mike was still solidly unconscious from the dose of magic jungle leaves. Anya was still mumbling like an Eastern European madwoman. And the rest of us had far more questions than we'd ever have answers.

"Is anyone hurt?" I asked.

Mongo said, "Mike's breathing is slow, and his heart rate is around thirty, so he's not doing great."

"How about the rest of you?"

Shawn held up a thick, black, wormlike creature. "I plucked three of these things off of me, so I recommend checking yourselves."

In seconds, seven American barbarians and one undeniably Russian non-barbarian were completely naked on the bank of a river, somewhere in the middle of the Amazonian rainforest, plucking leaches from each other like mother apes picking mites from their babies.

Under normal circumstances—whatever those are—the scene would've been hilarious, but laughter wasn't a luxury we could afford in the moment.

Reclothed, we struck out, roughly paralleling the river to the southwest as the sun battled its way across the horizon somewhere behind us and fought bravely to pierce the nearly impenetrable shield of foliage overhead.

We made slow progress and rotated through positions carrying Mike. Both the pace and the task were exhausting, so I called the team to a halt.

When Disco and Singer lowered the litter to the jungle floor, Mike stirred and groaned. The rainforest was as bright as it would be at any point in the day, but we remained in the shadows. Mike let his eyes roam our faces, but recognition wasn't there.

I laid a hand on his arm. "Relax, Mike. You're in good hands. You were injured, and we're carrying you out. Just stay where you are."

He rolled onto his side and studied the world and people around him. "Injured how?"

"You wouldn't believe me if I told you. Are you in pain?"

"No. I'm sleepy, though, and I can't really focus." He planted a hand on the mossy ground and tried to push himself to his knees. The attempt was noble but unsuccessful.

"Just stay down," I said. "We'll get you to a hospital as soon as we can."

"What happened to me?"

I produced a rolled ball of leaves. "We'll talk about that when you're feeling better. For now, chew on this, but don't swallow it."

He scowled. "What? Why?"

"It's a natural painkiller. It'll help you sleep."

"Who are you people?" he asked, still drowsy.

"Just chew on this. We'll get you to a doctor a lot faster if you'll sleep."

"I think I can walk."

I held him in place on the litter. "It would be better if you slept. Maybe you can walk next time you wake up."

Resistant to chewing the leaves, he shied away, but I stuck the ball into his mouth with my thumb. "Chew, but don't swallow."

He reluctantly obeyed and was soon back in what I assumed was a peaceful sleep.

Mongo knelt beside me. "What do you think about trying to get a call to the ship? Maybe Skipper can contact Gun Bunny and get her to fly out here and pick him up. I'm worried about him."

I laid a hand against Mike's face. "Does he feel hot to you?"

Mongo nodded and said, "That's what I mean. He's not doing well."

"Do we have any antibiotics?"

"I pumped him full, but short of opening that wound back up and cleaning it from the inside out, we're fighting the clock."

True to her word, Anya hadn't left my side since we climbed from the river.

I asked, "How's your English now?"

"I feel better," she said. "You want for me to climb tree again, no?"

"Can you?"

"I can maybe try. You will catch me if I cannot, yes?"

"Hold that thought," I said. "How far are we from the river?"

Mongo said, "I can hear it, so we're close. What's on your mind?"

"We might be able to pick up a satellite from the river if there's a break in the trees."

"It's worth a shot," he said. "If it works, you'll be able to get a solid position fix, too."

"Let's go."

While the remainder of the team rested, hydrated, and pulled security, Mongo and I headed for the water. Anya lumbered along as if tethered to my hip.

I motioned toward Mike as he lay lifeless on the litter. "Stay with him. We'll be right back."

"But you made me promise to never leave you," she argued.

"That's not exactly what happened, but I think you're sane enough to survive on your own for a few minutes."

"But you will come back to me, yes?"

I chuckled. "Just stay with Mike and make sure he doesn't wander off."

Mongo was right about our proximity to the river. I was pleased to see a sweeping horseshoe with a wide-open view of the sky above the river's bend only a few hundred yards away.

From the bank, I drew my sat-phone and unfolded the antenna. Within two minutes, the signal strength indicator showed contact with two satellites, and I'd never been happier to know we were under the watchful eye of the orbiting robots.

Skipper's voice felt like a warm security blanket wrapped around me. "Chase! Where are you? Are you okay?"

"You've been taking lessons from Penny on how to shove as many questions as possible into one sentence, haven't you?"

"I'm serious," she said. "We expected you in Tapauá by now."

"We ran into a little snag. Anya got shot by a poison dart and taken hostage. Mike took an arrow in the shoulder. And I learned to communicate with some tribesmen who've probably never seen anything like us before."

"You've had quite a night, then. Is Anya okay?"

"She's still a little loopy, and I think she may have forgotten how to speak English, but she's going to be okay. Mike, on the other hand, is not. We've got him knocked out on a homemade litter, but he's burning up with fever, and we really need to get him to a hospital."

"Where are you?"

"I was hoping you could tell me."

She rattled off a lat and long, but I said, "How far from Tapauá are we?"

"Six miles in straight-line distance."

"That's at least six hours carrying Mike. Do you have comms with Gun Bunny?"

"I do," she said. "Should I send her?"

"Affirmative. Get her here as soon as you can. Is there a decent hospital in Tapauá?"

"Stand by."

I waited, and she returned in seconds.

"She'll be there in less than fifteen minutes. Is there a place for her to land?"

"She'll have to hover over the river. There's no LZ in sight. What about a hospital?"

"I'll tell her," she said. "There are two hospitals, but there's likely nobody in either one of them who speaks English."

"That should make things interesting. I guess we'll have to rely on medicine being a universal language."

"Good luck with that."

"Does either of the hospitals have a helipad?"

"I'll find out."

While waiting for her to come back onto the line, Mongo checked the sky, and I asked, "Do you hear the chopper?"

"Not yet. I'm just wondering how tough this is going to be."

"It won't be easy, but I think there's plenty of room for her to get in, don't you?"

He studied the tree-lined riverbanks. "She can get in. The question is, can we get Mike into the chopper without drowning him or ourselves?"

"How deep do you think it is?"

"There's only one way to know."

He shucked off his gun belt and body armor before wading into the black water. Six shuffling steps later, he disappeared, and I tossed off my belt and armor. Fortunately, he reemerged before I jumped in.

"Wasn't expecting that," he said as he shook his head like a dog.

I said, "I guess it's at least seven feet, huh?"

He swam backward toward the center of the river. "It's deeper than that, but I'll check the center. If I can find a sandbar, that'll make it a little easier."

Skipper came back. "Chopper's airborne, and I found a helipad at Hospital Comunitário Santa Madre."

I said, "I don't know what that means, but I trust you."

Mongo swam back ashore and climbed the bank. "It's no good. It's at least ten feet deep all the way across."

"I wish we had a hoist on the chopper."

He wiped the water from his face. "You've got me and Shawn. We're better than any hoist. If you can get Mike above the skids, we'll be able to haul him in."

"It's worth a shot," I said. "Get the others, and I'll wait here for the bird."

He trotted off to the east, and I watched the Huey top the trees to the west. I yelled into the sat-phone over the roar of the approaching rotors. "She's here. I'll call you back from the air."

Before I thumbed the button to end the call, Skipper said, "You never answered my question. Is everybody else okay?"

"We're a little beat up, but we're good."

Gun Bunny came to a hover on the opposite side of the river and flashed her landing light in my direction. I waved and signaled for her to hover over the water, and she slowly brought the chopper forward and began her descent. As she drew within feet of the water's surface, spray flew in every direction, turning the air into a water-filled tornado. I studied the situation, but no matter how I approached it, there was nothing good about my terrible plan.

Mongo emerged from the jungle with the rest of the team in tow, just in time to see the torrent of water and wind beneath the Huey.

He said, "That doesn't look like much fun, but I guess we have to try, huh?"

"If we want Mike to live, we don't have a choice."

"All right. Here goes nothing."

He grabbed Shawn and swam to the center of the river. They fought the swirling wind and spray for several minutes before they climbed onto the skid and made their way into the cabin of the chopper. After a few seconds of rest, Mongo waved for us to bring Mike into the water.

Being the tallest two behind Mongo, Gator and I gripped the litter and waded into the river.

I yelled over the noise of the hovering Huey. "This is going to suck, but we've got to get him above the skid. Can you do it?"

He nodded, and we began our swim.

The wind blew against us using Mike's litter as a kite and pushed us back, no matter how hard we clawed at the water. We fought until we barely had the strength to stay afloat and propel ourselves forward. Singer and Kodiak dived in and swam out to add some muscle to our effort, but even with their added strength, we couldn't win the battle against the wind. We each took a corner of the litter and swam Mike back ashore.

I sat in the shallow water at the bank and studied the situation. There had to be a way to get Mike aboard that helicopter without drowning him.

The task of holding a five-thousand-pound machine in a hover only inches above the water is torturous, so Gun Bunny pulled up and climbed above the trees to catch her breath.

I looked up at Disco, the best pilot I've ever met. "Got any ideas?"

"How about a SPIE?"

"Why didn't I think of that?" I said. "Call 'em up and see what they've got up there."

He drew his radio and made the call to the Huey. A few seconds later, a length of rope fell from the chopper and dangled fifty feet beneath the belly. A second piece of rope fell to the river's surface and slowly floated downstream.

I didn't have to ask. Kodiak volunteered by stroking away from the shoreline like an Olympic swimmer. He was back in less than a minute and turned the retrieved rope into a Swiss seat for himself and a more elaborate harness for Mike, who'd be little more than a ragdoll on the lift.

Between the roar of the rotor and the wind, it was impossible for Mike to sleep through the experience. The look on his face said he was confused, disoriented, and maybe even a little scared.

His eyes darted wildly. "What's happening?"

"Trust us," I said. "We're getting you out of here."

Kodiak knelt beside our victim and asked, "Have you ever done a SPIE—a Special Patrol Insertion/Extraction?"

"Once," he said. "But I didn't love it."

Kodiak laughed. "You're not going to love this one, either, but it's our only way out of here. I'm taking you with me. Don't try to extend your arms. Just relax and let me do the flying."

With their harnesses tied and clipped together, Gator and I helped Kodiak and Mike to the edge of the water.

Mike was practically dead weight, unable to support himself. He said, "I don't feel so . . ."

What happened next was far from pleasant for any of us to watch, but Kodiak got the worst of it. When Mike stopped retching, Kodiak unclipped himself and slid into the water. After a quick bath, he was back.

"Don't do that again, kid. That's nasty."

Mike tried to wipe his mouth with spaghetti arms. "Sorry. I didn't mean to."

"Just turn your head next time."

I waved for Gun Bunny to move in, and she did exactly that. She brought the dangling line directly into my hand, and I tied a bowline in the end. After we clipped Mike and Kodiak to the line and backed away, I signaled for Gun Bunny to climb, and she eased away from the bank.

Kodiak and Mike left their feet and rose into the air below the Huey. A thousand thoughts poured through my mind in that moment, but the one I couldn't shake was hoping the natives were hidden somewhere in the trees, watching the man they'd try to kill—and then tried to heal—fly away into the heavens beneath a machine they'd never be able to describe to the rest of the tribe.

Chapter 25
The Right First Name

As the whop-whop of the Huey's rotors softened and finally disappeared, I said, "We're six miles from Tapauá. Do you guys want to wait it out and fly or hoof it?"

"We can make that in just over an hour if the terrain doesn't turn nasty," Singer said.

We struck out at the fastest pace we'd made in the previous two days. I pulled rear guard with Disco just in front of me. He was in great shape, but his age alone made him our weakest link.

"How's the pace, old man?"

"Just try to keep up," he said over his shoulder.

As we grew closer to the city, the jungle seemed to sense the necessity to open herself and allow humanity to encroach. Nature's acquiescence to man's insistence gave us the room to turn our fast-walking pace into a light jog, and we covered the six miles with ease. By the time we reached the edge of the city, Disco and I were winded, but the rest of the team seemed ready for another six miles.

Our sat-phones celebrated their clear view of the sky over the city of Tapauá. But as welcome as the satellite reception was, five fully armed, filthy commandos wouldn't likely receive a warm welcome on the streets of the city.

Gun Bunny answered promptly. "Go for air."

"It's Chase. How'd it go at the hospital?"

She said, "I think it was the first time they'd ever had anyone delivered on a rope, but they put him on a gurney and took him away. I left Mongo there with him, but Shawn's still with me. Should we come pull you out of there?"

"I hope they can work through the language barrier," I said.

"I think Mongo had that under control. He apparently found a common language with one of the hospital staff. I can be back on site in ten minutes if you need a lift."

"We're at the eastern edge of the city."

"Wow, you must've double-timed it. Shoot me your location, and I'll hop over and grab you. I don't think you need to be walking down Main Street with M4s across your shoulders."

I sent her our coordinates, and she appeared in no time.

We climbed aboard, and she touched us down on the parking ramp of the airport that was definitely not what I expected. Half of the runway seemed to be constructed of something resembling extremely low-quality concrete, and the other half was red clay. There were no hangars, but a few small buildings dotted the southern boundary of the aerodrome.

As the rotor spun down, Gun Bunny pulled off her helmet and leaned toward me. "Not exactly LaGuardia, is it?"

"I'd say it's a little more like Heathrow. Have you made any friends yet?"

She pointed toward a block building with a tin roof a few hundred feet away. "There's a shower in there, and you guys could definitely use one. The locals seem friendly. Nobody's asked any questions yet, and they were happy to take good ol' American dollars for all the gas I could carry."

We took advantage of the showers, and clean, dry clothes felt like a gift from Heaven. Without intentionally doing so, we drifted off to sleep in the awkward collection of chairs scattered around the building. But a few seconds into my slumber, I jerked upright with the realization that no one was pulling security, and Ronda No-H—our CFO and the best door gunner on the planet—pressed her finger to her lips and whispered, "Barbie and I've got you. Get some rest."

Barbie—AKA Gun Bunny from her days as an Apache pilot in the Army—had never worked with us on a ground operation, but she'd pulled our butts out of the fire more times than I could count. Knowing those two were standing guard allowed me to relax enough to drift back into the sleep my body needed so badly.

* * *

Once rested, we huddled up, and Mongo joined us.

"How's your paratrooper?" I asked.

"He's not mine. You're the one who adopted him."

"Regardless, how's he doing?"

"Not great. He's in pretty bad shape. The language is a hurdle, but it appears they're trying to decide where they can send him."

I said, "I thought you found somebody who speaks English."

"There are a few techs with some English, but I haven't found a doctor or nurse yet. From what I can piece together, they're leaning toward Hospital Israelita Albert Einstein in São Paulo."

"Einstein?" I asked.

"I don't get the connection. That's just what I picked up. I think we should let his wife know what's going on."

"Is it that serious?"

He nodded slowly, and I turned to Disco. "Can that dirt runway out there support the Gulfstream?"

"Sure, but you and I are the only two who can fly it."

I opened my sat-phone and had Skipper on the line in seconds. "Who do we have who speaks Portuguese?"

She said, "I'm not sure, but I'll find out. Do you need an interpreter?"

"No, we need a medical escort. Mike's not going to make it if we don't get him out of South America."

"Why do we need a medical escort who speaks Portuguese? Why not just load him up and bring him to the States? Who cares what their diagnosis is?"

"Give me a minute to think." A thousand thoughts cascaded through my head, but every one of them kept leading me to Emory in Atlanta or UAB in Birmingham. I didn't need an instant plan. I only needed to get the right ball rolling in the right direction, so I pointed to Disco. "Take Gun Bunny, and get the *Grey Ghost* here double-quick."

He and the Huey pilot hopped to their feet, and they were airborne almost before I stuck the phone back to my face. "Any luck with a Portuguese speaker?"

Skipper said, "Not yet, but I'm working on it."

"Start with Dr. Shadrack's staff. If we can get somebody on the phone with the doctors here in Tapauá to make them understand we're taking Mike to the States, that'll solve the initial problem."

"I'm on it," she said. "What else do you need?"

"That's it for now. As soon as Gun Bunny gets back, we're heading for Belo Monte. We're ninety-nine percent certain that's where Hunter and the natives are headed."

Skipper paused for a moment and finally said, "I know you're the boss and all, but I've got a thought."

"Let's hear it."

"What if we notify South-Wind Ventures about Mike? He's their responsibility, right?"

I said, "Under better circumstances, I'd say yes, but if I'm guessing correctly, they're going to hang him out to dry, and if he doesn't make it, that solves their PR disaster."

"I get it," she said, "but we could dangle the bait and give them a chance to do the right thing."

"I agree in concept, but I've seen these guys in action down here. If they send Smith and his team to snatch Mike out of the hospital, nobody will ever see him again. I like the way you're thinking, but we took responsibility for him when we nabbed him, so we're going to treat him like one of us until this is over."

"You're the boss. And the computer found a Portuguese speaker, but you're never going to believe who it is."

"Come on," I said. "We don't have time to play games."

"Dr. Masha Turner."

"That's perfect. And the fact that her first name is Doctor makes it even better. I'm putting you on with Mongo. Get the two of them on the same line, and work out what we need. Make sure she emphasizes being a doctor. She doesn't need to mention that she's not a medical doctor."

"I'll make it happen," Skipper said. "Where do you want to take him?"

"Find us a doctor willing to take the case and a hospital with a bed. Get Dr. Shadrack involved if necessary. He's got a lot of contacts in that world."

"I'm on it."

I handed the phone to Mongo and passed the baton. With Mike's situation well on its way to being handled, focusing on finding Hunter was my number-one priority.

Leadership, I've learned, is little more than crisis management without allowing anybody to see the torrential storm raging inside my skull.

I gathered my thoughts and restarted our briefing. "We're going to be down a man. Disco's going to fly Mike to the States to keep him alive while the rest of us find Hunter."

Mongo said, "Doesn't the *Ghost* require two pilots?"

"It does," I said, "but I'm not leaving this country without Hunter. Disco is more than capable."

"Fair enough. What's the plan at Belo Monte?"

I pulled up the map on my tablet. "It's less than ninety miles to the village from here. It appears on the chart as being east of the river, but I don't believe that's right. There may be a settlement with that name east of the river, but I expect to find our target well west of the water."

The team studied the satellite imagery on the tablet, and Kodiak said, "It looks like getting wet is our only insertion."

"Maybe," I said, "but if we can find a man-sized hole in the canopy, we can fast rope or rappel in. Getting out will be the challenge, but we've proven we can pull that off, even if it requires a little acrobatics."

I tossed a balled-up napkin at our Russian. "How are you feeling?"

"I am better now after rest. Did you kill person who shot me with dart?"

"Did you want me to kill him?"

"No. I hope you did not. I will go back and kill him when this is finished."

I wanted to believe she was joking, but I couldn't make that stretch. "Maybe we can give him a pass this time. What do you think?"

She glared back at me. "When do you give pass to man who tries to kill you?"

"You tried to kill me in the lagoon on St. Thomas a few hundred years ago."

"This is not true," she demanded. "I only made you submit to my will. If I were trying to kill you, you would be already dead."

"Submit to your will, huh? Was it your will for me to shoot you in the foot?"

She jabbed a finger toward me. "That was not necessary."

"It seemed pretty necessary to me at the time. I was seconds away from drowning."

She chuckled. "I would not let you drown, Chasechka. You were rookie intelligence officer back then. I had so much to teach you."

"Oh, is that what it was? You were conducting a training class?"

She smiled. "Being teacher for you was very nice time for me."

I shook a finger. "Nope. We're not going down that road. We're here to find Hunter, and that's what we're going to do."

* * *

Disco brought the *Grey Ghost* to a dusty stop on the clay end of the single runway and taxied to the parking apron. To my surprise, the fuel truck had the correct nozzle to gas up the *Ghost*, and we took on every ounce he could squeeze into the tanks.

Skipper called with the best news I'd heard in days. "I just got off the phone with Masha and the surgeon. You made a good call getting Mike out of there. He'll be packed and ready for shipping. They're going to deliver him to the airport by ambulance, and they sound quite happy to dump him on somebody else."

"Outstanding," I said. "Disco will have him on the ground six hours after the ambulance shows up. Where should he take him?"

"Shuttlesworth. An ambulance from UAB will meet them on the ramp. Dr. Shadrack arranged for a physician friend of his to take the case, and they just happened to have an available bed."

I felt the tiniest hint of relief. "You do remarkable work, Skipper. There's just one more thing . . ."

"Name it."

"Find a way to get Mike's wife from Georgia to Birmingham. They should be together during this."

She giggled. "It's already done, and I charged their hotel room to your card."

"Of course you did. Thank you for taking care of everything. As soon as Gun Bunny gets some sleep after she gets back, we're moving to intercept Hunter. I'll call before we blast off."

* * *

The ambulance arrived with Mike strapped securely to a gurney, and we carried him up the boarding stairs and locked the bed into the hardpoints just behind the main cabin.

I climbed into the cockpit with Disco as he programmed the navigation system and checked the weather to the north. I said, "Are you sure you're going to be okay by yourself?"

He laughed. "Sure, as long as the FAA doesn't catch me flying forty thousand pounds by myself."

"We'll break you out of aviation prison if it becomes necessary."

"Thanks," he said. "That's reassuring. What do you want me to do when I drop him off?"

"I want you to get some sleep and then get back here. We'll need a ride home when we find Hunter."

He glanced across his shoulder, apparently to make sure no one was listening. "What do you think the chances of finding him are?"

"One hundred percent," I said. "Failure is *not* what we do."

Chapter 26
Right Here, Right Now

We were awake and chomping at the bit to fly when the eastern sky showed her first glimpse of light the following morning. The Huey was fueled, and a thorough preflight inspection was complete. Barbie climbed into the cockpit and slid onto her well-earned throne of the right seat. Her experience and skill made her the default aircraft commander, but it was her fearlessness under fire that earned her the ultimate respect of every member of the team.

Comms checks were complete, and Skipper was on the line. She said, "Remember, guys. We'll have good comms as long as you're on the helo, but once you're under the shade of the trees, they'll be choppy at best."

I cast a glance at Mongo, and he gave me a wink, so I said, "Now that we've got the drones, we can fly a remote antenna our big brain built. That won't keep us in constant contact, but if we get ourselves in a bind, we'll at least be able to shoot you our position."

She said, "That sounds good. What's the plan for the Huey while you're on the ground?"

"Ideally, we'll find an LZ nearby where she can stage until we're ready to run."

Skipper said, "I've been combing through the satellite imagery, and I haven't found anything within twenty miles of Belo Monte except the river."

Gun Bunny said, "It's only eighty miles from here, so if all else fails,

I can stage back here at Tapauá. With the bladders, I've got twelve hours of fuel, so the autopilot and I can loiter all day if necessary."

I said, "We can plan and talk all day, but that's not getting us any closer to Hunter. So, let's roll."

Both sliding doors were secured open so the team could sit on the deck of the Huey with their boots on the skids and scan the landscape for any sign of our brother. I planted myself in the left seat, but I didn't plan to touch the controls.

With the full team and extra fuel bladders aboard, we were heavy, but the Huey was more than capable of climbing away at a thousand feet per minute.

Within seconds, we were west of the city of Tapauá and soaring across the jungle at a hundred twenty miles per hour. Every inch of the massive rainforest looked like every other inch in all directions, with the exception of the winding river cutting its way through the landscape like an enormous snake patrolling for her next victim. I forced myself to believe we wouldn't end up in the mouth of that ancient serpent.

"There's the cut," Barbie said with an outstretched finger.

"That's Belo Monte?" I asked.

"According to the chart, it is."

I studied the tiny opening in the jungle canopy. "Let's give it a look."

"Do you want the controls?"

"No, just put us in a gentle left turn about five hundred feet. We don't want to scare anybody."

She said, "Your flying isn't that scary."

My head and my heart needed that little moment of levity, so I enjoyed it without retaliating.

Soon, we were in a sweeping left turn around the opening in the trees. I leaned as far left as the harness would allow and examined the scene. "That's no native village."

Mongo said, "I was about to say the same thing. Those are real buildings, not huts. This isn't the place."

I said, "Track west in long S-turns, and let's see what we can find."

Barbie turned westward and set up the perfect search pattern, giving excellent visibility to both sides of the chopper.

I said, "We're looking for anything man-made, so keep your eyes open."

Approximately fifteen miles west of the river, a glint of light flashed from the trees out the left side of the helo, and I asked, "Did anybody else see that?"

Shawn said, "I caught a reflection at nine o'clock and eight hundred meters."

"Me, too."

Barbie said, "I didn't see it. You have the controls."

I slid my feet onto the pedals and my hands around the collective and cyclic. "My airplane."

"Your airplane," Barbie echoed.

I lowered the nose and turned left until we were bearing on the momentary flash of light. I'll never know what made me give the order, but something in my gut made me call, "Get on the gun, Ronda."

"Ready on the gun," she said.

The order changed the tone aboard the Huey. If we'd been alert before, we'd become über-aware of every movement below the skids. The muscles of my shoulders and neck tensed as we approached the spot where we'd seen the flash.

Ronda called, "Tallyho! Eleven o'clock, two hundred meters. It's camo netting."

I broke right just far enough to set up a long left turn, then I glanced backward to see three M4 barrels protruding from the fuselage just ahead of Ronda's M134 Minigun.

My mind reeled. *What could possibly explain camouflage netting in the middle of the rainforest? What have we stumbled upon, and who's trying to hide it?*

I was fixed on the object, but whoever placed the netting knew what they were doing. Nothing about the silhouette gave any hint of what was hidden by the green net.

I continued the left turn with my focus entirely on the ground and the Huey an extension of my feet and hands. "Anybody got the angle to ID that thing?"

The answer that echoed through my head was the last thing I could've expected to hear at that moment.

"Incoming! Four o'clock, three hundred meters."

Suddenly, my attention was back inside the cockpit, and Ronda No-H yelled, "Come about, and bring me to bear!"

I crushed the right pedal and slammed the cyclic into my right thigh. The helicopter spun just as I'd commanded, and Ronda's General Electric Minigun was coming through what had been our three o'clock position only seconds before.

Several muzzle flashes sparked in my periphery, and what had been a peaceful flight ten seconds before turned into an airborne assault. The Minigun belched its deadly roar, sending 7.62 x 51mm projectiles into the jungle at five thousand rounds per minute. The riflemen behind me added their weapons to the fight, and Barbie said, "We're hit! Partial hydraulic failure."

The fight was on my side of the airplane, but I was far from qualified to fly a failing helicopter under fire only feet above the treetops, but surrendering the controls would put Barbie at a decided disadvantage since she couldn't see the ground fire from the right side of the cockpit.

I gripped the controls. "Call hydraulic pressure and report additional damage."

The flashes from between the trees didn't stop, despite the hail of lead we were pouring onto the scene.

Ronda's calm voice came. "Break off and bring me back in from the east. Ready grenades."

Oh, I like it, I thought as I turned to the east and accelerated.

The maneuver would make the shooters on the ground believe we were bugging out, but in seconds, we'd change their minds for the rest of their lives . . . no matter how short that time would be.

Half a mile from the site, I said, "Hold on. We're coming hard about."

I pulled the cyclic into my lap and stomped the left pedal. My previous turn had been aggressive, but that one was enough to scare a drunken crop-duster.

We rolled out of the turn, bearing directly on the site, and I set the speed for the perfect gun run and aerial bombardment. Ronda pressed the trigger and steered the screaming gun into the trees. Tracer rounds reported the trail of bullets and looked like fireworks spraying from the left side of what had become our aerial gunship.

A glance backward gave me a view of a dozen fragmentation grenades falling from the hands of the team on the left side. Even from within the roaring Huey, the thunder of the grenades exploding below echoed through my skull.

We flew over and past the shooters on the ground, putting them astern far enough to assess our condition before making another run at them.

"Report damage," I said.

Singer answered, "We're leaking something that looks like hydraulic fluid into the cabin from overhead, and one of the fuel bladders is pierced. Nobody's hit."

Barbie said, "We're a wounded goose. We can't—"

Somebody yelled, "RPG! Seven o'clock!"

I threw the controls to the right in a desperate attempt to avoid the rocket-propelled grenade racing its way through the air.

Barbie yelled, "Dive!"

Without thinking, I simply obeyed and shoved the cyclic forward. For an instant, I levitated out of my seat, and Barbie ordered, "Hard right and climb!"

The maneuver planted my butt firmly back into my seat and slowed the Huey dramatically.

A glance out the left side gave me a view of the RPG still flying and climbing into the distance.

196 · CAP DANIELS

"I have the controls," Barbie said.

I offered no resistance.

She lowered the nose and built airspeed as we maneuvered farther away from the site.

She said, "Where there's one RPG, there's always another."

I scanned the panel filled with red lights that were warning of low hydraulic pressure and a dozen other calamities we didn't have time to deal with. "We've got to get out of here."

"Where do you want me to go?" Barbie asked. "The river's our only shot at saving the chopper."

We set a course directly for the river, and Anya said, "Look at top of tree at nine o'clock. Is maybe person who shot me with dart."

I wasn't certain I'd heard her correctly, but my head turned involuntarily, and to my absolute disbelief, a tribesman who looked a lot like the last natives we encountered sat in the top of a massive tree, waving his arms.

This keeps getting weirder by the minute. Did somebody give the natives automatic weapons and RPGs?

"We need to be on the ground," I said.

Barbie answered, "Yeah, I know. I'm working on it."

"No, I mean we need to be on the ground *right* here, *right* now."

"Why?"

"Because we just found Hunter."

The next voice I heard was Singer's, but it was far from his calm, confident baritone. It was as close to panic as I'd ever heard from him. "RPG, three o'clock close! Brace!"

Barbie shoved the controls in a thousand directions in a desperate effort to evade the helicopter-killing airborne grenade only feet from the fuselage. I spun in my seat as I tried to get a glimpse of the incoming round, but before I could focus, the Huey shuddered and bucked like a rodeo bull just before it began its death spin.

Barbie wrestled the controls. "You're getting your wish, Cowboy. We're going to the ground *right* here, *right* now. The tail rotor's gone."

We were riding a five-thousand-pound meteor on a collision course with an awning of trees a thousand miles from everywhere.

The world outside my windscreen was a blur of green spinning out of control, but the hardcore aviatress beside me continued her mortal combat with the machine that was doing its best to fall apart in her hands.

The spinning didn't stop, but it slowed as she lowered the collective, taking some of the torque out of the main rotor system. In my mind, the lowered torque meant only one thing—the torque went the lift, and we were falling like a rock. Nothing could be done to save the aircraft, and only mercy from above could save the lives inside.

Chapter 27
Do an E.T.

Terror comes in countless flavors, and as we plummeted toward the trees in a spinning, dying helicopter, I may have tasted more of them than at any other moment in my life. Time, in some way that's impossible to explain or comprehend, passed with immeasurable speed, while at the same time, almost froze in place.

Although confined in the cockpit of what would likely become my coffin, I imagined the faces of the family and team behind me, and I remembered with perfect clarity every battle we'd fought side by side and every fleeting moment of perfect peace we'd shared when the bullets weren't racing toward us at supersonic speed.

Gator's youth reminded me so much of my own when I was little more than an incompetent student of a world that I called home. I remembered every lesson Clark Johnson taught me as I grew and failed and thrived and won and lost. In that instant, I was both elated that Clark wouldn't share my coming fate and also saddened that we wouldn't lay down our lives on the same bloody soil, serving the ultimate duty of mankind.

I didn't have to see Singer's lips to know he was whispering to the God to whom he had devoted his very soul.

Shawn, although I'd known him for the shortest time of any brother-at-arms, had become an enormous part of me and the team with his skill, strength, and fortitude. He would die alongside warriors he already loved and respected just as much as we felt for him.

Mongo, a giant in every way, was no doubt calculating angles and directions that were most likely to provide even limited security from the coming collision with trees, earth, and eternity. But he would not place himself in those positions; instead, he would place as many of those around him in the places where they could possibly survive while he sacrificed himself so they might live.

I could envision Kodiak's unruly hair and beard swaying with the spinning chopper as the acceptance of his racing fate lay before him. His final thoughts would likely be about the sour taste of failure to complete his final mission of finding and evacuating Hunter.

Then, she came as I knew she would. Anya's face flashed before my eyes far too quickly for me to see or feel the physical beauty, leaving instead my sadness that she would never know the fullness of the freedom she never truly experienced. Somehow, I believed she would welcome the end, knowing she had perished among fighters of limitless skill and devotion, just like her.

As if she were part of me rather than another person so far away, I felt more than saw the wife to whom I would always owe my sanity and ability to do what had become my life's work. Without the support I felt, heard, and tasted from her, being what I was meant to be would've been impossible. She didn't need me. She was independently successful in every way without anything I provided for her. My very heart reached through the miles, desperately longing to find hers. I would likely depart this life without her by my side, and my greatest regret as I passed into eternity would be not touching her face one last time and hearing her laughter wrap around me before my body returned to dust.

As for me, the reality of death's cruel hand grasping for me didn't come. Although frightened and emptied by the coming aftermath of the inevitable crash, my soul was at rest, believing something far better waited on the other side of that minuscule point in time and space separating the quick and the dead . . . a point through which we must all pass.

I gripped my seat in an involuntary reaction to the situation. There was nothing my hands could do to make Barbie's wrestling match with the controls a winnable bout.

Will we be found?

Will anyone ever know our ultimate fate?

Will Hunter survive?

Will Penny spend the remainder of her life searching for the truth of my end?

The first of a thousand points of contact came, and with it, the truth of our dire condition. The skids brushed into the treetops, parting branch from limb and limb from trunk as the energy of the flying machine was transferred into the arms of the trees and ultimately down the trunk and into the waiting earth below.

The dense canopy absorbed us as if we were a stone falling into still water, and our spinning slowed even more. The thrashing, tearing, and shredding I expected didn't come. Instead, the sounds of breaking timber and metal sliding through vegetation filled the air.

Time reclaimed its cruel throne, returning the hands of the clock to their endless resilience. We penetrated the treetops and emerged with three dozen feet remaining between us and the floor of the rainforest. The darkening world before me was still framed inside the limits of the windscreen, but it was out of focus and chaotic. The inertia of our spin proved itself to be a formidable force, but the resistance of everything around us fought in earnest to further slow our corkscrew path through the trees.

The Van Horn composite main rotor blades disintegrated as they struck the unyielding trunks of mahogany trees, sending strips of carbon fiber exploding in every direction. Finally, the spinning ceased, leaving only a vertical component to our fate. We were going in, and we were nothing more than unwilling spectators in our own mortal demise.

Once again, time seemed to lose its hold on me, and the scene I perceived slowed as if caught by some unseen, all-powerful hand until the corpse of the Huey came to rest six feet above the forest floor, suspended and trapped by intersecting trees forming the cradle into which we'd fallen.

I was alive, or at least I believed that to be the case. The pair of turbines above and behind my head still whistled as they continued to do exactly what they'd been designed to do. Just like the men and women around me, they would fight and stay the course until the final ounce of passion and drive leaving their bodies was extinguished.

As I tried to take full measure of the world around me, I found my right arm clamped in an immovable vise. Nothing hurt, and I felt no blood, but trying to move my arm was like forcing the sun from the sky. Afraid of what I might find when I looked down to assess the condition, I cast my eyes downward with dread and fear. When I discovered what bound me to the seat, I was both relieved and even amused. I followed the line of the fingers, hands, and arms that were clamped around my wrist to find the blue eyes of the first woman who ever loved me as a man. Those eyes stared up at me with an intensity I couldn't understand until her lips formed the words, "I did not want to die without holding to you, my Chasechka. I will let go, but not for another moment, please."

A part of me in which I hold no pride appreciated the gesture and the sentiment, but I had responsibilities beyond those of the Russian's desires. My eyes met Barbie's, and she pressed her lips into a single thin line before offering a nod as she shut down each of the Huey's systems as if we'd made a normal landing in the middle of a perfectly flat runway.

I thumbed my harness, allowing the straps to retract and free me from my binding to the seat beneath me. As I turned to face the cabin, Anya's fingers melted from my arm, and the faces of my team stared back at me in perfect silence.

Forcing the words to come, I asked, "Is anybody hurt?"

No one spoke, but each of them shook their heads as if unable to open their mouths. Words, in that moment, weren't necessary. The fact that we hadn't perished, as fate seemed to demand, spoke volumes without any of us adding a whisper.

A moment passed as the reality of the incident overtook us, and one by one, we shifted our weight, slowly at first, testing the strength of the cradle under us. Shawn was first to leave his seat. He stepped lightly from the cabin and onto the left skid. The remains of the helicopter didn't budge, so he leapt to the ground waiting below. Following his lead, each of us traced his steps and found ourselves unscathed.

Barbie stood in awe as she studied the carcass of her beloved Huey suspended above our heads. She looked between me and the chopper and said the last thing I could've ever expected. "Next time, let me do the landing, okay?"

As much as we needed the comic relief, we had serious work to do.

I spun and gave the order, "Set perimeter security. Gator, get back up there and offload the gear."

Shawn, Kodiak, Singer, and Mongo moved to cardinal directions, and I positioned Ronda No-H to the northwest and Barbie to the southwest. We'd received the incoming fire from the west, so covering that sector was crucial until we could reclaim our gear and move on the offensive.

Gator scampered up the limbs and back into the belly of the Huey. He tossed gear, and I caught every piece, sorting it as I went. When the cabin was empty, we broke down security and claimed our individual gear. Gator rigged gun belts for Barbie and Ronda and unbagged a rifle for each of them.

I said, "Welcome to the infantry, ladies. No more air cavalry for you. Now, you're knuckle-draggers like us."

Ronda scowled. "Let's see if you boys can keep up."

We broke off into teams of five and four and moved parallel with fifteen to twenty yards between the two columns. Aside from giving us the ability to visually cover more ground as we moved to contact, the formation could save half of the team should one element befall an ambush.

Jungle warfare is as much a game of psychological operations as it is putting lead on target. If I could make the opposition believe we were a larger, heavier unit than we were, I could change not only their strategy, but also their mindset. I loved any advantage, as long as it were mine.

The jungle was silent again, and I didn't like anything about it. If I could command the monkeys to chatter and the birds to squawk, our movement would be much easier to conceal, but I'd never possess such power.

The crash was disorienting enough to allow questions of direction to float into my head and cloud my perception, but I forced back those emotions as we drew closer to the site of the ground fire.

Indicators of previous fire are great tools to identify a battlefield, but in small-unit skirmishes, those indicators are often difficult to identify. Empty shell casings concentrated in one position are telltale signs of a previous firing position. In our case, it wasn't enemy brass on the ground that gave away the fight. It was the wide swath cut by the massive firepower of Ronda's M134 Minigun. The scars were unmistakable, and they gave me the reassurance that my internal compass was still well calibrated.

Just as I was celebrating my small victory for finding the spot from which we'd been attacked, a short burst of automatic rifle fire cut through the air, and Kodiak radioed from the element to our right. "Contact, one o'clock . . . engaging. Flank from the left."

I motioned for my team to advance thirty yards to avoid firing through the other team. Once well clear of the other half of our team, we turned and closed on the position of the newest firefight. Our team was using short bursts of automatic fire coupled with focused semi-automatic fire. My element held our fire and continued flanking to the left of Kodiak's team, using the distraction of the gunfight to cover our movement.

As we advanced through forty yards, the gunfire was well off to our right.

204 · CAP DANIELS

That's when I broke radio silence. "Sierra One is on the left flank at twenty yards."

Kodiak said, "Hit 'em hard, One."

My five-person team focused full-auto fire directly into the area where the enemy fire was originating. We burned through a lot of ammunition, but saving ammo at the expense of our lives didn't make any sense.

After thirty seconds of sustained heavy fire, each of the weapons belching incoming fire was quieted until the fight fell silent.

As quietly as I could, I said, "Sitrep."

Kodiak answered quickly. "No casualties. We're closing from the front."

"Roger. We'll close from the left."

Feigning death to lure an enemy closer was a common tactic of seasoned guerilla fighters, but I suspected we weren't facing anything close to special forces operators. If they were South-Wind Ventures commandos, we definitely had the upper hand based on Mike's assessment of their qualifications.

Taking a human life is never a thing done lightly for any of us, but the bodies we discovered cut down by our fire had initiated the fight, and shooting at us rarely ends well for the aggressors.

We collected IDs and photographed everyone we found, then we scavenged their ammo and moved their bodies to one central location.

With the site secure, I said, "Set security. It's time to do an E.T. and phone home."

Chapter 28
Once and Never Again

Mongo rigged the antenna to the drone and found a hole in the tree cover barely large enough to fly through, giving the antenna a clear view of the sky.

Unlike Skipper's typical answer when I'd been delinquent in checking in, her tone was somber and dripping with concern. "Op center."

I said, "No casualties, but we lost the Huey."

"How did you lose a helicopter?"

"South-Wind shooters took out the tail rotor with an RPG."

She groaned. "South-Wind? How did they get an RPG?"

"Down here, everything's for sale," I said. "They had two. The first one missed, but they got lucky with the other one."

She said, "I was tracking you before you went down, and it terrified me when I lost you."

"We're all good, and we put down the aggression from the South-Wind guys. Three of the bodies are Smith, Vinny, and Bobby, but they had reinforcements. There are eleven total. I'll send you their IDs when we finish."

She asked, "Do you want me to contact South-Wind again?"

"No, we have to take advantage of their ignorance. There's no way they could know their guys are down, so we want them to keep believing their shooters are still working."

"Good idea. What's your plan now?"

"The ultimate plan hasn't changed. We're still getting Hunter out of here, but we'll need a ride. And if I'm right, I know exactly where we can get one."

"That sounds sketchy, but I like it. How can I help?"

I said, "I'd like for you to keep tabs on Mike. Put a couple of guys on his door, and ID everybody who comes and goes. South-Wind is spending a lot of money and men trying to stop us. I don't want them to get to him."

"I'm on it. What else?"

"That's all from here. Do you have anything else?"

She said, "Yeah, how's Gator?"

The question caught me off guard. "I told you we're all okay."

"I know, but this is his first really nasty operation. I just wanted to make sure he was living up to your expectations."

I tried not to smile. "Something tells me that's not all you're asking."

"Chase, stop it. I worry about you guys. You know that."

I couldn't resist poking the bear a little more. "You didn't ask about anybody else."

"Let's change the subject. When can I expect you to check in again?"

"That depends on how successful my next short-term mission is. I'll brief you if it works. Expect less than four hours if it goes well."

She was suddenly all business again. "Roger that. Do you need a position fix?"

"No, the sat-phone will pick it up from the drone antenna. Anything else?"

She said, "No, that's it from here."

"All right. Stand by for a minute."

I tossed the sat-phone to Gator. "Here. She needs to talk to you."

He caught the phone. "Me? Why?"

"Just talk to her."

He stuck the phone to his ear and walked away from the gathered team.

Mongo beat me to the punch. "We're going after the other helo, aren't we?"

I said, "That's exactly why you're second-in-command. I've been thinking about it, and that camo netting has to be covering a helicopter. We just need to find it."

He said, "Kodiak marked it from the air, and we've already plotted a course."

"You guys deserve a raise."

He scoffed. "It's awfully convenient how you forget about those promises when it's time to run payroll."

Ronda No-H cleared her throat. "I heard him say it, so don't worry. I'll hook you up when I cut the checks next month."

"We can always count on you," Mongo said.

She lowered her head. "I don't know about that. I should've taken out the second RPG gunner."

Mongo shot me a look, and I stepped closer to our CPA and door gunner. "Don't beat yourself up. Most of those bodies over there are full of your bullets, not ours. Without you, this thing would've been a lop-sided train wreck, and we'd likely be full of bullet holes ourselves."

She said, "Thanks, but I know I could've done better. I'll be honest. I was on my heels a little. I wasn't expecting incoming ground fire."

"None of us expected it, but we were ready to dance when the music started."

Gator stepped behind me, slipped the phone into my hand, and whispered, "Thanks for that."

I turned so only he could hear me. "Don't make me kill you in your sleep. Got it?"

I don't know what I expected him to say, but his answer proved that he was turning into exactly the man I'd want to see in Skipper's life.

He looked squarely into my eyes. "Yes, sir."

I gave his shoulder a squeeze. "Come on. Let's go find ourselves a magic carpet."

We followed Kodiak's lead and waded through the jungle until we reached the spot he marked from our flight.

He shrugged. "It should be right here."

"Don't panic yet," I said. "Let's find another break in the trees and get a good position fix."

Mongo launched the drone and said, "I'll get us a position fix, and I can probably find the objective.

"Why didn't I think of that?" I asked to no one in particular.

It took our Goliath less than ten minutes to spot the camo netting. "Found it. Follow me."

He led us directly to the mysterious position where the netting hopefully covered what we needed. We approached cautiously with rifles at the ready, just in case anyone was guarding the site. Fortunately for us, we didn't encounter anyone else who needed a bullet in his head. The site was empty except for the camo netting and whatever waited behind it.

I pulled a pair of stakes from the soft soil and lifted the edge of the netting. When I ducked inside and got my first glance, I'd never been happier to see any machine anywhere on the planet. I stuck my head back outside the netting. "Let's get this camo down. We just hit the jackpot."

It took fifteen minutes to pull the stakes and wrestle the netting down.

Ronda studied the helicopter. "What is it? A baby Chinook?"

Barbie slid a hand across the fuselage. "It's a Boeing Vertol One-Oh-Seven, the civilian version of the CH-Forty-Six Sea Knight."

"Here's a much better question," I said. "Can you fly it?"

Barbie examined the opening in the trees above us. "I can fly it, but flying it through that hole is another question entirely."

Nothing inside my head allowed me to believe I could fly it in a thousand-acre open field, let alone through a hole that was barely large enough for the rotors. "Do you want to try it empty first?"

"Nope. I want to do it once and never again."

It took only a couple of minutes for everybody and every piece of gear to find a home on our newest asset, even if we "borrowed" that asset without asking for permission.

When I settled into the cockpit, the panel and controls weren't entirely foreign to me, but the tandem-rotor system was unlike anything I'd ever flown. The four-hundred-page, two-volume pilot's operating handbook was conveniently located in a slot beside the cockpit seat, so Barbie and I spent twenty minutes learning everything we could from the printed material.

Finally, she closed the book and sighed. "What do you think, Flyboy? Wanna give her a go?"

With the checklist book spread out on my lap, we carefully stepped through every line, word by word. The turbines fired up with textbook temperatures, and every needle was in the green within seconds of starting the fires. The rotor system took longer to come up to speed than the Huey, but the Vertol was a lot more machine than the destroyed chopper a couple miles away.

Barbie situated herself and adjusted the pedals to bring them to her boots. "Let's make her light on the wheels."

"I'll follow you through the controls, but I'll stay out of the way."

Barbie nodded like a bull rider ready for the chute man to open the gate, and the ride was on. She pulled enough pitch to take half of the weight from the landing gear and gently moved the controls to get a feel for the chopper's temperament. Nothing misbehaved, so she pulled enough pitch to raise the nose gear off the ground. The enormous chopper was docile and responsive, so she landed the nose gear and said, "Let's do it."

"Make it happen, Captain."

She smiled. "It's been a long time since anybody called me Captain." Her expression turned to stone as she set the throttle and gave the gauges one last look before taking the new toy for our maiden voyage.

I let my hands hover near the collective and cyclic and my feet rest just above the pedals. Barbie lifted the collective and brought the ship barely above the ground, then she hovered motionless for a moment before letting the gear settle back to the jungle floor.

"What's wrong?" I asked.

She lifted her hands from the controls. "Nothing, but I want you to give it a try."

I took the controls and brought us to a similar hover as she had, and I was surprised how forgiving the helicopter was. My confidence swelled.

"Do you want to do it?" Barbie asked.

"Negative. You have the controls."

"Not yet," she said. "Put her back on the ground."

I landed, and she asked, "How'd that feel?"

"Not bad."

"Good. I have the controls."

I echoed, and she brought us back to a low hover. There was no room for any excess movement, so the climb-out would be almost vertical . . . hopefully.

After rising out of ground effect, the Vertol exhibited her first bit of misbehavior. We drifted backward a few feet before Barbie arrested the motion and continued the climb. Once we climbed through the canopy without incident, she lowered the nose, giving us our first taste of forward motion.

"Nice work," I said.

"Thanks. Not bad for my first tandem-rotor takeoff, huh?"

I was in awe. "Are you saying you never flew the Chinook?"

She let a smile cross her face. "I've never even been inside a Chinook."

"We'll make that our little secret, okay?"

She winked. "Great idea."

Sixty seconds later, we resumed the search pattern we'd been flying before our encounter with the RPG.

Before we covered more than a few miles, Singer stuck his head into the cockpit. "Tallyho! The village is at eight o'clock and a mile."

Barbie brought the Vertol around to the left, and we caught our first glimpse of the opening in the trees.

I turned to face him. "Good eyes, sniper. Let's see if they roll out the red carpet for us."

Chapter 29
Full Circle

Barbie flew a wide arc around the partially exposed village and through the irregular tops of trees. Although I couldn't see the crew behind me, I was confident everyone was focused out the windows, and as much as we wanted to recon the site, I'm sure we were all looking for our bearded brother somewhere below the trees.

When our first circuit was complete, I hadn't seen anything resembling an American. The grass huts scattered across the site in a haphazard arrangement looked as if they'd been dropped from the sky and landed in utter disorganization. I found the wide-eyed faces of natives peering skyward impossible to ignore. Their gazes appeared more curious than angry. No one fired an arrow or threw a spear, but I had little faith that condition would survive after we touched down. To them, we were foreigners from a world they'd never know. Even though we meant them no harm, it was perfectly understandable why they would mistrust us. The more I pondered their lives, the more I envied the simple existence and wondered if I would ever step from my world of chaos and conflict and into such simplicity and peace.

"How close do you want to be?" Barbie asked.

"What are our options?"

She pointed to several openings in the trees. "Pick one. I haven't seen this many LZs anywhere else in this country."

I motioned to the south. "Let's see what we have down there. I'd like to put a little distance between us and the village so we aren't eating arrows as soon as we land."

"You got it."

She turned southward and slowed. The gentle breeze from the northeast wasn't blowing hard enough to make landing a challenge, so our direction wasn't critical.

"How about there?" she asked.

"I like it. There's plenty of room, and it looks relatively flat."

"I agree. You have the controls."

I threw up both hands. "Oh, no. Not me."

She ducked her chin. "What are you going to do if I take an arrow to the eye down there? You have to learn to do it, and you picked the spot. That means it's your turn to make it happen."

I placed my feet on the pedals and took the cyclic and collective in my hands. "Stay on the controls with me. I've never flown anything like this monster."

"You'll do fine. Just remember there's no yaw, so fly it like an airplane without the necessity of forward speed."

I positioned us in line with the opening and flew my approach, allowing the Vertol to slow as the treetops grew nearer.

Barbie said, "Bleed off a little more airspeed, and think about touching down at treetop level. We'll hover there and step down, okay?"

"Got it," I said as I brought us to a hover roughly at the top of the trees.

She said, "Good. Now, step it down a quarter of the way to the ground and establish your hover again."

I did as she said and practiced two more touchdowns before hovering only inches above the earth.

She said, "Now, land it nice and gentle. You'll feel the wheels touch, but there's quite a bit of slack in the suspension, so fly it all the way 'til the full weight is on the gear."

It wasn't perfect, but I made the landing without losing any of the big pieces.

Barbie punched my arm. "See? You don't need me at all."

We lowered the rear ramp and ran through the shutdown checklist. By the time the rotors stopped spinning, the Vertol's cabin was empty, and my team had established a security perimeter.

With my boots firmly back on the ground, my mind went to work. Part of me wanted to stow the rifles and proceed toward the village in the most peaceful posture we could pull off, but I didn't have that luxury. If South-Wind had troops in the jungle, they likely had them in or near the village, as well. Facing an enemy who wielded automatic rifles and RPGs required that we be at least equally well armed. We wouldn't fire on the natives unless it became absolutely essential for survival, but South-Wind drew first blood, so I owed them no such courtesy. I would meet aggression with superior aggression, skill, and firepower. They made the rules. I just played the game they brought to the party.

I took a knee beside Mongo. "Put your drone in the air and get us a little intel."

He unpacked the football-sized device and let it fly from his hand. The performance of the miniature machine was impressive by any standard. It topped the forty-foot trees in seconds and began a pre-programmed search grid with its camera scanning the ground in high-definition as it progressed toward the village.

Upturned faces greeted us on the tablet mounted to the controller, but none of those faces belonged to Hunter or anyone who looked remotely like him.

As the scene on the tablet opened up, revealing the village, even more eyes peered skyward, but there was still no assault coming from any of the faces that seemed enraptured by the flying device.

As fascinated as the natives seemed to be with our drone, I was equally mesmerized by them. Their postures and expressions drew me in as if I were somehow tied to them by an invisible, unbreakable bond piercing time and space. Perhaps it was admiration I learned from my parents' respect for such people tucked away in corners of the world so few people would ever see.

I wondered what I could do to make their lives better. I could give them every dollar in my bank account, but those dollars would be nothing more than meaningless paper in their hands. I could give them weaponry to protect themselves, but the noise of the rifles would demolish the stealth the people used to their enormous advantage. I could abandon my life and devote what remained of it to teaching the natives everything I knew about God, but that wasn't my calling. It was Hunter's calling, and by answering his electronic cry for help, I believed I was fulfilling my purpose with a determination just as powerful as the drive that pulled Hunter into the depths of the jungle in service to God. Perhaps I was pawing to justify my existence, but if I let Hunter die in that jungle, he'd never be able to deliver the message—the only message of cosmic and eternal consequence in existence. I believed supporting that mission was as equally noble and essential as the delivery itself.

I pulled my head from the clouds and said, "Let's move. I'm on point."

We formed a column and walked toward the village with determined caution. Although I couldn't see them, I felt their watchful eyes on me from every direction. The stealth of the natives was unmatched by anyone I'd ever encountered, but I didn't believe they wanted to hurt us. We would've been an easy target if they chose to loose their arrows, but those arrows didn't come.

With the village in sight between the trees, I held up a fist and brought our formation to a stop. The team closed on me and mirrored my posture.

Singer was first to speak. "I counted ten, and all of them were armed."

"Were they threatening?" I asked.

He sighed. "Would they be alive if I thought they were threatening?"

"Fair enough." I pulled my rifle's sling across my head and handed the M4 to Mongo. "I'm going in alone. Don't kill anybody who hasn't killed me. Got it?"

Mongo said, "No, Chase. That's not how this works."

I met his gaze. "The natives aren't going to hurt me, but keep your eyes open for South-Wind operators. They're the dangerous ones out here."

"*We're* the dangerous ones, but we won't let South-Wind—or the natives—hit you."

I stood, dropped my gun belt, and took my first steps without a weapon in days. I felt lighter in every way, not just unburdened of the weight of the weaponry. I felt safe and curious and unstoppable. Warriors throughout history have stepped from the light and into eternity as they bore such feelings in the face of adversaries they failed to recognize as deadly. I prayed I wouldn't add my name to that list in the coming minutes.

I walked from the tree line and into a world so distant from mine in every way. The ground was worn smooth from the bare feet of people who'd never see a world beyond their own. It would've been impossible to sneak up on them, so I was under no illusion of surprise. I merely stood and waited for them to emerge and confront me.

My wait was brief.

Four men, lean and strong, stepped in front of me. Two of them held spears, and the others carried bows, but none of them raised a weapon.

They spoke in calm but curious voices.

"*Tee-muyah din ki-eep et ah-oohna.*"

I ached to understand them. I wanted their words to filter through the air and morph into a common language, but such a miracle was not to be. I needed them to understand that I was no threat, so I knelt with one hand on my thigh and the other pressed to the center of my chest. As accurately as I could, I repeated the phrase the tribesmen had spoken to me in the last encounter. "*Tu-Tu Non Cataan.*"

Although I had no idea what the words meant, their reaction was both surprising and a bit concerning. Three of the men knelt, matching my posture.

The fourth man stepped toward me and seemed to turn my statement into a question. "*Tu-Tu Non Cataan?*"

I nodded, but I didn't speak as he slowly moved toward me until our faces were only inches apart. He let out a low hiss, but it didn't feel like a threat. When the sound ceased, he stepped back, held his palm high over his head, and blew air through his lips in a buzzing sound. "*Tawn new-whe?*"

I mimicked his action and said, "Yes, the drone was mine. Drone . . . Drone."

He never blinked, but forming the words seemed to be painful for him. "*Dah . . . row . . . nah.*"

Just as he'd done, I waggled my hand above my head again. "Drone."

His second effort was less agonizing for him. "*Drooh-nah.*"

I nodded. "Yes. Drone."

Extending a hand behind myself, I motioned for someone to bring me the drone. I prayed it wouldn't be Mongo. Those guys didn't need to meet our giant yet.

I was pleased when Singer came forward in slow, deliberate steps and placed the drone and controller in my hand. I laid the small flying machine on the ground between me and my new friend. He leaned down to examine the drone, but he didn't reach for it. After he'd seen it from every angle, I lifted it and held it toward him. He extended a hand and allowed his fingertips to brush against the plastic body and propellers.

He smiled, and I touched one of the propellers with my fingertip and gave it a spin. Once the plastic blade circled twice and stopped, I motioned toward his hand and pointed to the propeller.

He looked into my eyes and then back at the drone before pressing a timid finger against the blade and giving it a push. It turned once, and he laughed.

The gravity of my situation was impossible to process. I was kneeling in front of a man who knew nothing about me, and I knew even less about him. We had no common language, no common history, and no common life experience, but I had made him laugh. The moment was one of the most powerful of my life, and I never wanted it to end, but finding Hunter remained paramount among my intentions.

I motioned for the native to step backward, but he didn't understand, so I changed tactics by turning ninety degrees to my left and placing the drone back on the ground. The man reached for it again, but I motioned for him to stay back. He seemed to understand.

With his hands and mine well clear of the four propellers, I pressed the controls to start the small electric motors and set the props in motion. They spun at high speed and buzzed a high-pitched whine.

The man leapt backward, so I shut down the motors and held up both hands in a comforting gesture. He stared at the now-still machine and wouldn't look away.

I started the drone again, but I didn't let it remain at rest, bringing it to a hover a few inches above the ground.

The fascination on his face was beyond description. He circled the hovering drone first to the left, and finally to the right, then whispered, "*Tu-Tu Non Cataan.*"

He reached for the drone, but I didn't want the propellers to cut his hands, so I pressed the control to climb the drone, and it rose a few feet above our heads.

As he watched, I moved beside him. With the control raised in front of him, I demonstrated how to make it climb and descend several times. Then I took the demonstration further than I originally intended.

I took his finger and gently placed it on the control stick. Together, we pressed his finger upward, and the drone rose. He jerked his hand away and laughed like a child before turning back to his friends, who were still kneeling behind him. The linguistic exchange was animated and melodious like nothing I'd ever heard.

When he turned back to me, the look on his face was unmistakable. He wanted to do it again, so I placed the controller in his hands and pulled mine away. His eyes darted between me, the controller, and the hovering drone. When I smiled and nodded, he pressed the stick upward and quickly released it. The drone rose several feet and hovered again. The elation on his face was indescribable, but what happened next moved me beyond anything I'd ever experienced.

He laid the controller on the ground and slid his hand inside a leather pouch hanging from his waist. When his hand emerged again, I couldn't believe my eyes. He held up the flint and steel I'd given the other tribesman two days before, and it was my turn to be fascinated beyond words. I'm certain the surprise shone on my face.

The man pressed the steel against the flint and stroked it until orange sparks flew from the end. He smiled and pressed the tool into my palm, then moved beside me and showed me how to hold the two pieces. Finally, he gripped my hands and demonstrated how to spark the starter.

I was almost in tears as I stared at the initials carved into the side of the steel. The C and F that I'd ground into the surface years before stared back at me, and for the first time in my life, I fully understood the true meaning of full circle.

Chapter 30

Spoils of War

I had more questions than I could count, but only one of them would ever receive an answer. I wanted to know who the man in front of me was and why the man to whom I'd given my fire starter raced through the jungle to give it to him. I had to assume the man before me was of some importance within the community; otherwise, he wouldn't possess my flint and steel.

The second question was a little easier to ask, but it would take some time and significant patience. I'd proven the process worked, but I had an entirely new audience. Just as I'd done on my first experience with the first native I met, I slowly drew my phone and pointed it toward my face. I snapped a picture and turned the screen toward my new friend.

Just like his friend two days earlier, his face exploded in disbelief. He touched the screen and then gently pressed his fingertips to my face. "*Lad min woo.*"

I was tempted to echo the words, but there were too many possibilities of what the phrase could mean. Instead, I remained still and allowed the man's wonder to grow. When he seemed to accept the technology, even though he couldn't understand it, I took his picture and handed the phone to him.

I expected him to touch his face after seeing his image on the small screen, but it didn't happen. He pointed the phone toward his three kneeling comrades, and a few seconds later, he turned the screen to face himself, but only his image was visible.

I was probably breaking every ethical rule of clinical psychology by introducing ultra-modern technology to a primitive tribe in the farthest reaches of the Amazon jungle, but I'd happily surrender my license to practice psychology for the experience in which I was immersed.

He would likely never figure out how to take a picture of his friends, so I intervened by moving his finger above the button to take the shot. Together, we pointed the lens toward his men, and I encouraged him to touch the button. He did, and the previous wonder in his eyes doubled.

Staring at the picture he'd taken, he laughed with unequaled exuberance. He took the phone to his friends and showed them the first, and likely only, picture he'd ever take. Slowly, the realization overcame each of them, and they sat in what appeared to be complete disbelief. As much as I enjoyed the moment, it was time to play my ace in the hole.

When I held out my hand and wordlessly asked for the phone, he seemed to understand and placed it on my palm. I flipped through the pictures until Hunter's face appeared on the screen, and I handed the device back to the man. The glee in his expression morphed into gloom, and he whispered, "*Tu-Tu Non Cataan.*"

I motioned toward the heart of the small village. The man appeared frightened and dismayed, but he took my hand and turned away.

I imagined the anxiety of my team lurking in the edge of the tree line as they watched me walk away with the man. I trusted him, and I prayed the team trusted my judgment in what may have been the most critical moment of the operation.

The man I was beginning to consider a friend led me deeper into the village until we came to a teepee-shaped tent with a thin stream of white smoke trailing from the top. He opened the panel woven with vines and leaves and pulled it aside. Although he made no effort to step through the opening, he placed a hand on my back and pressed me toward the darkened interior.

The emotion roaring in my chest felt like thunder as I stooped and moved through the small opening. As my vision adjusted to the absence of light, a silhouette formed before me until I could make out the details of Stone W. Hunter's profile lying motionless at my feet.

I threw myself to my knees and planted two fingers against Hunter's carotid artery on the side of his neck. In the first seconds of my probing, I couldn't be certain if I was feeling my pulse or his. Finally, I calmed my breathing enough to confidently feel the rhythmic thud of my brother's heart, and I sent up a beseeching silent prayer before saying, "Hunter, it's Chase."

He didn't move or make a sound, so I laid my hand against his healthy shoulder and shook him gently. "Hunter, it's me, Chase."

Still, he showed no reaction, but his pulse and respiration continued as if driven by a force stronger than any of us.

Although I felt anchored to him, I forced myself to squeeze back through the opening of the teepee, and I raised a hand against the glaring sun shining through the clearing above the village. My mind roiled trying to come up with a way to tell the natives I needed to bring the rest of my team to retrieve Hunter. Nothing was coming to me, but as my eyes adjusted to the light, I was amazed to see the entire team kneeling in a semicircle surrounded by tribesmen.

"Hunter's in there, but he's unconscious. Bring the helicopter. We've got to get him out of here."

Barbie and Ronda leapt to their feet and ran toward the helo.

Mongo stood with his kit. "Let me have a look."

A moment of amusement rushed through my head at the thought of the giant forcing himself through the small opening in the teepee. He made it, but it looked like ten gallons in a five-gallon bucket.

I followed him inside and held a light above Hunter as Mongo took his vitals and began the examination. Halfway down his body, the wound became apparent. The bullet's entry point was red and inflamed with a ball of leaves pressed inside.

Mongo said, "That looks familiar."

"It sure does," I said. "That might explain him being unconscious. Where's the exit wound?"

He rolled Hunter onto his side and probed at his back before shaking his head. "It's still in there."

My heart sank, and the darkness inside me roared as I hoped it had been my bullet that cut down the man who put a round in Hunter. My head rang with the fury of a thousand raging, war-torn bells as I fought to calm my rage.

The Vertol's rotors thumped, growing louder and offering a measure of relief for the anger churning in my chest.

Hunter's presence in this foreign world represented the epitome of selflessness and subservience, but the servants of gold-hungry, prospecting narcissists had left a bullet in a man who represented nothing beyond goodness and mercy.

I stepped back through the opening and found the team constructing a litter of two bamboo poles and a collection of shirts. The group of natives had grown until it looked like the whole village was gathered to watch the spectacle.

As Barbie descended to land at the edge of the village, the gathered faces turned to watch in awe. She put the Vertol on the ground with the ramp wide open and facing the center of the village.

I said, "Let's get him out of there."

Kodiak and Gator stepped through the opening with the litter. A moment later, the end of the makeshift stretcher came through the opening, and I took the bamboo shafts in hand. I stepped backward as Hunter's head appeared through the hole, and when Singer caught the foot end of the litter, we moved with determination toward the chopper.

As we climbed the ramp into the cabin, Ronda was putting the finishing touches on a well-padded nest for Hunter. We carefully laid him on the bed, and I scampered back down the ramp, where the village waited with curiosity and wonder pouring from every face.

I needed to tell them goodbye, but I didn't know how. It soon became obvious that words from me weren't necessary.

The man who'd flown the drone and taken pictures with me took my shoulders in his hands and pulled me toward him. He pressed his cheek to mine and chanted a melodious incantation. When he finished, he took a short step backward and took my hand in his. He placed my palm against his chest and his against mine. "*Tu-Tu Non Cataan ooh tee ku Tu-Tu Non Cataan.*"

He wouldn't understand my words, but perhaps the sentiment would come. "I'll always remember you, my friend. Thank you for caring for my brother."

Mongo was the last man on board, and I slipped between the seats to take my place beside Barbie. Before I was strapped in, we were airborne and climbing to the northeast. Instead of playing copilot, I became the communications officer and got Skipper on the sat-com.

"We've got him! He's gutshot but appears stable. I need you on the horn with Disco. Have the *Grey Ghost* ready for immediate takeoff. We'll be on deck at Tapauá in thirty minutes."

She said, "I've got him on the line and patched in. Say that again."

I reissued the order, and Disco said, "We're full of fuel and ready to fly. Where are we going?"

I said, "Plan for UAB, but we'll reassess once we get Hunter on the *Ghost*. Depending on his condition, we may head for Miami."

He said, "We can make either one nonstop. I'll be standing by and ready to fly."

With the coordination complete, I scanned the panel and checked our position. We were making a hundred sixty knots, but it felt like we were in slow motion.

"Is this all she's got?" I asked.

Barbie said, "At this weight, this is the best we can do."

"Push it," I said.

She squeezed four more knots out of the machine and asked, "Are we just going to abandon this thing after we land?"

"I haven't thought about that. Do you want it?"

"You'd better believe I want it. It would be a huge upgrade from the Huey, but it may not fit in the hangar on the ship."

"The ship is in dry dock," I said. "Can you get the helo to Pascagoula?"

"Oh, yeah, but I'll need Ronda."

"When you drop us at Tapauá, make it happen. You're in charge of the hangar deck redesign. I'll make the money available, and you can build whatever you want."

"I like the sound of that," she said. "Can Skipper handle customs and immigration? Sneaking a stolen helicopter into the country isn't exactly kosher."

"It's not stolen. It's the spoils of war. To the victor go the spoils, and we're the victors."

The Tapauá airport came into view, and the demeanor of the cockpit turned professional. We landed with the ramp down and as close as possible to the *Grey Ghost*.

The team had Hunter aboard and nestled into one of the plush, fully reclined seats before I left the cockpit of the Vertol. I left plenty of cash with Barbie and Ronda and climbed aboard the *Ghost*, but there was no time for goodbyes. I trusted the two of them to manage the long flight without any direction from me. My responsibility lay aboard the Gulfstream, and I wouldn't sleep until Hunter was in the capable hands of a world-class surgeon somewhere inside the States.

I took my place beside Disco in the cockpit. It looked like a spaceship compared to the Vertol, but I felt far more at home on the flight deck of the *Ghost* than I'd ever feel at the controls of anything with rotors.

As we put the Brazilian rainforest and my indigenous new friends astern, the sky welcomed us as if sharing the burden of carrying Hunter into home's waiting arms.

Chapter 31

Crayon Scribbles

We touched down at the Birmingham Shuttlesworth Airport in Alabama and taxied to the FBO, where the UAB ambulance waited with the rear doors wide open and a pair of medics flanking a gurney. By the time our wheels stopped rolling, the hatch was open and the stairs were deployed. Mongo cradled Hunter's unconscious body in his arms and descended the stairs in four strides.

The doors of the ambulance closed with Hunter and me ensconced inside with one of the paramedics. I briefed Hunter's medical history, and the tech started a fresh IV. I expected excellent service from everyone under the UAB umbrella, but the ambulance crew exceeded my expectations. We ran with lights flashing and siren blaring on our way to what I considered one of the premier medical facilities in the world.

The reception inside the hospital was at least as efficient as the ambulance ride. I carried the best insurance policy money could buy on every employee, contractor, and associate of my organization, and Hunter would always fall into the fold, regardless of his chosen profession and position on Earth. I would care for him as long as we both were breathing, and I prayed that period would encompass decades to come, but every minute he spent outside an operating room was one minute closer to his earthly demise.

I planted myself in a chair beside his bed inside trauma room eleven, but I hadn't had time to get comfortable before a man in his forties, wearing green scrubs and a surgical cap, stepped through the curtain. The nurse who'd situated Hunter in the space handed a tablet to the man, and he scanned the screen without a word.

After several seconds, he said, "GSW. All right, let's take a look."

He ignored me but not the nurse. She was obviously essential to his process. Their perfect, coordinated movement reminded me of how my team and I moved through targets with surgical precision at the muzzle of a rifle.

She cut away Hunter's shirt and pulled back the material as the man leaned in and pulled an overhead light into position.

He looked up at me almost instantly after beginning the examination. "What the hell is that?"

I wanted to have a good answer, but the best I could do was offer the only explanation I knew. "It's a ball of medicinal leaves from the Amazon."

He frowned and cocked his head. "You plugged a gunshot wound with something you ordered from Amazon?"

His question stumped me for a moment before I put it together, but I finally said, "No, it was from a tribal medicine man in the Amazon Rainforest."

"A medicine man?"

"Yes. It has a numbing effect, and—"

He held up a hand. "That's enough. Forceps."

The nurse slapped the curved tool into his outstretched palm. Seconds later, the ball of leaves landed in a plastic bottle, and the man said, "Figure out what that is."

The nurse was replaced by a technician who was rolling a portable ultrasound machine, and almost in no time, Hunter's gut was displayed in black and white on the screen.

The man in scrubs said, "Hold there and print it."

The technician pressed a series of keys, and the contents of the screen appeared on an extruded sheet of paper.

The ultrasound tech left, leaving the man I assumed to be a physician, Hunter, and me alone in the trauma room.

He didn't offer to shake, but he said, "I'm John Pade, chief trauma surgical resident. Who are you?"

I respected his no-nonsense approach, so I didn't waste his time. "I'm his brother."

"I see. Well, your *brother* has a bullet lodged between his fourth and fifth lumbar vertebrae."

"You can remove it, right?"

"I could, but I won't."

"Why not?"

"Because I'm a trauma surgeon, not a neurosurgeon. When was he shot?"

I stared at the white tiles beneath my feet and realized I had no idea what day it was or how long I'd been in the jungle. "At least a week, maybe more."

"You don't know for sure?"

"No. It's a long story. He's a missionary in Brazil. I'm a . . ."

"You're a what?"

I stammered. "I'm a . . . a recovery specialist."

He rolled his eyes. "Okay, Mr. Recovery Specialist Brother. We're going to prep Mr. Hunter for surgery. Someone will show you to the waiting area and the shower. I recommend the shower sooner rather than later."

I couldn't remember the last time I felt clean water on my skin, but the thought of leaving Hunter's side felt like stepping off a cliff. "I'll stay with him until you move him into surgery."

"Did you come straight here from the jungle?" he asked.

"I did."

"I'll be blunt. If you get the bacteria that's all over you in that wound, there's no surgeon in this hospital—or anywhere else for that matter—who can keep your brother alive. Go shower and find some clean clothes."

* * *

By the time I finished my shower and pulled on a set of borrowed scrubs, the rest of the team had shown up, and they smelled just like I had twenty minutes earlier.

"What's the word?" Singer asked.

"It's not good," I said, and laid out the details as I knew them. "It'd probably be a good idea for you guys to check into a hotel and get cleaned up. Hunter will be in surgery for a while, but I'll let you know if I hear anything before you get back."

No one argued, and I settled into an ugly, uncomfortable chair in the typical surgical waiting room. A pot of hours-old coffee and its odor lingered on a corner table beside a telephone with no buttons. The ubiquitous silenced television hung from a complex contraption in the corner opposite the coffee pot and phone. No remote seemed to exist, so I flipped off the set with the push of a button on the side.

Just before the chair had time to send that prickly sleep feeling down the backs of my legs, a young woman with a child in tow materialized in front of me. "Are you Dr. Fulton?"

I looked down at the scrubs I was wearing. "No, ma'am. I'm not a . . ."

She said, "I'm looking for Dr. Chase Fulton. I'm Carmella Perry."

I was sleep-deprived, hungry, worried about Hunter, and apparently incapable of completing a three-piece puzzle. "Yeah, I'm Chase Fulton, but I'm not a doctor here."

Carmella said, "I'm Mike Perry's wife."

The puzzle instantly fell together in front of me, and I hopped to my feet. "Oh, yes, I'm sorry. It's been a long . . ."

She pulled the little girl closer beside her. "I'm a little confused about what's going on. Someone who works for you set it up for us to get here. I think her name was Elizabeth, but I don't remember for sure."

I motioned toward the bank of miserable chairs. "Of course. Have a seat, and I'll tell you what I know."

The little girl, who I assumed to be Madeline, squeezed beside her mother and played with an electronic device of some kind while I told the most convoluted story I'm sure her mother had ever heard.

When I finished, Carmella said, "That's the same thing Mike told me, but it still doesn't make any sense. Why would South-Wind do that? They've been good to us."

"The only answer I have is greed. When the love of wealth outweighs the value of human life, people are capable of committing and justifying unthinkable horrors."

She pressed a hand against her stomach and stared at her feet for a long moment. "Thank you for what you did for Mike. The money . . . We can't pay it back if Mike isn't working, though, and I'm—"

"It's not a loan," I said. "It's payment for Mike's work. Without him, we wouldn't have found Hunter." I paused and glanced toward her stomach. "And congratulations on the good news."

She blushed. "Mike doesn't know yet."

"He probably does," I said. "It's pretty obvious from the look on your face."

She smiled. "Maybe, but he's on a lot of meds, so he's been a little out of it. That guy who works with you—I think he said his name is Singer—he's with him right now."

I checked my watch and flicked a piece of jungle mud from the face. "Where are they?"

She said, "I left them alone in the room. He was talking to Mike about God, and I thought it might be best if I let them have time alone. I've been praying for Mike since the day we met. You probably don't know what happened to him when he was a kid."

I grimaced. "He told me about the counselor at the camp. It's unthinkable."

She swallowed hard. "Yeah, it is, but blaming God isn't the answer."

"So, you're a believer?"

She squeezed her daughter to her side. "Yes, and I've tried for years to get Mike to come to church with us, but after what happened to him . . ."

"I understand, and there's nobody better at answering those tough questions than Singer. He's a remarkable man. But I've got a question that's going to sound strange."

She tilted her head. "Okay."

I cleared my throat. "Did Singer smell bad?"

She giggled. "Smell bad? No, not at all. What kind of question is that?"

"Never mind," I said. "He must've found a shower. Would you mind if I went down to see Mike for a minute?"

"I think he'd like that. Even though he's on the pain meds, he obviously has a lot of respect for you."

I didn't want to leave the buttonless telephone, but I had to know if Singer was fertilizing the seeds I'd sown two thousand miles away in a jungle full of death.

I followed Carmella and Madeline down the hall and into an elevator. When we got to Mike's room, she pointed at the door. "They're in there. I'm going to take Maddie to get a snack."

I reached to knock, but I saw a sliver of light filtering through the jamb, so I pressed the door inward a few inches and leaned against the frame.

I wish I could've heard the whole conversation, but I was only privy to the final few minutes of the most eternally consequential conversation of Mike's life.

His voice sounded clear and not remotely influenced by medication. "But you guys do what's right because you're good people. That doesn't have anything to do with God."

I could almost hear Singer's smile in his soft, confident response. "Do you remember when your little girl showed you the first thing she ever drew on paper?"

"Huh?"

Singer said, "It was probably scribbles in crayon colors on a piece of paper. Do you remember that?"

Silence consumed the moment until Mike said, "Yeah, I guess so. We probably stuck it on the refrigerator or something."

"Could you tell what it was?"

Mike chuckled. "No, but it didn't matter. I was proud of her for trying to draw whatever it was supposed to be, and I'm sure we loved it at the time."

"That's what we are, Mike. We're children of the most loving Father in existence. No matter what we do, it's going to look like crayon scribbles in God's eyes, but He doesn't want us to paint the Mona Lisa. He wants and expects us to strive for perfection, but ultimately, He wants us to do His will because we love him. That's exactly what little Madeline did with that first drawing both you and she were so proud of. That's what a relationship with God is. It's a love so strong that we'll never fully understand it."

He paused only long enough to let the bullet hit its mark. "We're not capable of true goodness, Mike. Chase and the guys, and me, we screw up every day. We do stuff that disappoints God, but when it comes down to the true nature of our souls, we want to please Him, and we want Him to hang our crayon drawings on His refrigerator."

Mike said, "I don't know. It just seems too simpleminded, you know?"

"Is the love you have for Madeline simple?"

"No."

"No, of course it's not. But is her love for you simple?"

Another moment of silence passed, and Mike said, "Yeah, I guess it is."

"It is right now," Singer said, "but as she grows and learns and matures, her love for you will grow in depth and complexity. But she'll never be capable of loving you exactly the same way you love her. A father's love for his daughter is different than a child's love for her parents. That's the nature of love—especially God's love for you and me."

Mike said, "I'm in a lot of pain, and I really need to push that painkiller button. Could you maybe come back tomorrow so we can talk some more?"

My phone chirped in the pocket of my scrubs, and I slammed my hand against it so I wouldn't get busted listening in. After putting a few strides between me and Mike's hospital room door, I pressed the phone to my ear. "This is Chase."

"Hey, Chase. It's Skipper. I need to tell you something, but I don't really know how."

"What is it? Is it Hunter?"

"It's not about Hunter. It's about Penny."

"Penny? Is she hurt? What's going on?"

"No, she's not hurt. She's okay, as far as I know. It's just that when I got back to Bonaventure, there was a package addressed to Penny Thomas, not Penny Fulton."

"That's not a big deal," I said. "That was her maiden name."

"I know that, but the package is from Greg Shanks, an attorney in Tennessee."

"Okay, it's probably a contract for a movie she's working on. Her agent is in Nashville. It's not a big deal."

Skipper said, "It *is* a big deal, Chase. I didn't open the package, but I did a little digging. Greg Shanks is the senior partner in Shanks and Associates, the go-to law firm for high net-worth individuals seeking a divorce in the Southeast."

Chapter 32
No Matter the Storm

I knew all too well the taste of another man's bullet piercing my flesh and the scorching burn of a blade striking bone. I'd felt my body surrender to exhaustion and my will wither as I lacked the fortitude to stay in the fight, but nothing had ever driven me farther into Hell's gaping depths than Skipper's crushing blow.

I don't remember if I yelled, begged, or whispered, "Divorce attorney? You can't be serious."

"We don't know anything yet except that Penny received a package from this guy. We don't know the contents. Let's take it easy until we know more."

"Open it," I demanded.

"Open the package? Are you serious?"

"Yes. Get it, and open it right now while I'm on the phone."

She hesitated. "I don't know, Chase. I'm pretty sure that's against the law."

"I killed eleven people and stole a two-million-dollar helicopter in the last three days. Open the damned package."

She still didn't relent. "Why don't you call her and have a conversation? If I open her package, and it's . . . wait a minute. What if I called her? Maybe I could talk to her and get to the bottom of it. Maybe it's not what you think."

I took a long breath and tried to slow my thundering heart. "What does it feel like?"

"Feel like? What does that mean?"

"It means, what does the package feel like? Is it a box or a pouch? Is it rigid or flexible? What does it feel like?"

She said, "It's an oversized envelope, and it feels like it has a stack of papers inside."

My heart stopped, and my mind raced until Skipper said, "She's calling me."

"What?"

She repeated, "Penny's calling me right now. Do you want me to answer?"

"Yes! Answer and keep me on the line. I'll mute from my end."

"Are you sure? You can't burst into the conversation, no matter what you hear. Got it?"

"I can't make that promise."

She said, "Then I can't patch you into the call."

"Okay, I'll stay silent. Just do it."

The line clicked, and Skipper said, "Op center."

My wife's voice sounded stressed and foreign. "Oh, good. You're there. Sorry to call on this line, but it's a bit of an emergency."

Skipper's tone was cold, and to me, that sounded like loyalty. "What is it, Penny?"

"There's probably a package there for me. The tracking says it was delivered. Have you seen it?"

I willed Skipper to lie, but she wouldn't. "Yeah, I saw it. Why?"

"Oh, good. Chase isn't there, is he?"

"No, he's not."

Skipper's refusal to turn the conversation pleasant pleased me.

Penny said, "Good. You can't let him see the package, and don't open it."

"I don't keep things from Chase. You know that."

Penny groaned. "This time, you have to. It's really important."

"Then tell me what's in the package."

My wife let out an exasperated breath. "It's a surprise for Chase, okay?"

"He doesn't like surprises."

"This one is different," Penny said.

Skipper took a hard left turn. "Why didn't you ask if Chase is okay?"

"What?"

The best analyst—and little sister—on the planet said, "You only asked if Chase was here. You didn't ask if he was all right. That's not like you."

"Of course I should've asked. I was too worried about the package when I got the email notification that it'd been delivered."

"You still haven't asked," Skipper said. "But whatever. I'll tell you anyway. He's back in the States, and he's okay . . . physically."

"That's great. Thank you for letting me know. I'm sure he'll call me when he has time. Can you forward the package to me here in L.A.?"

Skipper grunted. "Not today. We're in the middle of an operation, and I can't leave the op center."

"Well, can you have someone do it, please? I can't let Chase see it yet."

Another conversational left turn. "When are you coming home? This *is* your home, remember?"

"What's going on with you?" Penny asked. "You're obviously upset about something."

Skipper stayed the course. "When will you be home?"

"I don't know, but definitely by the weekend. Why is that so important? You never ask me when I'm coming home."

Skipper said, "I just thought you might want to be here when your *husband* gets home from risking his life to save his best friend—someone else you haven't asked about. He's *not* fine, by the way."

"Skipper, what's going on with you?"

"I'm just thinking about Chase's well-being. That's one of my jobs, even though I'm not his wife. He's been through Hell and back in the past few days. I'm sure he'd like to hear his wife tell him how much she loves him and appreciates the kind of man he is."

Penny said, "Okay, this is getting weird. Is it Anya? Is she doing something I need to know about?"

Skipper didn't hesitate. "Anya can do whatever she wants, but Chase drew a line in the sand the day he became your husband. Nobody's allowed to cross that line—especially not her. He's the most loyal husband there is. What's in the package, Penny?"

My Hollywood wife said, "Look, if I did something to make you mad, you can just tell me what it is, and we can work through it. But *this,* whatever *this* is, is not okay."

I could think of a billion things that could've happened next that would've been perfectly reasonable, but none of those things happened. Instead, Anya Burinkova grabbed my arm. "My Chasechka, you must come. Surgeon is waiting to talk only to you."

I gripped my sat-phone as if I were trying to crush it in my palm and send everything in my mind crumbling to the floor in a thousand shards of plastic, but the phone was more resilient than my desire to destroy it. I wanted to jerk my arm from Anya's grip, both physically and metaphorically. I'd been under her spell for too many years, and that weakness was on the verge of costing me the one person I believed would endure, no matter the storm. My world was falling down around me, and not only was I powerless to stop it, but I was also incapable of picking up the pieces, even if any of them were big enough to recognize.

Hunter lay unconscious and beyond my reach inside the same building I occupied. A surgeon stood waiting to tell me of success or failure, victory or ultimate defeat. Thousands of miles away, my wife pressed a telephone to her beautiful face and argued with Skipper about a package that could contain nothing other than the end of my sanity. When that package was opened, the chain tying me to the only anchor that could hold me against a tide of ruin would be severed, and my ship would succumb to that tide and be tossed upon the rocks until the ship I had been was torn to unidentifiable shreds.

I could thumb the mute button and break my promise to Skipper

in a perfectly understandable betrayal, desperately attempting to preserve what remained between Penny and me. I could press the red button and pocket the sat-phone to stand before the surgeon who waited
impatiently for my ears and open heart. Or I could drop it all, walk
away, and disappear from the world that seemed to no longer need a
man like me, whose ideals were antiquated, whose allegiances were tied
with faded twine, and whose mind and body had been tattered and
torn until so little of who and what he'd once been remained. I had
nothing left to give, nothing left to sacrifice, and nothing worthy of
either.

The decision was made, and I slid the phone into my pocket and
my hand into Anya's. "Does the surgeon appear to have good news or
bad?"

She shrugged and stared down at our entangled fingers. "*On
vyglyadit ustavshim.*"

*Had she spoken the words in Russian, or had I only heard them in
the language that would never be my own?*

I let my hand fall from hers. "What did you say?"

She curled her fingers into her palm and caressed the flesh where
my hand had been only an instant before. "I said he appears to be
weary."

"Where is he?" I asked, fearing that not only the surgeon, but everything that existed, was a thousand miles away.

"He is inside room for waiting."

Correcting her English was a waste of time, effort, and sanity, so I
left Anya standing in the hallway as I became a blind man pawing for
the light and begging my legs to take me to the man who'd hopefully
saved Hunter's life.

My legs granted me the gift and carried me to the surgical waiting
room where the team had reassembled—clean, dry, and looking almost
like polite citizens of a society I only wished existed.

A man in brown scrubs with paper booties over his shoes and a surgical cap crumpled in his hand asked, "Are you Mr. Fulton?"

"I am."

He licked his lips as the expression Anya described as "weary" deepened on his unshaven face. "Mr. Fulton, I'm Doctor Conner, and I'm very sorry . . ."

I fell to my knees and felt my heart dissolve into molten lava as it filled the shell of my body from the inside. Tears wouldn't come no matter how I beseeched them to fall. What I had been was no more. What I desired was ancient and alone. What I felt was torture without end. What I deserved was to have every drop of pain I'd ever delivered upon another living soul explode into a torrent of agony too dark and too massive to survive, and wash over my corpse, carrying what I had been into the abyss beyond time and space.

Every point of light inside my world collapsed into a pit of darkness without depth or width or form—a darkness so black it seemed to hold the weight of all that had ever been, all of Creation, and the sum of every evil and hate—and every broken vow crushed me from both, without and within, until I believed I'd become the very essence of that boundless black void.

Chapter 33

IV Bags and Cheeseburgers

The next memory I had was standing in the office of South-Wind Ventures in Arizona with a pistol in each hand and the muzzle of each of those pistols shoved as far down the throats of Tommy Southard and Gary Windham as they would physically go. It wasn't anger I felt inside the shell of a man I'd become; it was righteous vengeance. I was the sword, the bearer of all that is due to those who would trade human lives for material wealth.

The terror in their eyes and trembling bodies was like fuel to the fire inside me. Knowing I was but an instant away from delivering the souls of the men before me into Hell's fiery depth brought me no joy, no relief, and no pleasure. It was nothing more than my duty, my solemn and eternal responsibility, to release the guillotine's weighty blade upon the necks of those delivered into my hands. Likewise, it brought me no sadness or guilt. It was simply a finite instant in an infinite expanse of time.

Without the curse of coming remorse or the freedom of satiated desire, moments were all I possessed—fleeting specks between ticks of the clock. I was no longer mortal man, but instead, I was time itself. I could grant the condemned a few seconds more of the life for which they would gladly trade every ounce of gold they plowed from the earth. I could just as easily deny them those precious seconds, and nothing would change for me. I was the truly condemned creature in the room, for Tommy Southard and Gary Windham would soon escape the mortal realm, and I would be left behind for all eternity to unleash what was deserved.

I heard everything: the rasping breaths they drank in like water; the leather of their seats parting under fingernails driven so deeply into the fabric that blood oozed from beneath each opaque surface; the metallic spring inside the pistols as they compressed; the firing pin sliding inside its cavernous sheath and falling against the primer of the round inside each chamber; the crack of that primer as it exploded, igniting the powder pressed tightly into the casing; the surrender of that casing when its projectile left the confinement of the brass that had been its home; the bullet rotating inside the barrel as it was driven forward with no possibility of recall. Destiny awaited the damned, and I had unleashed it upon them.

"Chase! He's not dead. Hunter's not dead, Chase. He made it."

I shuddered and forced open my eyes. I was still on my knees, trembling, quivering, and gasping. Sweat poured from my skin, and my body was consumed by the icy reality of where I was and why I was there. My body was still inside the surgical waiting room, still on the floor, and I was still unsure of who or what I was. Dr. Conner was kneeling in front of me with both of his hands grasping my shoulders. He was shaking me and still calling my name.

Nothing was real, and yet, everything was too bright, too vivid to be anything less. "What's happening to me?"

Dr. Conner aligned his face with mine. "Look at me, Chase. Do you know who I am?"

I nodded, and he said, "I need you to answer out loud."

"Yeah, I know who you are. You're the neurosurgeon."

"That's right. I'm Dr. Conner, the surgeon who removed the bullet from Mr. Hunter's spine. The surgery was successful. He's alive, but he's got a long road ahead before he'll walk again."

A wave of relief washed over me, but my uncertainty about what was real and what my brain was creating on its own still lingered.

The doctor patted the places where pockets should've been, but his surgical scrubs didn't have any. "Does anyone have a flashlight?"

Several hands appeared, holding flashlights of every size and shape. The everyday-carry selections of my team always included a small light of some kind, and I was amused by the comedy of the moment.

Dr. Conner chose one and shined it in my eyes. "Follow the light, but don't move your head."

I did as he ordered, and he doused the light. "Do you know what just happened, Chase?"

"I got a little overwhelmed and needed to take a knee."

He groaned. "I'm afraid it's a little more serious than that. I believe you may have just suffered a psychotic break. I'd like to refer you to the psych team and have someone take a look."

I shook him off. "No, that's not happening. I'm fine. I just need some sleep, something to eat, and some good news. You delivered the news, and I can handle the other two on my own."

Forcing myself to my feet, I stumbled onto a chair and searched the room for the person I needed more than anyone else at that moment, but he was already on his way to my side.

Singer took the seat beside me. "Where were you?"

Unwilling to admit the truth in front of Dr. Conner, I whispered, "A long way from here."

He said, "That's what I thought. Dr. Shadrack and Dr. Kennedy are on their way."

I didn't understand why our ship's doctor was en route, but Dr. Kennedy—the psychiatrist from The Ranch—would be a welcome addition.

"How long was I out of it?"

Our sniper said, "You weren't exactly out. You were talking and gesturing. It looked a lot like a bad nightmare, and it lasted four or five minutes."

"I can't believe I was out that long. Who called our doctors?"

He said, "I called Dr. Shadrack, and he called Dr. Kennedy. Our doc doesn't have privileges here at UAB, but Kennedy does."

Dr. Conner stuck his head into the conversation. "Mr. Fulton, we need to admit you and get started—"

Mongo stepped between me and the doctor. "That ain't happening. Have a nurse bring up a couple of bags of saline and a cheeseburger. I'll take care of the rest."

The doctor looked up at our giant. "I'm afraid that's not how things work here."

"That's fine," Mongo said. "I'll use my own bags of saline from my kit. We've been in the jungle pulling Hunter out. We're all tired, hungry, and dehydrated."

The surgeon cocked his head and furrowed his brow. "The jungle?"

"Yes, the Amazon. That's where Hunter got shot a week ago."

Dr. Conner continued the confused expression. "You moved him here from South America? That's not possible."

Mongo laughed. "Apparently, it is. He took the bullet six or seven days ago. A bunch of natives carried him over a hundred miles through the jungle and to a medicine man in another village, who packed him full of meds and stuck him in a sweat lodge 'til we got there and carried him out on a helo."

Dr. Conner shook his head. "That's impossible. If any of that had occurred, the bullet would've annihilated his spinal cord."

Mongo smiled and turned to our Southern Baptist sniper. "Explain miracles to this guy, Singer. He doesn't seem to believe the truth."

The doctor's look grew even more interesting. "What *are* you people?"

The answer came in unison so tight it sounded choreographed. "A family."

Dr. Conner knelt in front of me one last time. "Can you at least tell me what day it is?"

My family laughed, and Kodiak said, "There's a better-than-good chance that you're the only person in this room who knows what day it is, Doc. How about those IV bags and cheeseburger?"

"I can't help you with the burgers, but I'll see what I can do about a couple of bags of saline. Your *brother* will be in ICU when he's out of post-op. I'll send someone out to take you up there. Something tells me you're not leaving."

The surgeon disappeared through a door, and Mongo became my attending physician.

"What's going on, Chase? Why did you go down like that?"

I swallowed hard. "Penny wants a divorce, and I thought Hunter was dead. It was too much all at the same time."

"Wait a minute," he said. "What do you mean Penny wants a divorce? When did you talk to her? Did she tell you that on the phone?"

I shook my head and told them about the mysterious package at Bonaventure and Skipper's conversation with Penny.

"So, you listened in on the conversation, but you didn't say anything?"

I nodded, and he held out a hand. "Give me your phone."

"We're not calling her until I get my head straight," I said.

He stood. "I'll turn you upside down and shake you until your phone falls out, or you can give it to me. Pick one."

"Seriously," I said. "I don't want to—"

The biggest human I've ever known grabbed me by my ankles and yanked me from the chair. The phone hit the floor, and he kicked it toward Singer. He wasn't exactly gentle when he put me down, but that was the day I learned to give Mongo whatever Mongo wanted whenever Mongo wanted it.

Singer dialed and pressed the speaker button, but Mongo was clearly in charge.

He lifted the phone from Singer's hand the instant Penny answered. "Hey, I was hoping you'd call. I heard you were back in the States."

"Penny, it's Mongo. Why do you want a divorce?"

"What? What are you talking about? I don't want a divorce. Is this some sort of stupid boys' prank? If it is, it's not funny."

"Chase thinks you want a divorce."

She said, "No, he doesn't. Why would he think that? Put him on the phone."

I took the phone from Mongo's two-acre palm and switched off the speaker. "Skipper says there's a package at Bonaventure addressed to Penny Thomas from a divorce lawyer in Tennessee."

"Ah! That explains it. Skipper was a real witch on the phone. Chase, you know I don't want a divorce. That's ridiculous. I can't believe that thought would ever enter your mind."

"Then why are you getting mail in your maiden name from a divorce attorney at our house?"

"It's a contract, you silly thing. You know my agent is in Nashville. It's just a contract. Open it and see for yourself."

"I'm not back at Bonaventure yet. We're in the hospital in Birmingham with Hunter."

"So, is he okay?"

"Not yet, but he will be. Look, I'm sorry about this. I was—"

She cut me off. "Why didn't you call me the second you thought I wanted a divorce? Chase, I'm the happiest girl in the world, and I worship the ground you walk on. You know that."

"I'm sorry. I was just . . . afraid."

I could almost feel her delicate hands caressing my face. "It's okay to be afraid, but don't do it alone. I may be a thousand miles away, but I'll always come home to you."

"So, it's really just a contract?"

"Yes, it's really just a simple contract. You can open it if you want."

"How about you? When will you be home?"

She said, "I just happen to have access to a nice business jet. I can be there before you. Wanna race?"

"Let me check on Hunter, and I'll meet you at home tomorrow

night. If I'm not mistaken, I think I still owe you a honeymoon, Mrs. Fulton."

"You're not mistaken, Mr. Fulton, and I have it on good authority that you're a man of your word. You promised me we'd have one, and I think it's time. Don't you?"

"I could use a break from these sweaty hairy dudes, so yeah, I think it's time."

Chapter 34
Mistaken Identity

The IV bags never materialized, but I downed half a gallon of water at Mongo's insistence. "It's not as good as an IV, but at least it'll get some hydration in you. I don't want to see any more of that craziness out of you. I can deal with blood and guts, but I'm not so good with crazy."

"What would I do without you?" I asked.

He laughed. "You'd get along just fine, but you'd get your butt kicked more often."

Although he wasn't bearing any IV bags, a nurse finally appeared and surveyed the room. "Oh, boy. There's a bunch of you. We moved Mr. Hunter into post-surgical ICU, but I can only bring two at a time to see him. Dr. Conner said one of you was his brother. Which one?"

Every man's hand went into the air, and Anya almost raised hers.

The nurse laughed. "Well, it's quite a family he's got. Pick two, and come with me."

Singer took my arm. "Are you good?"

I stood. "Yeah, I'm all right now."

The nurse led us through the door and down a hallway. "Don't expect Mr. Hunter to be a hundred percent. He's awake and alert, but he's on some serious meds, and the nerve block hasn't worn off yet."

He entered a four-digit code—that I memorized—into a panel beside a pair of electric doors, and the motor whirred, opening both doors at once.

We continued following until the nurse stopped at room number seven, and I had a silent moment celebrating the irony of that particular room. Since the day I met Stone W. Hunter, it had been a running joke that we'd always answer "seven" if we didn't know the real answer to any question. There could've been no better room choice.

When we walked into the room, I wasn't prepared for what waited on the inside. Hunter was positioned on a device that might qualify as a hospital bed in some other universe, but in Birmingham, Alabama, it was a torture device. His torso was clamped into a clamshell contraption that was connected to the bed. An IV fed into the back of each of his hands, and an oxygen cannula lay under his nose. From the appearance of the framework, he could move his head and arms but nothing else.

A smile and look of recognition radiated from his battered face. "Hey, guys. When did you get here?"

I stepped beside him. "The same time you did, brother."

"That's a cool coincidence," he said through the narcotic haze he seemed to enjoy.

"Do you know where you are?" Singer asked.

"Yeah, but I can't think of the name. Can you?"

Singer said, "You're in Birmingham at UAB. Do you remember what happened?"

Hunter's eyes floated, and he finally said, "Somebody burned . . ." He seemed to drift off for a moment as if reliving the horrific fire in the jungle. "Then . . . then they murdered Litinday."

"Litinday?" I asked. "What does that mean?"

He stared up at me as if I'd asked what a saltshaker was. "You know Litinday. She was Toogah's daughter. They killed her."

I said, "Yes, we know about the murder, but we didn't know her name."

Hunter narrowed his gaze. "Were you there?"

"We were there after you sent the distress signal from the top of the ridge in the tree."

He smiled. "So, it worked . . . yeah?"

"It worked," I said. "And we came to find you."

He drew in a long breath and slowly let it escape. "Why did they kill Litinday?"

I said, "They wanted the tribe to move off that land. They were prospecting for gold."

"Who?"

Uncertain how deeply I should dive into the murky pool with him, I tried to imagine the roles being reversed. I would want every morsel of information I could get, and there was no doubt Hunter would want the same.

"It was a company called South-Wind Ventures out of Arizona. They buy the rights to mine for gold in the Amazon."

Hunter furrowed his brow. "They killed a baby to get gold?"

Singer took the floor. "It was a miracle you survived. You took a bullet to the gut, and it lodged against your spine."

"I remember. It sucked, and I didn't have a rifle. I should've listened to Chase. He tried to make me take a kit, but I wouldn't listen. That's me . . . not listening. It's what I do sometimes." He lay in silence for a moment, staring into the ceiling. When he returned, he asked, "Did you find them?"

"Who?" Singer asked.

"The people who killed Litinday. Did you find them?"

Singer glanced at me, and I said, "Yes, we found them."

Hunter closed his eyes as if in silent prayer. "You killed them, huh?"

It was my turn to take a long breath. "They attacked us. We had no choice."

"Did anybody get hurt?"

"We picked up a kid from the South-Wind team who didn't belong. He's a former paratrooper. You'd like him. If we hadn't found him, we never would've found you."

"Did he get hurt?"

"Yes, he did. He took an arrow. A big one. He's alive, though, and he's here at UAB recovering."

"Maybe I could meet him," Hunter said.

"Maybe you could."

His eyelids shuddered several times until he let them close. The conversation was over, or so I thought.

Hunter whispered barely loud enough to hear. "Tu-Tu Non Cataan."

I froze. "What did you say?"

Hunter tried to smile. "It's their word for God."

I was instantly covered in goosebumps and barely able to stand. "Say it again."

Hunter licked his lips. "Tu-Tu Non Cataan. They'd never heard of Jesus, of course, but they inherently knew there was a God. They called Him Tu-Tu Non Cataan."

"You learned their language," I said. It was meant to be a question, but it came out as a statement of fact.

Hunter smiled again. "Some of it. It's really pretty simple when you listen. They're good people."

I said, "They called me that name."

"What name?"

"Tu-Tu Non Cataan."

The drug-induced smile that had been in place suddenly melted away. "When you came to get me, how did you get there, and how did you carry me away?"

"We crashed the Huey after the South-Wind guys put an RPG through the tail rotor. After the fight, we took their Vertol."

"A helicopter," Hunter whispered. "You flew away with me."

"Yes, we did," I said. "Why does that matter?"

Singer gasped. "Oh, no."

"What is it?" I asked.

Singer said, "They think you're God. They think you came and took Hunter away into the sky."

Hunter closed his eyes again. "I have to get back down there. I have to make them understand."

I laid a hand on his arm. "Take it easy. You're not going anywhere soon. The surgeon said you've got a long road to recovery."

He said, "You don't understand. We made so much progress, but we told them how Jesus would return one day and take His children to Heaven. Think about what you did down there."

I mouthed the words, "I came from the sky and took you away with me . . . back into the sky."

"Yeah, you did," Hunter said. "They don't understand what a helicopter is. Think about how it looked to them."

Every second I spent with the natives flooded through my head, and I replayed every word they spoke.

"What does *Tee-muyah din ki-eep et ah-oohna* mean?"

Hunter frowned. "Say it again, but slowly."

I did, and he sighed. "I don't know. It's something about fear or being afraid. When did you hear that?"

"It's one of the first things the natives said to me when I came to the village where we found you. They said it right after I told them I was Tu-Tu Non Cataan."

Hunter said, "They were asking if they should be afraid of you."

"What about *poon poon boondy*?"

Hunter asked, "When did you hear that?"

"They took Anya after knocking her out with a poison dart. When they gave her back, they called her *poon poon boondy*."

His smile returned. "That's funny. They don't really have numbers in their language. One is *poon*. If they mean two, they say *poon poon*. Three is *poon poon poon*. See?"

"I get it, but what's *boondy*? There's only one Anya."

Hunter almost laughed. "*Boondy* means wife. They must've believed you had two wives, and Anya was number *poon poon*."

"That's ridiculous," I said. "You're making that up."

"I'm not smart enough to make that up."

It was Singer's turn to steer the conversation back in the direction he believed was most important. "Do you think you can make them understand that Chase isn't Tu-Tu Non Cataan?"

"Yeah, I can make them understand, but they probably think I died, so when I go back, that's going to be tough to explain."

We had put Hunter through more than he needed in one conversation, so I said, "I'm going back to Bonaventure to meet Penny, but I'll be back tomorrow or the next day. We're not going to leave you here alone."

Barely awake, he whispered, "I'm not alone."

I nodded toward the door, but Singer said, "I'm going to stay a little longer if you don't mind."

* * *

I fell asleep seconds after my head hit the pillow, and I dreamed of dragging Tommy Southard and Gary Windham through a mile of broken glass, but I didn't have any more thoughts of being the mystic harbinger of righteous punishment. The broken glass thing wasn't punishment. It was carnal weakness and my inability to turn the other cheek. I'd work on that, but not before breaking a little glass.

With the exception of Singer and Mongo, who stayed behind with Hunter, the team climbed aboard the *Grey Ghost* and blasted off for the fifty-minute flight back to Bonaventure. Gear needed to be cleaned and repaired, and the same was true for each of us.

I had a cup of coffee with Dr. Fred Kennedy, the psychiatrist from The Ranch. It took an hour to tell my story, but only an instant for him to make his diagnosis.

He said, "Make a list of the people in this world who are under the same or greater amounts of stress than you."

"That's ridiculous," I said. "Everybody handles stress differently."

He snapped his fingers. "Look at you, all learned and stuff. You've been studying."

"Cut it out," I said. "Where's this going?"

He slid a sheet of paper toward me. "You don't have to make the list. I already did."

I lifted the paper and flipped it over. "It's empty."

"That's right. Nobody in the world bears the same stress level as you. I told you the day we met that you were stepping into a world unlike anything you could imagine. Part of that world, at your level, is enough stress to cripple an elephant. I'm surprised this was your first episode. You're a psychologist, so tell me about a psychotic break."

I spit out the textbook answer. "A psychotic break is a sudden loss of touch with reality, often characterized by hallucinations and delusions."

"Does that sound familiar? How about when you were on your knees in that hospital, fantasizing about shoving a pair of pistols down a couple of throats in Arizona?"

"I didn't have a psychotic break. I'm not schizophrenic or bipolar."

He leaned back in his chair. "That's why you're a psychologist and not a real doctor, like me. Psychotic breaks are *often* symptoms of severe mental illness, but not always. I agree with your assessment, though. It most likely wasn't a full-blown psychotic break. It was more likely a stress-induced mental breakdown."

"That's not a clinical diagnosis," I said. "There's no recognized medical definition of 'mental breakdown.'"

"You're right again," he said, "but that doesn't mean you didn't have one. You're psychologically and psychiatrically healthy. There's nothing wrong with your brain . . . with the possible exception of that unnatural fascination you have with Eastern European blondes."

"That's not fair," I snapped. "It's not unnatural. Everybody knows they're some of the most beautiful women in the world."

"Okay, I'll give you that one, but back to my point. There's nothing wrong with your noggin. You'd just been told that the wife you adore wanted a divorce and your best friend was dead. Even a healthy brain like yours can't deal with that level of acute stress in the same instant."

"So, how do I keep it from happening again?"

"I'm going to write you a prescription," he said.

I protested. "You know I can't take mood-altering drugs. I have a top-secret clearance and a license to fly. I can't afford to lose either."

He pulled the blank sheet of paper from beneath my elbow and scribbled something before signing his illegible name at the bottom. When he slid it back toward me, I expected something in Latin, but instead, it just said "vacation."

As quickly as he'd arrived, Dr. Kennedy was gone, and I was left sitting alone at the kitchen table with the package that had caused so much trouble. I pushed it in circles with a big wooden spoon and came to realize that I didn't care what was inside. My *poon boondy* would be home later in the day, and I couldn't wait to hold her in my arms and never think about that unopened package again.

My phone chirped an hour before sunset, and I answered without checking the caller ID. "This is Chase."

Penny said, "I just wanted to make sure you were home."

"I am. We got here this morning about ten. When will you be home?"

She said, "Soon. In fact, if you'll walk down to the dock, I'll meet you there."

I tossed the phone onto the table and bounded down the back stairs and onto the lawn, where my beloved gazebo waited patiently for my return. It would have to keep waiting. Penny was more important.

I trotted down the slope and onto the dock protruding into the North River. It was slack tide, so the dark water lay motionless except for a few ripples around insects that had just become snacks for hungry baitfish. The tranquility of the moment was almost magical, but the anticipation of Penny showing up overshadowed nature's evening show.

Why she wanted me on the dock was a mystery, but I had solved all the mysteries I could handle for a while. I would simply sit on the bench at the end of the dock and wait.

Two minutes into my impatience, the sound of an aircraft I didn't recognize cut through the still evening air, and like every boy who loves flying machines, I turned my attention skyward. I couldn't instantly identify the odd-looking machine, and that made it even more fascinating.

I studied the lines and silhouette. Two massive engines rested high on a pair of wings elevated above the fuselage, and that's when it hit me. I knew exactly what the mysterious flying machine was. It was a blast from the past—a throwback to a magical time in aviation when designers weren't afraid to think outside the box, and pilots weren't afraid to strap themselves to anything with wings and take it for a ride.

The beautiful machine flew a low pass over the river and executed a graceful teardrop turn over Cumberland Sound. As the majestic old girl aligned herself with the river, the pilot pulled the throttles back and let his airplane glide onto the water and finally settle into her new role as a temporary boat. The pilot was good. He handled the massive craft with finesse until he shut down the engines and let her drift alongside the Bonaventure dock.

The hatch opened, and a man in his sixties emerged wearing a WWII–era flight suit. He tossed a line onto the dock, and I made it fast around a cleat.

The pilot tipped his hat. "Sorry to drop in unannounced, but you're Chase Fulton, aren't you?"

"I am."

He stepped from the hatch onto the dock and stuck out a hand. I shook it, and he said, "Nice to meet you, Chase. My name is Greg Shanks."

A chill ran down my spine as I recalled the return address on Penny's terrifying package.

Nothing made sense, and I fought off the urge to take a knee in preparation for another episode. "What can I do for you, Mr. Shanks?"

"You can offer me a bathroom and a cup of coffee before we take your nineteen-forty-four PBY-Five-A Catalina for a ride."

I was speechless and frozen as my beautiful wife stepped through the hatch. "Surprise."

I stammered and pointed between the airplane and the house. "This is . . . the contract . . . is this? You can't be serious."

Penny leapt into my arms and kissed me as if I'd just come home from the war. Perhaps I had.

When she finally stepped back, she asked, "Do you like it?"

"I can't believe you did this. How? I mean . . ."

She giggled. "I'll take that as a yes. It's not just any PBY Catalina. It's the one Dr. Richter flew after the war in nineteen forty-five, and Greg has all the paperwork to prove it."

Epilogue

Penny hadn't lied. The package did contain a contract, but it wasn't a production deal. It was the purchase contract for the PBY. Over the next several weeks, Greg Shanks and I flew over a hundred hours together. I finally learned how to operate the 1200-horsepower radial engines of the PBY and land her without jarring the wings off. In return, I taught my new flying buddy how to strap on the P-51 Mustang and grease every landing. We had the time of our lives, and Greg took me through the twenty-year restoration project of the Catalina after he bought it in pieces from a museum's warehouse in California.

By the time I logged enough hours in the Catalina to satisfy the insurance company and feel safe, it was time for sea trials aboard the RV *Lori Danielle* after her refit in Mississippi.

She performed beautifully, but she had lost four knots of speed. The extra weight of the transfer pool and the redesigned hangar deck cost us a few knots, but the sacrifice of speed was well worth the reward. Dr. Masha Turner enticed three breeding pairs of vaquitas to join her aboard the ship. Two of the pairs enjoyed a fourteen-thousand-mile voyage from the Gulf of California to the exact same latitude off the coast of Kuwait City in the Persian Gulf. The geographical similarities between the waters of Western Mexico and the Persian Gulf were perfect for relocation of the six vaquitas. Just as they could swim six hundred miles south out of the Gulf of California and into the open waters of the Pacific, they could make the same southbound swim from the Persian Gulf into the placid waters of the

Arabian Sea. Whether the relocation would be successful in saving the species would require decades to determine, but I was proud that our ship could play a role in such a momentous project.

The third pair of vaquitas found a home with the Scripps Institution of Oceanography at UC San Diego, where they would be treated like royalty and given every opportunity to produce the offspring that might one day be the catalyst for returning the species to a flourishing population.

Our mandate, and the nature of the world in which my team and I lived, demanded the destruction of life at times, so possibly playing a small role in the rescue of the vaquitas gave my mind and heart reason to rejoice.

In typical Stone W. Hunter fashion—and perhaps with a helping hand from above—our favorite missionary recovered at a pace unbelievable to most of the physicians around him, but none of us was surprised. He returned to the rainforest to continue his work with the indigenous tribes, but on his second trip to the Amazon, he went a little more well prepared. Dr. Mankiller developed a satellite repeater built into a solar-powered drone so Hunter could contact the outside world from anywhere on the planet. And although I doubted that he'd ever pull another trigger in anger, Hunter built four battle rigs, including rifles, pistols, body armor, and enough ammo to start a war. I believed without any doubt that he would accomplish the mission he set out to do and continue his work as long as he lived. Part of me envied his faith and devotion, but knowing and following our calling is where true satisfaction and fulfillment live. He was serving his, and I was serving mine.

Mike Perry recovered from his arrow wound and subsequent infection. Singer spoke with him every day in the hospital as if he loved him more than he loved himself, because that's exactly how Singer lives his life. When the former paratrooper was finally released from the hospital to return home to Georgia, he attended church for the first time with Carmella and Madeline. After a few weeks, he joined the church and was baptized in a nearby river, just as John baptized Christ two thousand years ago. He stayed on our payroll, but he'd never be a member of the team. Instead, he became the security manager for WORD, the Worldwide Organization of the Redeemer's Disciples. Mike returned to the Amazon at Hunter's side to make sure nothing like the fire and Litinday's brutal murder ever happened again.

The ship's refit included facilities to operate and manage the deep-sea remote exploration autonomous manned utility platform, or DREAMUP. Mongo devoted himself to the design, construction, and testing of the astonishing device, alongside Dr. Mankiller. Everyone on the team believed the DREAMUP would become an integral part of our seaborne operations for years to come.

Tommy Southard and Gary Windham abandoned their offices in Arizona and vanished into hiding somewhere. Their bankroll was more than sufficient to facilitate their disappearance and a comfortable life in exile, but I had a warship and a team of commandos who had no understanding of the concept of giving up. I would find them, and they would stand trial for their crimes, even though my fantasy of dragging them through glass still lingered.

And after too many years of delays, I finally kept my promise to go on a real, uninterrupted honeymoon with my one and only *boondy*.

Author's Note

Well, that was quite an adventure. It took me almost three years to write the manuscript for *The Opening Chase*, book #1 in this series. Looking back now, that seems unbelievable. I've learned to write at a much better pace since then. Among other things, Stephen King is famous for his motto, *Numquam dies sine verbo*. I'm a simple guy from East Tennessee, so Latin ain't my bag, baby. I do, however, know enough to translate that one for you. It means "Never a day without a word," and I like it. I shoot for 2,500 words per day, every day. I hit the 2,500-word goal on the days when I write, but it isn't always possible to write absolutely every day. Real life gets in the way.

I've now written thirty-eight full-length novels, and this manuscript is the first one I actually wrote every day without missing a single day—and that included two weeks on a cruise ship in the Caribbean. As it turns out, they have Jack Daniel's and a few quiet spots on that ship where a scribe like me can get a little work done. I wrote this one in twenty-nine days, and that's a record for me. The story fell out of my head so quickly that I could barely type rapidly enough to keep up. It was a fascinating experience for me, and I hope you felt the pace and excitement throughout the story.

There are writers who scoff at novelists like me who write quickly. They believe time equals quality. The longer it takes to write the story, the better the story will be. Perhaps for some writers, that's true, but not for me. My stories feel more solid and consistent when I write quickly. I immerse myself in the action and drama, and I live my life inside the story when I'm writing every day. Actors often talk about getting into character and staying there throughout filming. Maybe that's what happened for me in this story. I'm pleased with the final product, and I hope you are, too.

Now, let's talk about how this one came together. The inspiration for this story came in the form of two aerial photographs taken by a drone in the Amazon Rainforest. In the pictures, a few indigenous people without clothes are looking up at the buzzing drone. In one of the pictures, they're simply looking, but in the other picture, they're armed with bows and spears aimed skyward. My brother, Dave, showed me the pictures while he and I were on a sporting-clays outing in Northeast Georgia. The missionary group he's part of took the pictures. I was immediately mesmerized, and a thousand storylines flooded my mind. I wanted to know what would happen if an isolated tribe of people met a team of missionaries and collided with a band of greedy, trigger-happy bandits. *The Calling Chase* is the result of that question, and this time, the good guys won, but I fear that isn't often the case. Greed is a powerful motivator, and darkness in the hearts of men often pours out upon the innocent.

Let's move on to something a little more pleasant, like Dr. Masha Turner and her beloved vaquitas. We met Masha a few books ago at the Ocean Reef Club Airport on Key Largo. If you remember, she's the niece of Hank, the airport manager, who is an old friend of Dr. Richter's. I liked Masha back then, and I wanted to find a spot for her in future stories, so I chose this one to reintroduce her. I hope we'll see more of her, but I can't make any promises. As far as the vaquitas are concerned, they are absolutely real, and the statistics I quoted in this story are also painfully real. They're one of the most endangered species in the world, and they're fascinating. I encourage you to do a little research of your own when you're looking for something interesting.

South-Wind Ventures is, of course, fictional. However, the name isn't entirely made up. When Melissa and I were conducting sailing charters before you turned me into a successful novelist, we named our business South Wind Sailing. So, instead of picking on someone else's business name, I used ours. Thanks to you and a few million of your reading friends, our days of running boats for other people are long gone. Thank you for rescuing me from a life of repairing diesel engines that I don't understand and standing at the helm through wind and rain. Writing is a much more comfortable gig, and I'm deeply appreciative for the freedom to be your personal storyteller.

Some of you may have scoffed when you read that there are gold prospectors in the Amazon Rainforest. They, just like the tribesmen, are absolutely real. I don't have any evidence that they commit atrocities like burning villages and murdering babies, but I needed a dramatic background, so I wrote those horrific events. If you'll think back a few hundred years, you'll remember the Spanish sailing back and forth across the Atlantic with ships full of gold, silver, and gems from South America. That treasure hunt is still happening, but we don't use sailing ships and conquistadores anymore. It's a little more sophisticated these days, but perhaps still a bit savage at its core.

One of my favorite lines in this story is when Chase refers to Anya as his Russian Zacchaeus while she was in the palm tree. After I wrote that line, I couldn't stop singing that silly little song I learned in Sunday school. Then I couldn't stop singing it in a Russian accent. Then somebody heard me, and it got stuck in his head. It's the little things that I love most.

Oh, yeah . . . We were going to talk about the trees. I'll confess that I didn't know there were palm trees in the Amazon Rainforest, but after a little research, I learned the specific palm tree I used, the *Euterpe precatoria*, is the most common tree in that particular rainforest. That's either absolutely true, or I made it up. You'll have to do some digging on your own to find out which.

Here it is, the part I'll never stop saying, no matter how many times you've heard it. Truly, sincerely, and completely, I treasure each of you, not as fans, but as friends who enjoy my stories. You've given me the best job I've ever had, and I'll never be able to adequately thank you, but I'll do my best by creating the strongest and most enjoyable stories I'm capable of producing because that's what you deserve. By the time you read this note, I will probably have another story in editing and on its way into your hands. Until then, I wish you the greatest happiness, joy, and success, however you define any of those.

Cheers,
Cap

About the Author

Cap Daniels

Cap Daniels is a former sailing charter captain, scuba and sailing instructor, pilot, Air Force combat veteran, and civil servant of the U.S. Department of Defense. Raised far from the ocean in rural East Tennessee, his early infatuation with salt water was sparked by the fascinating, and sometimes true, sea stories told by his father, a retired Navy Chief Petty Officer. Those stories of adventure on the high seas sent Cap in search of adventure of his own, which eventually landed him on Florida's Gulf Coast where he spends as much time as possible on, in, and under the waters of the Emerald Coast.

With a headful of larger-than-life characters and their thrilling exploits, Cap pours his love of adventure and passion for the ocean onto the pages of the Chase Fulton Novels and the Avenging Angel - Seven Deadly Sins series.

Visit www.CapDaniels.com to join the mailing list to receive newsletter and release updates.

Connect with Cap Daniels:

Facebook: www.Facebook.com/WriterCapDaniels
Instagram: https://www.instagram.com/authorcapdaniels/
BookBub: https://www.bookbub.com/profile/cap-daniels

Also by Cap Daniels

The Chase Fulton Novels Series

Book One: *The Opening Chase*
Book Two: *The Broken Chase*
Book Three: *The Stronger Chase*
Book Four: *The Unending Chase*
Book Five: *The Distant Chase*
Book Six: *The Entangled Chase*
Book Seven: *The Devil's Chase*
Book Eight: *The Angel's Chase*
Book Nine: *The Forgotten Chase*
Book Ten: *The Emerald Chase*
Book Eleven: *The Polar Chase*
Book Twelve: *The Burning Chase*
Book Thirteen: *The Poison Chase*
Book Fourteen: *The Bitter Chase*
Book Fifteen: *The Blind Chase*
Book Sixteen: *The Smuggler's Chase*
Book Seventeen: *The Hollow Chase*
Book Eighteen: *The Sunken Chase*
Book Nineteen: *The Darker Chase*
Book Twenty: *The Abandoned Chase*
Book Twenty-One: *The Gambler's Chase*
Book Twenty-Two: *The Arctic Chase*
Book Twenty-Three: *The Diamond Chase*
Book Twenty-Four: *The Phantom Chase*
Book Twenty-Five: *The Crimson Chase*
Book Twenty-Six: *The Silent Chase*
Book Twenty-Seven: *The Shepherd's Chase*
Book Twenty-Eight: *The Scorpion's Chase*
Book Twenty-Nine: *The Creole Chase*
Book Thirty: *The Calling Chase*
Book Thirty-One: *The Capital Chase*

The Avenging Angel – Seven Deadly Sins Series
Book One: *The Russian's Pride*
Book Two: *The Russian's Greed*
Book Three: *The Russian's Gluttony*
Book Four: *The Russian's Lust*
Book Five: *The Russian's Sloth*
Book Six: *The Russian's Envy*
Book Seven: *The Russian's Wrath* (2025)

Stand-Alone Novels
We Were Brave
Singer – Memoir of a Christian Sniper

Novellas
The Chase is On
I Am Gypsy

Made in the USA
Middletown, DE
19 July 2025